THE STAR OF THE DESERT

GORDON WALLIS

Copyright © [2020] by [Gordon Wallis]

All rights reserved.

No portion of this book may be reproduced in any form without written permission from the publisher or author, except as permitted by U.S. copyright law.

Contents

1. Chapter One: The Great Thirst, Namib Desert, Namibia, 150 Km East of Walvis Bay, 1868. — 1
2. Chapter Two: London, The Present Day — 5
3. Chapter Three: Windhoek, Namibia. — 10
4. Chapter Four: Wings Over the Desert — 14
5. Chapter Five: The Big Hole — 38
6. Chapter Six: Secrets — 54
7. Chapter Seven: Bad Penny — 74
8. Chapter Eight: Lucy In The Sky — 82
9. Chapter Nine: Strange Days — 92
10. Chapter Ten: Night Moves — 104
11. Chapter Eleven: Icarus Rising — 108
12. Chapter Twelve: Oom Piet — 115
13. Chapter Thirteen: Search and Rescue — 124
14. Chapter Fourteen: Temba Zulu — 128
15. Chapter Fifteen: Triggered — 133
16. Chapter Sixteen: Green — 148
17. Chapter Seventeen: Klopp — 151
18. Chapter Eighteen: Green — 155
19. Chapter Nineteen: Klopp — 157

20.	Chapter Twenty: Green	160
21.	Chapter Twenty-One: Klopp	164
22.	Chapter Twenty-Two: Green	168
23.	Chapter Twenty-Three: Klopp	174
24.	Chapter Twenty-Four: Green	177
25.	Chapter Twenty-Five: Klopp	180
26.	Chapter Twenty-Six: Green	183
27.	Chapter Twenty-Seven: Cape Town, Two Days Later.	190

1

Chapter One: The Great Thirst, Namib Desert, Namibia, 150 km East of Walvis Bay, 1868.

The mid-morning sun glinted harshly off the endless flat, featureless expanse of hard white sand that stretched away to the horizon in every direction. The old San bushman stopped in his tracks and brought his wrinkled brown hand up above his eyes to look for the distant hills he had been expecting to see since sunrise. Squinting his eyes from the glare he saw only the deceptive, shimmering liquid blue mirage that seemed to ripple and swell like water. He grunted in annoyance and shook his head as he removed the zebra-skin pouch from his shoulder and squatted down on his thin legs. Placing his powerful bow on the sand nearby he removed the quiver of poison-tipped arrows from the soft pouch before loosening the bark twine string that secured its contents. The rich aroma from the strips of dried Oryx meat filled his nostrils. The great bounty from the long hunt would feed both him and his wife until the moon was full once again. It was a smell that would usually please him, but this day his main concern was water. For three days he had chased the animal running through the day and only resting when the wounded Oryx bull itself rested. A lifetime of experience had taught him the patience and steely determination of the great hunter he was. *Or had been.* It was on the third day when the dose of poison from the arrow had finally beaten the animal and the old man had been able to make the kill. Now, five days later, doubt began to creep into the old man's mind and once again he heard the stern warning that he had been given by his wife the night before the hunt had begun.

"You are an old man now," she had chided him in the click consonants of the ancient Khoisan language. "Do not venture too far into the great emptiness. Water is plentiful and there are rabbits and other smaller animals here."

"I am a hunter," he had replied gruffly, "and as such, I will hunt."

The old man remembered those words as he removed the polished ostrich egg that contained his meagre supply of water. Feeling its weight, he shook it and heard the level of water was low. Still squatting on his bare feet, he looked towards the East where the mountains should be. *Perhaps that old woman was right? How can this be? Lost in the great emptiness.* Although his mouth was dry from running the old man placed the ostrich egg and the arrows carefully back into the soft pouch and drew the string. Once more he screwed up his wrinkled face as he stared towards the East.

"They must be there," he muttered to himself in a series of clicks as he began to run once again.

It was late in the afternoon and the sun burned the old man's bare back when finally, the distant mountains, tinged with purple, came into view on the horizon.

I knew it. He thought to himself. *That old bull had made a turn as it ran and led me astray. But now I see the mountains and after two days I will return triumphant. The old woman need never know.* But the old man was weakened and the straps of the heavy leather bag cut into his shoulders. He removed the small smooth pebble that he had held in his mouth all day to fight the thirst and it came out completely dry. *I must drink.* He thought to himself. *Walk now, enough running.*

It was as the sun was setting in a giant orange orb behind him that the old man first saw the isolated clumps of dried grass that grew above the rocky canyon. It had been the first sign of vegetation he had seen in eight days and instinctively he walked towards them. It was only when he reached the edge of the narrow canyon that he saw the scale of it. It stretched from the distant mountains to his left and as far as the eye could see to the right. Perhaps once every few years water would flow from the mountains and travel down the thin rocky river - bed that lay thirty metres below. In a lifetime of hunting in the great emptiness the old man had never seen this place and he let out a soft whistle as he stared down at the white sand and smooth blackened boulders below. *There will be water there.* He thought to himself as he wearily removed the bag from his shoulders and sat on the soft sand. After eating a stick of dried meat and drinking the last of the stale water from the ostrich egg the old man lay back and rested his head on the bag. *There will be sweet water.*

The old man awoke before the sunrise and his first thought was his great thirst. He pulled the wooden plug from the top of the empty ostrich egg and tipped it up above his mouth in the hope that there might be a drop left. There was none. He rubbed his eyes with his bony hands and sat to wait for the sun. It rose an hour later heralded by a spray of pink on the horizon to his right. Patiently, the old man sat until it had risen sufficiently for him to see the bottom of the thin canyon below. Wearily, and carrying his belongings, he began the descent down the steep rocky slope. It was when he was only five metres above the fine white sand of the dried river - bed that he saw what he was looking for. The dried twigs of the Bi Bulb were plentiful and stuck out of the sand every few metres. Thirty centimetres beneath the packed sand the coconut-sized tubers would be easily accessible to the old man and would provide bitter, but drinkable water. *I knew it!* He thought as he scrambled over the last remaining rocks onto the level sand below. Using a thin dried length of firewood from the pouch he squatted on his haunches and began to frantically dig around the tough twigs. The thick, crusted white layer of sand gave way and the work became easier. Finally, the digging tool struck something hard and the old man smiled a toothless grin as he reached into the hole. *Now I will drink!* He thought as his bony fingers scraped in the sand. But the smile on his wizened and wrinkled face soon turned into a frown as his fingers found an unexpected object where he had expected the life-giving tuber. Shifting from his haunches onto his knees, the old man forced his hand deeper into the sand to extract the object. It felt hard and slightly smaller

than a monkey orange. *It must be a stone. The water-giving plant will surely be there.* Eventually, after some effort, the old man lifted the object from the ground and held it in his hand.

It is unusual. He thought as he sat back on the sand. *Very heavy and with a strange shape and colour. I have never seen a rock like this.* The old man turned the stone in his small hand before tossing it into the air and catching it once again to feel its unusual weight. As the caked sand fell from the stone, he saw glints of sunlight sparkling from the exposed surface. But the old man placed no value on the stone for he was solely focussed on his great thirst.

"Hmm," he grunted as he tossed it onto the sand by his side and resumed digging in the hole.

Eventually, he found what he was looking for and after a few minutes, he triumphantly lifted the giant life-giving tuber from the sand. He spent the next hour crushing the inner flesh of the tough grey subterranean plant with the strange rock he had dug up and he drank his fill of the bitter water that flowed from it. When he was done he tossed the curious stone back into the hole he had dug it from and covered it once again with sand that had piled up near the hole.

Later that day the old man found a sipping well further down the ravine near a corner in the river-bed. Using the stick, he dug half a metre into the damp sand below and filled his ostrich egg by sucking the muddy water that accumulated into his mouth through a dried reed and depositing it into the egg. Once again there had been many of the strange stones, albeit smaller than the first, but as before he had ignored them. As the sun set the old man laid his head on his bag and chewed on a stick of dried meat as he watched the stars appear in the sky above. *Two days from now.* He thought with a smile on his wrinkled face. *Two days from now I shall return to the mountains and show that old woman I am still a great hunter.*

Four days later, in the cool of the early evening, the old man ambled up to his grass and reed dwelling in the mountains. There was a great tiredness in his eyes, but he hoped his wife would not see it in the light of the fire where she sat.

"Where have you been old man?" she said. "I thought your skinny body had dried up and blown away in the wind of the great emptiness."

"I am a hunter," he replied as he sat and removed the bundles of dried meat from his bag. "I have been hunting."

2

Chapter Two: London, The Present Day

The call came at 1.00 pm as I was about to leave my North London flat for the local supermarket. I was frustrated and had been waiting all day for a parcel I had ordered from eBay. The seller had told me he had shipped my order by first-class mail the previous day and guaranteed the package would be delivered. I had spent the morning pacing the flat waiting for the door buzzer to ring but until then it had been all quiet. The seller was a young man by the name of Martin Walter from South London. He worked as a driver for a popular courier company delivering goods mainly from Amazon. Martin Walter had a particularly high rate of non-delivery claims on his company record and I had followed him on his rounds for two days the previous week. In the event that the receiver of the package he was delivering was not at home, Martin Walter would leave said package along with a note in the doorway. However, what the courier company had suspected was true. After his shift ended at 2.00 pm each day, Martin Walter would re-trace his exact route from the morning through London on his motorcycle. Any packages that were still unclaimed on the receiver's doorstep would be lifted and bagged by Martin Walter and he would quickly move on to the next address. The full-face crash helmet he used prevented his face from being captured on any CCTV cameras. On a good day, he would return to his home in South London with five packages and he would have something similar to a lucky dip. A lot of the packages he lifted contained high-value items and by 8.00 pm that night, they would be listed for sale on his own eBay account. Martin Walter's industrious but criminal enterprise had been running smoothly for ten months and I was one of his newest customers. The blue tooth headphones I had paid him for had only cost me £55.00. A bargain price for an 'unwanted gift still in the original box'. But the delivery had failed to arrive and I was seriously considering leaving him negative feedback on his eBay account. The delivery would be the final nail in Martin Walter's coffin and the case would be handed over to the police. The job had been going on too long and I was anxious to wrap it up. I pulled the phone from my pocket and immediately recognized the number on the screen as that of the chief case supervisor from the head office of the insurance firm. I had been working with them on a freelance basis for over seven years and I was surprised to get a call rather than an email.

"Hi Diane," I said flatly.

"Oh, hello Jason," she said. "Hope I'm not disturbing you."

"Not at all," I replied. "What's up?"

"It's a bit unusual Jason but the board wants to see you," she said.

I stopped my pacing and looked out of the window at the rainy afternoon.

"The board of directors?" I asked.

"Yes," she said.

"Is there a problem Diane?" I asked feeling puzzled.

"No," she said. "I don't think so. It all seems a bit hush-hush, to be honest, but I think they have a job for you. I'd imagine it must be quite important."

"Any idea why they requested to see me in particular?" I asked.

"No," she said. "Sorry, Jason. They just asked me if I could get you down to head office as soon as possible. That's all I know."

I looked at the door buzzer and my watch in that order.

"That's fine," I said. "Tell them I'll be there by 2.30."

I said goodbye and hung up. The request was unusual, but I was suffering a serious case of cabin fever and the opportunity to get out of the flat was welcome even if it was raining. I dressed for the chilly October weather and headed out after locking the flat. The rain abated for the short walk to Seven Sisters tube station and I crushed out my cigarette before descending into the humid bowels of the underground. I took the Victoria line South to Green Park then changed to the Jubilee line, finally emerging at Canary Wharf station in the modern financial district of London. The rain had returned and I pulled my coat tightly around myself as I rushed towards the skyscraper that housed the offices of my primary employers. As I stepped through the giant revolving doors, I realized I hadn't set foot in the building for at least three years. All communication between myself and them had been through either email or the phone. I took the lift to the eighteenth floor and walked through the company doors to the reception desk. The smart young lady at reception spoke before I had the opportunity to introduce myself.

"Mr Green?" she said with her eyebrows raised.

"Yes," I replied.

"I'll just call Diane, she's expecting you," she said picking up a telephone

She spoke in hushed tones into the receiver and within seconds I saw the tall elegant figure of Diane emerge from her office down the corridor. She wore a tweed business suit and her heels clicked on the marble floor as she approached with a sense of urgency.

"Nice to see you again Jason," she said as she shook my hand. "Shall we go up? They're expecting you."

"Sure," I said as I followed out the door and back to the lifts.

"Any idea what's going on here?" I said as the doors of the lift closed.

"Not a clue, Jason," she said as she pushed the button for the twenty first floor. "But one of the directors has flown in from Scotland specially to meet you. It's all a bit rushed I'm afraid."

She tapped her waist impatiently and glanced at her watch as the doors closed. We arrived and walked through another reception area I had never seen and I followed Diane down a corridor to a door with a sign that read 'Boardroom' She opened the door after two quick knocks and I followed her into the room. At the far end of the long space was a polished ebony table surrounded by sumptuous chairs upholstered in green leather. The rain lashed silently against the wide windows obscuring the view of the other skyscrapers of Canary Wharf. Closer to the door a group of four men sat stretched out in easy chairs drinking coffee as they talked. The atmosphere was relaxed but I could tell they had been waiting for my arrival.

"Sorry gentlemen," said Diane. "Mr Green has arrived. I'll leave you now. Thank you."

The four men thanked her and then stood up as she closed the door behind her. One by one they introduced themselves amicably and shook my hand. All of them wore standard suits that one would expect from the executive board of a large international insurance company. The largest of them, a portly Scotsman by the name of Pritchard, spoke first after the introductions were over.

"I don't see the need to be too formal here gentlemen," he said in a broad accent. "Shall we all sit where we are?"

The three other men nodded and grunted in agreement while one of them pulled a chair out for me to sit on.

"Would you like a cup of tea or coffee Jason?" said Pritchard.

From his blotchy skin and red nose, I could tell he was a man who enjoyed his drink. However, his manner was pleasant and friendly enough and I accepted his offer of coffee. The other three men made small talk with me as Pritchard busied himself near the coffee machine. The main subject, unsurprisingly, was the weather. Finally, the cup was delivered and Pritchard wheezed his large frame into a nearby chair and smiled.

"Well Jason," he said still smiling. "I know I speak on behalf of everyone here when I say thanks very much for coming in on such short notice. We do appreciate it."

The others grunted and nodded in approval as they made themselves comfortable.

"No problem at all," I said openly. "What can I do for you?"

"Mr Green ... ah ... Jason," said Pritchard leaning forward in his seat "We know you have some experience working in Africa."

"Correct," I replied.

"Well, Jason. One of our international clients, Apex Resources, a diamond consortium, has been having a few problems with one of their operations in Namibia. Now the company has quite a few others, mines in The Congo, Zambia, and a small one in Botswana, but the one in Namibia is causing us quite a few headaches."

The other men nodded in agreement once again.

"What sort of problems are they having?" I asked as I sipped the coffee.

"Well in the past two years, there have been some very unusual claims. There have been several accidental deaths on the job. Now, this particular company takes work safety very seriously indeed and in the ten years they have been operating there has *never* been a death. On two occasions there have been claims for missing gems as well. There have also been cases of very expensive machinery inexplicably breaking. Claims and more claims. This mine is very remote and you can imagine security is extremely tight, especially when it comes to diamonds."

"I see," I said putting the cup on the table in front of me. "I'm guessing these claims are fairly substantial?"

The four men harrumphed and nodded their heads in concern.

THE STAR OF THE DESERT

"Very expensive claims indeed, Jason," said Pritchard. "The shareholders are quite concerned. So much so that we decided to ask you if you would go down there and ... cast an eye shall we say, on the operation for us. See if you can identify the problem."

The room fell silent and there was a look of hopeful desperation on the men's faces.

"How long would I go for if I agree?" I asked.

One of the other younger men spoke.

"As long as it takes to get sorted," he said. "We can't afford to lose this account but at the same time these claims are damaging us massively."

Pritchard spoke again in his broad Scots accent.

"I think you can see our predicament now Jason. It's pretty dire. We would also like you to take a good look at the mine manager. A German. Man by the name of Klopp. Heinrich Klopp."

Pritchard reached forward to the centre of the coffee table and pushed a thick file towards me. Printed in the centre of the cover were the words 'Apex Resources Namibia'.

"The people at the Apex head office in Antwerp swear by him," said Pritchard. "Say he's a great man who produces results. We are not so sure though."

"What have you heard about him that makes you unsure?" I asked.

"Nothing," said the younger man. "But he *is* the manager of Apex's most lucrative mine and the buck stops with him. Naturally, he would be the first port of call."

"Of course," I said. "And if I were to agree when would you want me to leave?"

The men all laughed politely and allowed Pritchard to answer.

"As soon as possible," he said. "I actually came down from Scotland today especially to see you."

He paused and looked me in the eyes.

"I guess it's time to cut to the chase," he said. "Will you do it, Jason?"

Fifteen minutes later I walked out of the giant revolving door on the ground floor of the building and stepped into the grey drizzle of the afternoon. After a short negotiation of my remuneration for the job, I was handed the file along with an open first-class ticket to Windhoek via Frankfurt for that very night. Martin Walter would be free to continue his petty thieving for the meantime. The job was on.

3

Chapter Three: Windhoek, Namibia.

It had only taken an hour to pack my bags and leave the flat. As usual, I packed the standard equipment and a few extras I thought I might need. The all-expenses-paid nature of the job allowed me to catch a taxi to Heathrow Airport instead of using the tube and I began to peruse the file as the car merged onto the busy M25 motorway in the evening drizzle. Apex Resources was, by all accounts, a model company that partnered amicably with the governments of the countries it operated in. The operations were as transparent as any diamond extraction outfit could be while at the same time maintaining the levels of security one would expect with such a high-value product. The production output from the Apex Namibia mine was of both industrial and gem-quality diamonds. Their discovery had been made by an independent prospector five years previously and samples of the gems had been offered to several mining houses in sealed packages and the claim was subsequently purchased through a secret ballot system in Antwerp, Belgium. The now extremely wealthy prospector had since moved on to other projects leaving Apex Resources to develop and exploit the deposits which were both alluvial and underground. The mine was extremely remote and difficult to access making the site an attractive one given the natural security afforded by the many hundreds of miles of desert that surrounded it. The company had built a compound and an airstrip on site and access for engineers and management was mainly by light aircraft while the labour force and equipment were transported 480 km West of Windhoek on rough and dangerous dirt roads. I pulled a map from the file and looked it over as the driver veered left off the motorway and headed towards the airport. I had been told I would be met by a company pilot at Windhoek International Airport the following morning and flown in a light aircraft to the mine with an ETA of about 11.00 am. I folded the map and replaced it in the file as the vehicle pulled up at the drop-off point near an overhanging roof to shield passengers from the weather. I paid using my card and the driver opened the boot to retrieve my luggage and thanked me as I made my way inside the building. Being late in the day the check-in and security process took a full hour and I had to rush to the gate to make my flight. The short hop to Frankfurt was over in a flash and I killed the next two hours drinking German beer in the Lufthansa lounge. Eventually, it was time to board and after making it through the gate I sat down in my window seat in the business class section at the front of the long-haul aircraft. I found the seat wide and comfortable as I settled in and continued reading the file while the plane taxied and eventually took off into the night. The details of mine manager Heinrich Klopp made for interesting reading. At 55 years old he had achieved a great deal firstly as an aircraft mechanic in the German Air Force and then later on in civilian life as a mechanical engineer. His career had taken him from his humble beginnings in Germany to management level in the giant gold mining conglomerates of Australia and South America. Shrewd, thorough, and of sober habits, his profile indicated a man whose priorities lay with his employer and his focus firmly on the smooth running and efficiency of his organization. I sat back after being handed a glass of whisky and ice by the flight attendant and stared at his picture in the file.

The man was slim but well-built with a full head of short-cropped grey hair. Although he was pictured with a half-smile, the lips were thin and with his light blue eyes narrowed in concentration, he appeared somehow humourless. It was clear the picture had been taken in a cold climate as the tight navy blue jacket he wore was zipped up to his chin giving him the look of a man with a military background. The face was perfectly symmetrical with wide cheekbones and a large forehead. I sighed as I placed the sheet of paper back in the file and stared out of the window on my left into the darkness. *All will be revealed Green. All will be revealed.* It was after dinner had been served that I finally put the file away. The turn of events had been sudden and unexpected and although I was pleased at the prospect of the change of scenery and the new job, I was feeling tired and warm from the drink. I decided to adjust my seat and watch a movie. I awoke at 5.15 am as the sun had just begun to show in a faint yellow glow through the window. During the night one of the attendants must have spread a blanket over me as I slept as I had no recollection of doing so. I reached to my left and retrieved the small water bottle that sat in a receptacle above the seat. As I drank, I stared at the glow of the rising sun and wondered what the day would have in store for me. In all my years in Africa, I had never set foot in Namibia and apart from the rushed browsing I had done in the airport, and what I had read from the file, I had very little idea of what to expect. It was after breakfast and coffee was served that the pilot announced we had begun our descent into Windhoek. I pushed the button to return the seat to the fully upright position and began to watch the scenery below. Even from the enormous height the sparse brown landscape stretched flat as far as the eye could see and changed very little in features or colour. Barren and parched there was little-or-no sign of human activity and it soon became clear that this was one of the least populated countries on earth. I sat in awe as the giant aircraft descended and the isolated sandy dirt roads of the ranches and cattle stations began to show between the scrubby camel-thorn bush. The outskirts of Windhoek were marked by a mountain range that rose up to the left. Ahead lay the faded tar strip of the lonely single runway of the international airport which seemed to disappear into insignificance in the vast emptiness of its surroundings. The plane passed it banking to the left before turning to face it head-on for landing. After a brief tilt of the left wing, the aircraft landed and the pilot welcomed us to Namibia on the speaker system. The plane taxied up to a wide and low single-storey building and came to a halt. *Jesus. Looks like you landed in the back of beyond here, Green.* There was no modern moving walkway through which to enter the building and instead, I watched as a white truck with a telescopic passenger boarding staircase drove up and positioned itself at the door behind me. Soon enough the seatbelt sign turned off and I stood up to retrieve my hand luggage from the overhead storage. Being in business class, I was one of the first to exit the plane and I was immediately struck by a wall of blasting dry heat. I glanced at my watch to see it was only 7.50 am. but the sun beat down on the tarmac and glinted in my eyes as I walked down the stairs. There was no bus for the passengers only a series of red plastic cones with airport workers standing nearby directing us to walk towards the main building.

Above me, the sky seemed bigger and bluer than any I had seen before.

The interior of the building appeared dark at first after the blinding light of the apron, but it was cool and modern and I followed the signs to the left that led to the immigration desks. The young man at the desk made a yawning enquiry as to the nature of my visit to which I replied I was on holiday. After flicking through my passport for a few seconds he brought his heavy stamp down onto one of the pages.

"Welcome to Namibia, Mr Green," he said.

"Thanks," I replied as I took my passport and walked off.

THE STAR OF THE DESERT

The baggage collection hall consisted of two small carousels in a large room surrounded by advertising for tourists. After what seemed an age one of them began to circulate and I stepped forward to await my luggage. Thankfully it was one of the first bags out and I walked off through the 'Nothing To Declare' doors under the scrutiny of some uniformed men. I felt their eyes on me as I walked, but thankfully I made it through to the arrivals hall without being searched. I was grateful as the surveillance equipment and the drone I was carrying would have surely raised some eyebrows. In desperate need of a cigarette I searched around for the nearest exit sign but my eyes settled on a young white man holding a piece of paper to his chest with the words 'Mr Jason Green' printed on the front. He wore dark jeans and a crisp white short-sleeve shirt with the blue and gold epaulettes of a pilot on each shoulder. He was tall and couldn't have been more than twenty-five years old with slightly long blonde hair and a cheeky look of permanent amusement on his face. I nodded at him as I approached and his face broke into a wide smile.

"Mr Green?" he said enthusiastically.

"That's me," I said holding my hand out to him. "Jason Green."

He took my hand in a vice-like grip and shook it vigorously all the while with a beaming smile.

"Danny Meyer," he said. "Pleased to meet you."

4

Chapter Four: Wings Over the Desert

"How was your flight?" he asked keenly as he beckoned me to follow him. "Not too bad thanks," I replied pulling my bag behind me. "I need a smoke, any chance we can stop for a moment?"

"Sure, certainly," he replied happily. "We'll just step outside."

I followed the young man out through an exit to a taxi rank. We stood in the shade of an overhanging roof and I pulled my cigarettes from my pocket. Once again, I was struck by the dry heat of the early morning.

"A bit warmer than London," I said as I lit up.

The young man laughed and looked up at the expanse of deep blue sky above.

"Oh ya," he said. "It's even warmer down by the big hole."

"By the big hole, you mean the mine?" I asked.

"Sorry, Mr Green, yes," he said with a brief frown. "I meant the mine. I'll be flying you down there today."

"Please call me Jason, Danny," I said casually as I exhaled a plume of smoke. "How long have you been flying for Apex?"

"Well I'm not on a full-time basis for them," he said. "I'm actually a freelance pilot but whenever Apex needs me, I get the call and fly in. Anyone or anything important that needs to get to or from the mine, I'm there. The rest of the time I fly charters for tourists mainly."

"Oh okay," I said casually.

"I might fly down to the mine once every two weeks?" he said. "It depends on Mr Klopp. He's the boss..."

THE STAR OF THE DESERT

I crushed out the cigarette in a nearby sandbox and gripped the handle of my bag in readiness to leave.

Without wanting to press the young man for too much information I glanced towards the car park and put my sunglasses on.

"Well," I said. "Shall we go?"

"Sure!" he replied happily. "Let's do it."

The fierce morning sun burned my neck as we made our way up a set of concrete steps and across a road towards a car park lined with blue shade ports. We rounded a row of vehicles and stopped at a red twin-cab Toyota Hilux pickup truck with raised suspension and a canopy on the back.

"Here we are," said Danny as he unlocked the vehicle. "Your bags will go on the back seat I think."

I opened the door and lifted my bags into the hot interior of the cab. Danny leant over and opened the passenger door as I closed the back. He watched as I got in the cab then pulled his own Rayban sunglasses from his top pocket and put them on.

"Right!" he said reaching for the ignition. "Let's go."

The moment he turned the key in the ignition the car's stereo burst into life and my ears were pounded with loud dance music. Danny quickly fumbled with the volume control and shut it off.

"Sorry, Mr Green!" he said with an embarrassed laugh.

"Jason, Danny," I said "Jason."

The young man's enthusiasm and happy-go-lucky attitude were somewhat endearing and I sat back comfortably in my seat as we pulled out of the car park onto the road towards the exit.

"So, we are going to Eros Airport," said Danny as he made a right turn onto a single-lane highway "It's about forty kilometres from here, close to town. From there we'll take off and make a short hop down to the mine. Takes about one hour fifteen minutes flying time."

"Okay," I said. "And how long is the drive to the mine?"

"Ah, I'm not too sure, Jason" he replied as he looked at his watch and shifted into fifth gear "Anything from eight to fifteen hours from what I've heard. A very rough road."

"But it is used from time to time?" I asked.

"Oh yes, it is" he replied "Labour, machinery, fuel. All of it comes and goes by road. Either from here in Windhoek or from Walvis Bay on the coast, depending on the dunes and the state of the road."

"And you've never driven it?" I asked.

"No," he replied with a grin. "No, I stick to the skies."

I nodded and looked around at the scenery. To the left was the line of mountains I had seen from the air. The rocky soil was brown and bone dry with scrubby camel thorn trees and covered with clumps of dry, sun-baked grass. To the right, the landscape undulated and dipped towards distant hills. I opened the window slightly to let in a breeze and sat back in the seat. Fifteen minutes later we climbed a hill and veered left and the small city of Windhoek spread out below us. It was a mixture of old German colonial buildings and modern medium-sized blocks. The traffic was orderly and the verges and pedestrian walkways were neat.

"Well," said Danny "that's our city."

"A lot smaller than I imagined," I said. "And cleaner."

"Ya," he replied. "Compared to a lot of other African countries Namibia is very clean."

Danny pulled up to a set of traffic lights and stopped before making a left turn to skirt the city below.

"I could give you a short tour but I'm afraid we're on a bit of a tight schedule," he said. "Mr Klopp is expecting us by lunchtime."

"Of course," I said "Another time maybe. Do you know Mr Klopp well?"

"Um, no not really," he said fidgeting with the steering wheel. It was as if my question had rattled him somewhat and he was unsure of what to say.

"Do you not know him, Jason?" he said.

"No, never met the man," I replied.

"Oh," he replied, "I naturally thought you were with Apex and knew him."

"Nope," I replied as I opened the window to let more air into the now stuffy cab. "No, I'm just with the insurance company. I've come down to take a look. That's all."

"Oh okay," he said cheerfully as he pulled up at another set of traffic lights, "Mr Klopp is a bit of a difficult chap."

"Difficult in what way?" I asked.

He shifted in his seat and once again I could sense his discomfort at my questions.

"You can talk openly with me Danny," I said casually. "I'm not connected to Apex Resources or Mr. Klopp in any way. I'm just an independent insurance assessor from London. That's all. And I'm interested to hear your thoughts especially now you say you're not connected to Apex either."

Danny turned and smiled at me and I could tell I finally had his trust.

"Well Jason," he said with a chuckle, "let's just say Mr Klopp is a bit of a strange one."

"Strange in what way?" I pressed him.

"Well to be honest I don't like the man at all," he said. "He is one of the rudest, most unfriendly clients I have ever worked for."

"Go on please," I encouraged him.

"Well you can hardly get a word out of him when you talk to him," he said. "I've tried on many occasions and it's like getting blood from a stone. He is a stickler for absolute neatness and punctuality, which is why I said I couldn't show you around Windhoek- and to be honest, as far as I can see, the staff at the mine hate him. They say he's a cruel man."

He paused and looked at the surrounding houses as we drove, then turned to me again.

"Not a very nice guy at all," he said with a half-smile. "Sorry Jason, but those are my thoughts."

"Not at all Danny," I said casually. "I appreciate the heads up."

The road swept down through a leafy upmarket residential suburb and once again I was struck by the orderly streets and cleanliness of the place. The houses and gardens were well-maintained and neat and the kerbs were freshly painted. It was quaint, charming, and unexpected at the same time.

"We're on the outskirts of town now," said Danny. "There are some shops coming up just ahead if you'd like to pick anything up before we fly out. How long are you going to the mine for?"

"I have no idea, Danny," I replied honestly. "My brief is simply to go to the mine and have a look. Is there nothing available there at all? No shops?"

"There is a small mine shop," he said. "You can get cigarettes and other basic goods there, but you will be put up in the managers' compound and will be eating there as well."

"Well in that case no," I said, "I think we're good to go."

"Cool," said the young man. "We'll head straight to the airport."

The road continued down through the suburb until it bottomed out at a small shopping centre where we took a left turn. To the right was a tall fence with a large flat expanse of grass beyond.

"This is Eros Airport," said Danny. "Most of the light aircraft traffic in Namibia transits through here."

The road stretched ahead for a kilometre and we drove along on the faded tar in the bright sunlight until we arrived at a large bricked gate with guards and a mechanical boom. Danny produced an ID card to a uniformed guard and the boom lifted and we drove in. A minute later we arrived at a car park behind a low white building with a control tower to the centre. On either side of the building were a series of light aircraft hangars that ran for hundreds of metres either way.

"Well, here we are," said Danny as he switched off the engine and opened the door. "I just need to make a quick call before we leave."

"No problem," I said as I got out of the car and retrieved my bags from the back seat.

I stood in the shade of a bird plum tree and lit a cigarette as Danny made his call. The dry heat of the day was oppressive but still a welcome change from the frosty London mornings.

A minute later Danny stepped around the rear of the vehicle with a weary smile on his face and spoke.

"Sorry about that Jason," he said, "My girlfriend insists I call her before and after every flight. She worries a bit too much."

"No problem Danny," I said. "Is she here in Windhoek?"

"No, she lives in Cape Town," he replied. "I'm from there originally as well. We've been together for two years now. Anyway, shall we go?"

"Let's do it," I said.

I pulled my bag behind me as we walked through the car park and into the cool interior of the building. It was brightly lit and air-conditioned, with signposts for the various areas and offices. I followed Danny past the Customs and Excise offices and he paused as we arrived at a small shop on the right.

"I think I'll pick up some water," he said. "Always a good idea when flying in the desert. I'll just be a minute."

"No problem," I replied.

THE STAR OF THE DESERT

While he stepped into the shop, I paused and looked around the building. There was a mixture of tourists and locals, some working, others waiting around for their flights. The atmosphere was quiet, relaxed and pleasant. Danny emerged a minute later carrying a plastic bag with six bottles of water.

"Well," he said, "we're all set. Shall we go?"

"After you," I said.

We walked through a set of double doors and emerged into a large open waiting room surrounded by floor-to-ceiling windows. Beyond that was a small area of green grass with a low hedge and then the apron of the runway. Parked on the apron were twenty or so light aircraft and a few helicopters. The sunlight flashed from the chrome fittings on the aircraft and Danny replaced his aviator sunglasses before stopping at a desk near the exit. He took a pen and a clipboard from the attendant and signed us both out before holding the swinging glass door open for me. We stepped out into the fierce sun and walked down a concrete walkway to the apron. The Cessna 172 Skyhawk was white in colour with a red ribbon painted on the sides.

It stood among many other light planes forty metres to the left of the airport building, bright orange rubber chocks wedged under its three wheels. The four-seat, single-engine, high-wing aircraft was new and I sensed Danny's pride in it as we approached.

"Here we are Jason," he said as he opened the door and pulled the seat backrest forward to enable me to load my bags into the rear, "I just need to make some pre-flight checks and we'll be off. Please, jump in and relax. The cabin will cool down once we're in the air."

The dark blue leather of the seat burned my skin as I sank into it in the cramped space of the cabin in front of the right yoke or control wheel. Beads of sweat formed on my forehead as I cast my eye over the myriad of dials and gauges on the control panel in front of me. Danny walked around the small aircraft making his meticulous checks and logging his results in a notebook as he went. When he was finally done, he removed the chocks, placed them behind his seat, and climbed in.

"Wow," he said as he buckled his seatbelts, "it's a bit warm in here!"

After flicking a few switches and tapping a few gauges he removed the radio headset that hung on the control wheel in front of him and placed it on his head and ears.

"You're gonna need to put yours on as well Jason," he said. "It'll get a bit noisy in here!"

I lifted the headset from the yoke and put it on my head. The black leather of the speakers burned my ears as they had been sitting in direct sunlight. Danny flicked another switch and suddenly I heard his voice loud and clear through the headset.

"That's better," he said, adjusting the microphone arm so it sat in front of his mouth. "Can you hear me?"

"Loud and clear," I replied.

"Good stuff," he replied "Right. Let's go."

Danny exchanged a quick word with the control tower and two men in overalls, who had been standing on the apron in front of us, stepped forward and began pushing the plane backwards by the wing struts. Once clear of the other aircraft on either side Danny turned the control wheel until we faced the runway. He gave a thumbs up signal to the two men who responded with a wave and walked off. After one final check of the instruments he pushed the starter button and after a few judders the engine roared into life and the propeller blurred in front of us.

Danny turned to look at me with a half-smile on his face.

"All buckled up?" he said into the microphone.

"Yup," I replied.

He pushed the throttle forward and the small plane lurched forward and trundled along the concrete towards the taxiway that ran parallel with the runway. I watched as another light aircraft came into land on my right and listened to the distorted chatter between the control tower and the other pilots on the headset. The trimmed grass on either side of the slipway was yellowed by the sun and ahead, beyond the perimeter of the fence, the morning traffic passed steadily on the road.

Eventually, we reached the end of the taxiway and Danny made the right turn onto the runway. After a brief pause and a quick word with the control tower, he pushed the throttle forward and the engine roared once again. The interior of the cabin became a vibrating cacophony of noise as the small aircraft trundled down the runway gaining speed. It was soon after we passed the control tower and the hangers to our right that we became airborne. Beneath us, the small quaint city spread out with its orderly tree-lined streets stretching away towards the distant hills. The engine strained as we gained altitude and Danny made a sharp left turn heading West in the direction we had taken off from. Within minutes we had left the city limits and ahead of us, a range of rocky hills and mountains spread out towards the horizon. Once we had reached an altitude of 10,000 ft Danny finally spoke.

"So we are in what is called the green belt," he said. "For the next 40 minutes, we will be travelling over this range of hills and mountains and then finally over a place called the Boshua Pass. Once we get past there it's as if the world literally drops away into the desert. If you look down to your right, you'll see the only road that leads to the coast. It's called the C28 and it goes all the way to Walvis Bay. That is also the only way in and out of the mine by road."

I looked down and saw the thin yellow strip that was the road winding through the rugged and parched hills below.

"You said greenbelt," I said. "It doesn't look very green to me, Danny."

"No" he said laughing "but believe me once we get past these mountains, you'll see the real desert."

I sat back in the now cool air of the cabin and gazed at the endless vista of rugged hills and mountains below. I was immediately struck by the isolation and loneliness of the landscape. It was almost as if no humans had ever set foot there. After flicking a few switches and checking some gauges Danny turned to me with a satisfied look on his face.

"That was thirsty work," he said reaching back behind the seat, "how about a drink of water?"

"Sure," I said. "Thanks."

He retrieved two bottles of water from his bag and handed one to me. We sat in the bright sunlight of the cabin and drank the water while listening to the constant drone of the engine in front of us. I spent the next fifteen minutes casually chatting to Danny about how he came to be a pilot working in Namibia. Originally born in Cape Town, he had taken flying lessons during his years at university, finally ending up working as a bush pilot in the Okavango Delta in Botswana. It was two years previously while taking a holiday in Cape Town that he had met his girlfriend Charmaine. Not wanting to be too far from her he had found the job working for the charter company in Windhoek and had been there ever since. The closer proximity of Namibia to Cape Town and the fact that he would often have to fly there to collect clients meant they could spend more time together. I could see his enthusiasm when he spoke of her and it was clear to me that the young man was very much in love. It was not long after that I noticed a strip of hazy whiteness on the horizon. It shimmered in the distance and at first, I had no idea what I was looking at.

"That's the desert up ahead Jason," said Danny. "We're coming up towards the end of the mountain range."

"Wow," I said sitting up in the seat to look. "It's vast."

"It is," he said as he fiddled with a knob, "you certainly don't want to get lost anywhere in Namibia, that's for sure."

The thin belt of whiteness in the distance grew larger as we approached. It stretched away to the horizon and merged with the pale blue sky in a milky haze. Apart from the odd black boulder at the foot of the hills, it was featureless and completely flat. I had never seen such a desolate and inhospitable place in my life.

"Okay Jason," said Danny "we are now flying over the Boshua Pass. Ahead you can see the drop off into the desert and from here on it's all flat until we get to the big hole."

"Amazing," I said into the microphone as I stared down at the spectacle, "and how long from here to the mine?"

"About forty minutes from here," he replied, "forty minutes across flat empty desert all the way."

"How many workers are at the mine, Danny?" I asked. "Permanent staff."

"I'm not too sure Jason," he replied, "maybe three or four hundred people. The labour compounds are down towards the actual mine, but we will be housed in the upper section where the managers stay. You'll see the layout clearly as we come in to land."

"We?" I asked. "Are you staying there as well?"

"Yes, just for tonight," he replied. "I'll be taking Mr Klopp to Windhoek tomorrow. It's the usual delivery of product from the mine. I take him every two weeks, drop him at the airport and then bring him back the following day."

"So, you actually fly the diamonds out?" I said.

"That's right," he replied, "every two weeks like clockwork. There is an armed guard in the plane with us and we are met at the airport in Windhoek by an armoured vehicle that transports Mr Klopp and the diamonds to a secure facility. From there the diamonds are flown out straight to Europe. Mr. Klopp will supervise the whole operation until the package leaves on the evening flight from Windhoek International Airport. The only reason I'm staying at the mine tonight is because you arrived today. Usually, I would leave early, collect Mr. Klopp and be back in Windhoek by lunchtime."

"And how are they actually transported?" I asked. "The diamonds that is."

"Well they are held in a sealed aluminium suitcase," he said matter of factly. "Locked of course and handcuffed on a chain to Mr Klopp's left hand."

"Really?" I said. "Sounds like some very serious security."

"Oh yes," he replied. "It has to be. The whole operation runs like clockwork and there is absolutely no room for any deviation or error. Like I was saying Mr Klopp is a real stickler for punctuality and routine."

I saw the frown lines appear on his forehead as he spoke.

"To be honest it's the one part of this job I don't like," he said.

"Working for the mine in general or just Klopp?" I asked.

He sat in silence for a few seconds and stared out at the blinding expanse of flat white sand below.

"Well," he said turning to face me. "Mr. Klopp yes. I'm sorry, this is probably too much information and is quite unprofessional of me to tell you."

"Not at all Danny" I replied. "Like I said I really appreciate the heads up. Thank you."

My words lifted the atmosphere somewhat and we both drank some water before I changed the subject. I asked him about the other aspects of his job. It turned out that he often flew air safaris and would travel the length and breadth of the country delivering clients to remote luxury camps from the enormous red sand dunes of Sossusvlei to the wooded camps of the Caprivi and beyond. Often he would end up flying into Victoria Falls in Zimbabwe where the tourists would finish their trips in a luxury hotel and after a night or two would connect to Johannesburg before flying home. More often he would take well-heeled travellers on two-hour excursions from the small coastal town of Swakopmund south east over the dunes and back up the coast where they would see the many old shipwrecks and massive seal colonies that dotted the desolate shoreline. The young man was quick-witted with a ready smile and eager to tell me about his job. He displayed even more enthusiasm when I asked him about his aspirations for the future. He replied by telling me his dream was to eventually become a pilot with an international airline and have a family.

He said he had his eye on a small holding in Stellenbosch where he planned to build a home in the Cape Dutch style and eventually settle down. His conversation was engaging and his enthusiasm infectious and I found myself liking him the more we spoke. Here was a young man with a bright future and his whole life in front of him, doing the job he loved and doing it well. I paused and looked around for any change in scenery or visible landmarks, but the desolate flat white landscape stretched out to the horizon completely void of anything. I found myself blinking at the glare even through my sunglasses. I turned in my seat to catch a glimpse of the mountains we had passed but they too were out of sight and I was suddenly struck by a sense of total isolation.

"There is just nothing here," I said quietly.

Danny heard my mumbling and replied.

"Yup, a whole lot of nothing," he said cheerfully.

The constant drone of the engine and the warm sunshine that washed through the windscreen began to make me drowsy and a few minutes later I felt myself beginning to nod off. I was awoken soon after by the crackle of the radio through the headphones and Danny's voice announcing to the Windhoek tower that he was beginning his descent to the Apex Mine. I blinked my stinging eyes behind my glasses and took a drink of water before speaking.

"Guess the long flight last night caught up with me there," I said. "I dozed off."

"No worries Jason," he replied. "Was only a few minutes and you didn't miss anything."

Danny adjusted the revs on the throttle and I began to feel the pressure in my ears change as we dropped in altitude. I sat forward in my seat and looked ahead for any sign of our destination but there was nothing but the flat expanse of pale emptiness we had been surrounded by since leaving the mountains.

"You'll see it soon enough," said Danny. "It's basically a thin dark line of rocky ground with a massive hole in the centre."

Sure enough, the faint image of the geographical fault in the landscape began to appear out of the blurry mirage in the distance. From above it looked like a crack in the earth, albeit a tiny and inconsequential one. As we approached, I saw that it was indeed a small thin canyon with a raised rocky edge that stretched out on either side like a jagged knife wound in the desiccated flesh of the earth. Ahead to the right, I noticed a plume of dust that rose from the flat expanse of sand before being swept to the right by the ground wind.

"That will be one of the service vehicles on its way to the mine," observed Danny. "Probably a fuel tanker. You should be able to see the road, or what they call the road shortly."

THE STAR OF THE DESERT

Sure enough, as we approached I saw the chrome glint of the fuel tanker as it powered up through the desert towards the landmark ahead. The track was barely visible in the sand and great clouds of dust billowed up behind the vehicle as it went.

"What a place to drive a truck," I said as we passed the lonely vehicle below.

"Dangerous as well," said Danny. "If these trucks break down it can be days before the driver is rescued. There is no cellphone signal or radio contact down there."

We soon passed the tanker and as we approached the canyon Danny made a sweeping left turn followed by another to the right which afforded me a view through the window. Like he had said there was no mistaking the fault in the earth below that ran from left to right. From above it appeared small and inconsequential. Basically, a thin rocky canyon with a slightly raised rim. There was absolutely nothing to indicate the treasures that were held beneath it. Danny dropped the revs further and finally, the mine and the compounds came into view ahead of us. The 'big hole' he had spoken of was a lot larger than I had anticipated. At roughly 70 metres wide, and perfectly round, it cut straight down into the rock below to a depth of at least 130 metres. Above it, to the right were two large industrial buildings clad and roofed with what looked like asbestos sheeting. Both buildings belched thick clouds of dust constantly. Directly to the left of the first building was a massive pile of red and green coloured rocks that were being fed into the building by a large yellow front-end loader. Each rock must have been at least two feet in diameter and from above it appeared that each load the truck delivered to the building would be at least two cubic metres in volume. To the left of the building was the opening to a shaft that I imagined would lead to the floor of the great hole. As we approached, I saw a large, low-profile articulated mine truck emerge from the shaft towing a full load of rocks and heading for the stockpile. On the other side of the building, a long conveyor belt stretched up from the ground level and entered the nearby second building near the roof. The entire length of the belt was clad in steel plate and I saw the razor wire that surrounded the support poles from the ground level up.

Danny made another right turn directly over the hole and I saw at least a hundred workers clad in blue overalls with bright yellow helmets working at the bottom. They swarmed over the rough rocks like ants, pulling a myriad of thick dusty pipes and cables and positioning their pneumatic drills in spots that had been pre-marked in pink spray paint.

"Well," said Danny into the microphone. "There it is...the big hole."

"That is quite something," I said gazing down to my right. "Where does the water for all of this come from Danny?"

"That comes from an ancient underground aquifer" he replied, dropping the revs of the engine further. "I believe they pump it up from three hundred metres below the surface. At first, when the discovery was made, the diamonds were all alluvial. Then Apex came in and cleared those out. Soon enough they realized that they actually originated from what's called a diamond pipe. An ancient volcanic formation that made its way to the surface millions of years ago. It was in that pipe that the diamonds were formed and the shape or outline of that pipe is exactly what you see below. Effectively they are blasting and digging directly into that diamond pipe, straight down, to get at the ore."

"And there's nothing else around it anymore?" I asked.

"Nope," he replied as he flicked a switch, "not anymore."

I lifted my gaze and looked ahead. On each side below were five neat rows of tiny two-room houses. Fabricated solely from sheet metal, they were positioned at the same level as the mine workings and I could only imagine the appalling conditions of dust and heat their unfortunate inhabitants would endure. To the centre of them was what appeared to be a mess hall. I imagined it would be where the labour force would have their meals. The entire area was fenced off and the perimeter had been planted with a row of fast-growing wattle trees to barricade it from the outside world. Beyond the trees was a tarred road that ran parallel to the boundary of the compound. It stretched away to the left and rose up to meet another fenced-off area with a guard house and a boom gate. The buildings above were freshly painted and much larger than the shacks afforded to the lowly labour force below. Tarred roads linked the various buildings many of which had green lawns and palm trees surrounding them. The buildings were dotted up the face of a natural hill that rose above the dust of the workings below.

"That's the management compound," said Danny as he banked to the left. "We'll be staying there I'm sure."

We crested the hill and made a right turn back towards the desert passing over an area the size of two football pitches that was covered in great piles of crushed stone. I imagined it was the mine dump where the processed material was brought after the diamonds were extracted. To the right of that a runway stretched out directly behind the hill where the management compound was located. A simple flat strip that had been graded from the desert, it looked rough even from above. I gripped the side of my seat as Danny skilfully brought the small plane down and landed. After a few hair-raising bumps and judders we were down and I could hear the millions of tiny stones of the runway under the wheels as we slowed to a taxi.

Up ahead to the right was a large aircraft hangar or workshop with aviation fuel bowsers and pumping equipment nearby. The apron in front of the building was paved with concrete and the small plane juddered again as it mounted the lip of it to park. To the left of the building, two black men stood near a dusty Toyota twin-cab pickup truck. The words 'Apex Resources' were emblazoned across the side of the vehicle in bright yellow lettering.

Both men wore khaki long trousers, short-sleeved khaki shirts, and sunglasses. On their heads, they wore the same yellow mining helmets I had seen the workers wearing from the air. The men waited until Danny had stopped the engine then began to make their way towards the aircraft.

"Well Jason," said Danny as he flicked switches and unbuckled his seatbelt. "Welcome to Apex Resources Namibia."

"Thanks, Danny," I replied doing the same. "A really interesting flight."

Once I had unbuckled my seatbelt I looked up to see the shorter of the two men had approached my side of the aircraft. He ducked under the wing and opened the door with a wide smile of perfectly white teeth. Immediately I was struck and overwhelmed by a rush of dry heat so intense it almost took my breath away. It was as if the air outside was the exhalation of a blast furnace. It radiated off the blinding white of the concrete and engulfed me completely.

"You must be Mr Green," said the young man still beaming and offering his hand.

He was well-built and handsome and his hand was dry and firm in mine.

"That's right," I said as we shook hands. "Jason Green, pleased to meet you."

The young man introduced himself as Temba Zulu, a foreman for the mine. His enthusiasm and immediate friendliness reminded me of Danny and I knew instantly that I would like him.

"Welcome to the Apex facility sir!" he said keenly, still shaking my hand. "Please allow me to help you with your bags."

I stepped out of the plane and stood in the sunshine near the wing. It was like stepping into a giant microwave oven. I stretched my arms and looked around. Apart from the mine dump to my right and the barren hill in front, the landscape was completely flat and featureless. The flat, cream-coloured sand stretched away to the horizons eventually coalescing with the blue sky in a blurry and confusing mirage. *Fucking hell!* Immediately beads of sweat formed on my arms and forehead as Temba pulled my bags from the back seat of the small plane. I walked to the front of the aircraft to meet Danny and the other man who were standing in the sun talking to each other.

"Jason this is Max Chawora, one of the foremen here at the mine," said Danny.

I walked up to the man and introduced myself. In stark contrast to the young fresh-faced Temba, he was a big man, well over six feet tall, and slightly overweight. His face and arms glistened with sweat and he appeared lethargic and slightly lugubrious in manner. After a brief mumbled welcome and a limp handshake, Danny spoke.

"Gentlemen I just need a few minutes to look over the plane and then we can go," he said.

"No problem Mr Meyer," said Temba who had arrived carrying my bags. "We will wait for you in the vehicle where it is cooler. Mr Klopp is expecting you for lunch, so we have some time."

Danny nodded and walked back to inspect the aircraft.

"Mr Green, please follow me," said Temba.

I followed him to the parked vehicle. He quickly opened the back door of the fibreglass canopy and placed my bags inside before opening the back door for me. The truck's diesel engine was running and it was a relief to sit in the cool of the air-conditioned cab. His inspection done, Danny made his way to the vehicle and joined me in the back seat followed by Max who sat in the front passenger seat.

Temba took his place behind the wheel then reached down to the footwell where he retrieved two yellow hard hats. He turned in his seat and handed them to Danny and me.

"Sorry gentlemen but it's the mine rules that everyone should wear hard hats," he said. "Of course, you don't have to wear them when you're in the management compound but it's regulation everywhere else. I also have these identity cards for you."

Temba reached into the centre console and retrieved two laminated cards attached to nylon ribbons.

"Mr Meyer your card is for access to the management compound and Mr Green I believe your card is for access to all areas," he said handing them to us

Danny and I put our cards around our necks and donned our hats.

"Now gentlemen I think we are good to go," said Temba.

After reversing behind the hangar, Temba took a left turn and headed down a dirt road that skirted the base of the hill. After a brief wave to an armed security guard, we set off leaving a plume of dust behind us. We passed a small building with a sign on the front that read 'Apex Store'

"This is our only shop here at the mine," said Temba. "It's not very well stocked but it does have cold beer."

"Good to know," I said.

The road led to a security fence with a boom gate and another armed guard. Temba stopped the vehicle and we were all made to show our identity cards to the guard who logged our names in a book. Once done the boom was lifted and we drove into the mine complex.

With the hill to our right, we drove along a graded dirt road passing numerous warehouses and storerooms. All appeared extremely secure and some had permanent guards stationed nearby.

As I had seen from above, the area had been planted with trees to give the inhabitants of the mine the impression that they were not in such a desolate place. We passed a few workers, all in blue overalls and all wearing the distinctive yellow hard hats. Temba waved to them as we passed while Max sat morosely in silence in front of me. Eventually, we rounded the hill and arrived at the tarred road I had seen from the air. It marked the boundary of the workers' compound and beyond that the actual mine workings. It was surrounded by a tall security fence with razor wire atop it and was lined with a row of green wattle trees. Temba took a right and drove up the tarred road until we reached another tall fence at the base of the hill on our right. Once again there was a boom gate with a guard present and once again our names were logged into a book before we could enter. The area on the other side of the gate was in stark contrast to the rest of the site. Green lawns stretched up the hill and palm trees surrounded the small neat houses that dotted the hill. An underground sprinkler system was operating and spraying a fine mist of water at various points up the slope. The bungalow houses, although quite small, were freshly painted and were fitted with satellite dishes and air conditioning. The tarred road wound up the hill giving a view of the mine workings behind us. We passed a building on the left with floor-to-ceiling glass windows to the front and a shaded veranda with an outdoor seating area.

"That is the mine management dining room," said Temba as we drove past it. "We will be meeting Mr Klopp there for lunch but first we will take you to your accommodation."

Temba parked the vehicle under a carport at the second building from the top.

"Now then gentlemen," he said, "this is your house. If you'd like to follow me, I will show you the facilities and let you settle in."

Danny, Temba, and I got out of the vehicle leaving Max in the front.

We retrieved our bags from the back and followed the young man to the front door. The main room was bright, modern and airy and it was a relief to step into the air-conditioned interior. To the rear of the room was a small kitchenette with shelves that appeared to be stocked with tea, coffee, fruit, and cereal. On either side of the room were two doors that led through to bedrooms with double beds and en-suite bathrooms. On the table in the centre of the room was a laminated piece of paper with a welcome message and the WI-FI code. There was a cream-coloured lounge suite and a flat-screen television mounted on the wall.

"Well gentlemen," said Temba with a smile, "I think everything is self-explanatory here and I hope you are happy with the house. Lunch is at 1.00 pm in the managers' dining room and Mr. Klopp is expecting you."

He glanced at his watch briefly.

"That's in just over an hour," he said. "Would you like me to pick you up?"

"No that's fine," said Danny as he drank from his water bottle. "We will walk down. See you there."

"Great!" he replied. "See you ."

With that, Temba left and closed the door behind him. I walked up to the window and looked at the view that spread out below me. The rolling green lawns stretched down to the security fence and beyond that, I could clearly see the glinting sheet metal houses of the workers' compound. Beyond that, the two processing buildings were visible along with the top of the 'big hole'. Danny walked up next to me and stood drinking water as he stared out at the view.

"It's quite something isn't it?" he said.

"It certainly is," I replied. "I never imagined I would see such a place let alone be actually working here."

"Ya!" he replied with a chuckle before turning to go and sit on the couch. "I need to connect to the WI-FI and call my girlfriend."

THE STAR OF THE DESERT

I took a seat on the opposite couch, opened my bag and began to page through the file I had been given. I spent the next forty-five minutes reading up on the brief history of the mine whilst Danny typed on his phone. Eventually, he sat up, looked at his watch, and spoke.

"I think we better head down to the dining room, Jason," he said. "It's almost time."

"Sure," I said putting the file away in my bag. "Let's go ."

We stepped out of the front door into the blazing heat of the day.

Temba had left a key in the door which I locked behind me and pocketed. We made our way past the shaded carport and onto the tarred road that led past the other buildings down towards the dining room.

"Have you ever had to stay here at the mine before Danny?" I asked as we walked.

"No," he replied. "Usually I'm here for no more than a couple of hours. Of course, I've been to Mr. Klopp's office and I've had lunch at the dining room a few times, but never stayed."

"The house is fine though," I said.

"Oh ya," he replied, "I expected no less. Mr Klopp runs a pretty tight ship here."

By the time we had made it to the shade of the acacia tree near the dining room both Danny and I were sweating profusely. Although tables and chairs had been placed under the shaded veranda it was clear that it was far too hot to even consider eating outside. As we approached the tall sliding doors of the front entrance a young black woman in a green and white maid's uniform smiled from behind the glass and slid them open for us.

"Hello Mr Meyer, welcome, how are you?" she said in a musical voice.

"Oh, hi Betty," said Danny as we entered the room, "I'm fine and you?"

"I'm very well!" she replied with a beaming smile and a curtsey. "You must be Mr Green?"

"Yes hello," I said shaking her hand. "Pleased to meet you."

The young woman closed the door behind us and we stepped into the cool bright interior of the building. Placed neatly through the room were six heavy teak tables with matching chairs. To the rear of the room, behind a counter, a pair of tall glass-fronted drink chillers stood packed with bottles of water and soft drinks. The fittings were expensive and the red-tiled floors were polished to a mirror finish. On each table were crisp white cotton tablecloths with settings for six people on each. Danny and I were led to the top table at the rear where we were invited to take our seats marked by specifically placed small laminated name cards. Danny and I had both been assigned seats near the top of the table and a quick glance at the name card at the head of the table left me in no doubt as to who would be sitting there. The card read 'H. Klopp. Mine Manager'. The room was somehow reminiscent of a Bavarian beer hall only with a lot less cheer. It appeared everything had been precisely placed and measured down to the perfect placement of the glittering cutlery that lay before us.

"This is very formal," I said under my breath to Danny. "Not what I expected from a mine in the middle of the desert."

He gave a half smile and looked nervously at the glass sliding doors to the front.

"Very German," he whispered, "including the food."

I nodded as the pleasant young woman who had welcomed us approached.

"Now gentlemen what can I get you to drink?" she said still beaming. "It is very hot today. I have still or sparkling water and a full selection of soft drinks."

"Do you have any beers, Betty?" I asked hopefully.

"Oh I'm sorry Mr. Green," she said apologetically, "Mr Klopp does not allow any alcohol on the mine premises."

"No problem," I said somewhat disappointed, "just a still water then."

"And I'll have the same," said Danny.

"Thank you," said Betty as she made her way towards the chillers, "Mr. Klopp will be joining you very soon."

I glanced at my watch. The time was 12.59 pm. The drinks were delivered and both Danny and I poured them into the polished glasses that stood in front of us. At the stroke of 1.00 pm, I heard the crunch of tyres outside the building. I turned to see a black Mercedes Benz 4x4 vehicle pulling in at speed to the carport in front of the outside eating area. The windows were tinted, so it was impossible to see the interior. Emblazoned in large white lettering on the driver's door were the words 'Apex Resources One.'

I watched as Danny turned towards the bay windows with a slightly concerned look on his face.

"Here he is," he muttered, "right on time as usual."

I watched as the driver's door opened and the man stepped out of the vehicle. In his left hand, he carried a light tan-coloured leather briefcase. He wore dark jeans with a light cotton blue check shirt with long sleeves. On his feet, he wore leather shoes the same colour as the briefcase. He closed the door of the vehicle and strode towards the sliding glass doors with an air of urgency and purpose. The atmosphere in the room changed the moment he walked in. Gone was the smile from Betty's face as she hurried to the chillers to retrieve a bottle of sparkling mineral water. The man was tall. Over six feet, with broad shoulders and bulging muscles beneath his sleeves. His square, tanned Germanic head sat on a thick neck with close-cropped blonde grey hair. He nodded at Danny and me where we sat but without a word made his way to the counter where he placed his briefcase neatly in the centre of the table and collected his water from Betty. Having collected the bottle, the man made his way quickly towards us. As he approached, Danny and I stood up to greet him.

"You must be Mr Klopp?" I said with a smile, offering my hand, "Jason Green, pleased to meet you."

He stopped at the head of the table and nodded curtly at me.

"Heinrich Klopp," he said brusquely in a deep voice with a strong German accent. "Welcome to the Apex Namibia facility, Mr. Green."

He took my hand eventually and gripped it just a little too tightly as he shook it. It was a clear show of dominance.

"You will have our complete cooperation whilst you are here," he said. "For whatever reason that may be."

His statement immediately told me that he resented my presence at the mine and it was clear that I was unwelcome. I smiled and made light of the fact that I had been sent there in the first place.

"Thank you, Mr. Klopp," I said cheerfully, "I'm certain my visit will be brief and I assure you I'll not get in anyone's way."

Once again the man nodded at me before turning to face Danny.

"Daniel," he said gruffly as he took his hand, "I believe you are our guest tonight as well."

"Hello Mr Klopp," said Danny quietly, "that's right. I'm in the same house as Mr Green."

"I see," said Klopp. "Well gentlemen. Let us sit down to lunch. My time with you is short as I have business to attend to."

We sat down together and again I was aware that the atmosphere was strained and uncomfortable. As he sat I saw a brief flicker of annoyance on Klopp's face as he looked down at the cutlery. One of the knives to the right of his place mat had been put down slightly off-centre.

A frown formed on his forehead as he corrected it then, satisfied, he proceeded to open his bottle of water and pour the contents into the sparkling glass in front of him. As if on cue, the now unsmiling Betty approached and he handed her the empty bottle without a glance. Klopp looked at me with his cold piercing blue eyes. The rims of his eyelids were bright pink and his eyelashes were pure blonde. It was as if he was trying to measure me in some way. I smiled dumbly and looked to my left out the window towards the workings.

"Quite an operation you have here Mr Klopp," I said cheerfully, trying to break the awkward impasse.

My statement appeared to annoy him somewhat and he responded immediately.

"Yes, Mr. Green," he said sarcastically, "It is *quite* an operation."

Jesus Christ, what a piece of work! I thought.

Danny and I lifted the neatly folded napkins and placed them on our laps. The uncomfortable silence continued for what felt like ages until Klopp spoke once again.

"I believe we are having bratwurst for our luncheon today gentlemen," he said to no one in particular. "Is that correct, Betty?"

"Yes, Mr. Klopp," replied Betty from behind the counter as she busied herself.

"Hmm," said Klopp. "Excellent!"

At that moment another vehicle pulled up to the car park outside. I recognized the vehicle as the one that had collected us from the airstrip. This was confirmed when both Temba and Max walked in.

"Good afternoon," they said in unison as they removed their yellow hard hats.

It came as a surprise to note that instead of sitting at our table the two black men took a separate table on the other side of the room.

Danny and I both greeted the men while Klopp sat in silence staring into space. The fact that they were separated from us was a clear indication of either seniority or racism.

Either way, it was interesting to note and I remained a silent observer.

The strained atmosphere and awkward silence in the room continued until the door at the rear opened and Betty emerged carrying a tray laden with silver serving dishes. Her face was unsmiling until she saw the two black men on the other side of the room. Upon seeing Temba her face lit up briefly and once again I saw her smile. The gesture was returned by the young man and I knew immediately that there was a connection there. She made her way directly to our table and proceeded to place the various serving dishes in the centre.

All the while Klopp watched her like a hawk as if he were trying to pick out any fault with her service or delivery. My training had taught me to read people and I could tell that she was afraid of the man. Once she had finished setting the table she stood back and spoke.

"Please enjoy your lunch," she said nervously.

"Thank you, Betty," said Klopp as he lifted the top from the bigger serving dish.

Betty backed away and turned towards the kitchen door once again.

"Hmm," said Klopp as he looked at the sausages, "köstlich! Or delicious ... in English."

He proceeded to pile his own plate with the sausages followed by a generous helping of mashed potatoes and sauerkraut. He nodded to Danny and me to serve ourselves and began eating. I waited while Danny silently loaded his plate and then did so myself. Soon after, Betty emerged from the kitchen carrying a tray loaded with glass serving dishes. She made her way across the room towards Temba and Max and once again I caught the spark of familiarity between her and the younger Temba. The two men sat in silence as she placed the dishes on their table and then walked back behind the counter to wait.

Although the atmosphere at our table was strained and uncomfortable, the food was excellent and I made a few attempts at polite conversation.

Most of these attempts were responded to by Klopp with grunts or monosyllabic replies as he ate his meal vigorously and noisily. Although I tried my best to keep an open mind, I found myself disliking the arrogant, rude man. *Danny was right, the man's a prick.* Upon finishing his meal, Klopp placed his cutlery neatly in the centre of his empty plate, sat back and wiped his mouth daintily with the white napkin. Betty immediately approached and graciously removed his plate.

"Jawohl!" he said in his booming voice, staring ahead into space, "excellent Betty!"

"Thank you, Mr. Klopp," she replied meekly as she backed away.

It was then I noticed that in his top left pocket, he had four identical Parker pens. I knew they were identical as I could see the black enamel bodies of the pens through the cotton material of his shirt. It puzzled me as to why the man would carry four identical pens, but I quickly decided that perhaps the ink in each was a different colour and there must be some reason for it. I put the thought out of my mind and made another attempt at conversation.

"Well that was delicious Mr Klopp," I said cheerfully. "Thank you"

"Hmm," he responded. "Mr Green I believe that at 3.00 pm, our foremen will be giving you a tour of the facility. It will give you some time to rest."

"Thank you," I replied politely. "I look forward to it."

"I believe that head office has deemed it necessary for you to have an 'all access' pass," he continued with a hint of bitterness in his tone. "For what reason I do not know, but as I said, you will have our full cooperation."

By then the man's sarcastic tone and demeanour had begun to annoy me and I looked him in the eye as I spoke. He held my stare with his cold piercing blue eyes and I could see that by doing so I had rankled him. It was a direct challenge on my part and by then I was beyond caring.

"Thank you again, Mr. Klopp," I said sweetly, still holding his gaze.

The big man bristled and I saw Danny visibly shrink at what was clearly a passive confrontation.

Eventually, Klopp had had enough and as he stood his chair scraped noisily on the tiled floor.

"You will excuse me, gentlemen," he said gruffly, "I have work to do. Goodbye."

Danny and both stood to bid the man farewell as did Betty, Temba and Max. We sat down as he left the building and opened the door of the black Mercedes. Danny looked at me with raised eyebrows as if to say *I told you so*.

"Christ," I said to him under my breath, "What a prick!"

He responded by nodding knowingly as he finished the last of his water. The meal finished, we both stood to leave and after thanking Betty we passed the two foremen who were still eating.

"See you at 3.00 pm Mr Green," said Temba who stood as we passed.

"Thanks, Temba," I said. "See you then"

Danny and I stepped out into the blazing dry heat of the afternoon and made our way up the tarred road towards our cottage.

"Now I understand what you were talking about Danny," I said as we walked.

He chuckled quietly and shook his head in exasperation.

"Ya," he said. "Good old Mr. Klopp."

It was then I noticed the black Mercedes had been parked under a shade port near the house at the top of the hill. The surrounding garden was plush and dotted with cycads and palm trees. A gardener wearing the blue overalls of the mine was busy placing sprinklers and working on a rock feature.

"That must be his house," I said quietly.

"Yup," said Danny lethargically. "That's Mr. Klopp's house. King of the castle."

By the time we had made it back into the air-conditioned interior of the cottage my back was damp with sweat. I stood at the bay windows and stared out at the little green oasis I had found myself in. *A little green oasis in the middle of a vast baking hell hole.* Danny immediately slumped on the couch, flicked the television on and began texting on his phone.

"Hope you don't mind Jason," he said from behind me, "I think I'm gonna have a quiet afternoon here."

"Not at all mate," I replied still staring out the window. "You carry on. I'll sit with you for a while and then go on this tour that Klopp has arranged for me."

I walked back to take my seat on the opposite couch and pulled the file from my nearby bag. *Might as well read up as much as you can Green.*

5

Chapter Five: The Big Hole

The claims that Apex Resources Namibia had made with the insurance company were numerous and unusual, to say the least. In the past year, three men had inexplicably fallen into the mine and the subsequent payouts to their families had been huge. On another occasion, one man had apparently disappeared into thin air and his body was never found. It had taken six months for the Coroner to finally produce a death certificate and the whereabouts of the body was still a mystery. Of note was the fact that the missing man was one of the senior managers in the diamond sorting section. A highly-paid and well-respected job. These unfortunate incidents were in stark contrast to the high standards of safety that prevailed in the other mining operations owned by the Apex Group. There had also been several accidents involving hugely expensive vehicles and equipment. One morning, eight months previously, a dump truck valued at over $700,000.00 had been found smashed at the bottom of the access shaft to the mine. The security detail assigned to that section of the mine were dumbstruck and baffled as to how this 'accident' had actually happened. It was finally decided that one of the workers had somehow gained access to the yard in question and had managed to drive the massive vehicle down the shaft. After duties and shipping, the claim had cost the insurance company over $1400,000.00 to replace said vehicle. Added to all of this was the murky issue of minor discrepancies with the actual output of product from the mine. On more than one occasion there had been 'anomalies' with regard to the actual weight in carats of diamonds shipped to Antwerp. I took a deep breath and put the file back in the bag. I walked up to the bay window and stared out once again at the rolling green lawn and the crude, industrial complex below. The scene was buzzing with activity and dusty mechanical productivity. *Keep an open mind Green. It's clear you're not welcome but remember you are here on behalf of the insurance company. Not Apex and certainly not Klopp. You do your job and you go. Simple.* Temba arrived at 3.00 pm on the dot. I donned my hard hat, grabbed a day bag and made to leave.

"The truck is here Danny," I said. "I'll see you later."

"Oh right," he said. "See you later Jason. I'll be here"

I stepped out into the fiery afternoon sun and walked towards the parked vehicle. Max alighted and offered me the front passenger seat while he took his place in the back. Temba was full of smiles as usual and greeted me with enthusiasm as I took my seat in the cool air-conditioned cab.

"Mr. Green, I have been told to take you wherever you want," he said, "Is there anywhere you'd like to go first?"

"Well I'm in your hands Temba," I said. "Why don't we start with this great hole you have dug in the desert?"

"Certainly," he said as he started the engine. "We can start there."

We took the short drive down the hill through the green lawns and past the dining room building until we reached the security gate at the bottom. The guard nodded as he lifted the boom and Temba took a left turn down the road that ran parallel to the line of wattle trees with the workers' compound beyond. Soon enough we arrived at another checkpoint on our right and once again our identity tags were checked and logged by a guard before we could make the turn and enter. Immediately upon entering, we were driven directly through the centre of the workers' compound. On either side were the rows of galvanized tin shacks I had seen from the air. Here there were no trees or manicured lawns. Apart from a small satellite dish on the roof of each dwelling, there appeared to be no comfort or respite from the burning orb of the sun above. It was a place of work and nothing else. Dusty, desolate, and brutal.

Upon passing the rows of shacks we came up to what looked like the communal mess hall. Behind the building, I saw several people busy offloading foodstuffs from a refrigerated truck. The thick cardboard-covered slabs of meat were frozen and the khaki-clad workers formed a human chain as they moved the stock into the working end of the building.

"This is the workers' mess hall, Mr Green," said Temba. "They are busy preparing tonight's meal."

"I don't see many workers around," I said as we drove past.

"Most of them are in the mine now," he replied. "Preparing for 6.00 pm when we blast."

"I see," I said.

"We blast every day at 6.00 pm. sharp," he continued. "The dust settles during the night and then we remove the ore the following morning for processing."

"And this happens every day?" I asked.

"Every day without fail," he said proudly. "Here there are no weekends or holidays. The workers come in for three-month shifts and then have one month off to go to their families."

We carried on down the dusty road and passed a small building on our left that had a large red cross painted on each wall.

"This is the mine clinic," said Temba. "Any illness or injury is treated here."

I found myself marvelling at the stark contrast between where I had just been and where we were then.

Whereas the managers' compound had been a lush green oasis with manicured lawns and palm trees, this place I could only describe as a dust-covered dystopian hell hole. I had to remind myself that this was a working mine and not a place designed for aesthetics or beauty. Looming up ahead were the two huge asbestos-covered buildings I had seen from the air. Both towered ominously with their tall bleak facades belching dust and smoke and I could hear and feel the crushing and grinding of the raw rocks as we approached.

"We are going to drop Max at the crushing plant," said Temba as we pulled up to the heavily guarded gate to the complex. "He has some work to attend to. We will continue around to the mine."

Temba stopped the vehicle near the gate to the complex and we both bade farewell to Max as he alighted into the cloud of fine dust that we had created. He closed the door with a grunt and made off towards the boom. Temba took a left and drove parallel with the tall electric fence that skirted the boundary of the crushing plant.

We passed a large factory structure with massive hoists and gantries on our left that served as a workshop and I saw several parked articulated underground mine trucks and a team of mechanics working on a front-end loader. We carried on skirting the fence until we had passed the boundary of the crushing plant and ahead of us lay the rockstrewn rim that marked the surface of the diggings. Temba parked the vehicle nearby and turned in his seat to speak.

"Right Mr Green," he said. "We can take a short walk from here and you will be able to see down to the bottom of the mine."

"Great," I replied as I opened the door. "Let's go take a look."

The afternoon sun burned fiercely above and a hot blast of wind blew in from the east as we picked our way through the boulders towards the rim of the big hole.

"There is a steel rope barrier at the edge, Mr. Green," said Temba as we walked. "But I would ask you to please stay well back from the edge. It is quite dangerous."

"So I've heard," I said quietly as I stepped over a boulder.

Eventually, we crested the rim of rocks and the staggering scale of the enormous hole in the earth below opened up in front of us.

"Good Lord," I whispered to myself.

"Impressive isn't it?" said Temba with a note of pride in his voice.

"It's so much bigger than I thought," I said, as we approached the steel rope that hung from iron bars drilled into the rock at the edge.

Immediately I realised that what I had seen from the air earlier in no way was a true representation of the scale of what lay before me. Seventy metres across and a hundred and thirty metres cut and blown straight down into the rock. It was as if a perfect cylinder of the world had simply been removed. We stepped cautiously up to the steel rope and stared directly down to the workings below. The sound of multiple hydraulic drills and compressors filtered up and the workers below swarmed around like ants as they raced to meet their drilling targets for the day. The surface at the base of the hole was a mess of giant jagged boulders and dust. Great tangles of dusty pipework and cables spewed out of the access shaft like spaghetti and I was instantly in awe at the astounding lengths men would go to get to the tiny, seemingly inconsequential stones. I pulled the pack of cigarettes from my pocket and lit up as I gazed into the giant gaping cavity in the earth.

"Explain to me what is actually going on down there Temba," I said.

"The men are drilling," he replied pointing down. "They will drill two-metre holes in the rock everywhere you see the pink circles marked in spray paint. The drilling must be complete by 4.00 pm after which the equipment will be removed and the blasting teams will come in and lay the charges for the explosives. At 6.00 pm a siren will sound all through the mine and then we will blast.

The dust will be allowed to settle overnight and then the workers and the trucks will return the following morning to remove the ore and begin the process once again. This procedure is followed every day at exactly the same time without fail."

"That's astonishing," I said quietly as I stared down in amazement.

Temba laughed in delight.

"Thank you, Mr Green," he said "We are very proud of our work."

I stepped back from the steel rope and looked around at the moonscape of rock and dust. The wind that blew in from the east felt like a hair dryer.

"So," said Temba. "Where would you like to go next?"

"Perhaps we can take a look at the crushing plant?" I said crushing out the cigarette.

"Certainly," he replied. "We can take a look and I will explain as best as I can. Unfortunately, I cannot take you into the sorting facility though. I'm not authorised for that area."

He pointed at the identity card that hung around my neck.

"Of course, you are authorised for all areas," he said, "but I'm sure Mr Klopp will take you there in due course."

"That's fine," I said as we began the journey back to the parked vehicle, "let's just do a general tour of the mine for now."

The air-conditioning in the cab of the vehicle was a blessed relief from the heat and dust. Temba reversed and we made our way back down the dirt road towards the workshop and the crushing plant. When we arrived, he pulled up just short of the security gate and parked leaving the engine running. The tall, ominous, asbestos-clad building emitted a thunderous noise and spewed dust from every opening. Giant yellow loaders fed it constantly with rock and the sound of their engines mingled with the deafening racket from the building.

"So the entrance to the shaft is over there," he said pointing to the left. "The ore comes out on articulated underground trucks and is dumped near Crusher Number One. From there it is delivered using front-end loaders and the processing begins. Once the rock has been reduced to a size of roughly 20cm it travels up a secure conveyor to Crusher Number Two. That area has the highest security on the mine as it's from there that our actual product is extracted and sorted."

"And how is this all powered?" I asked as I stared at the scene.

"We have a huge diesel power plant near the mine dump," he replied. "We will see it as we continue our tour."

"Okay right," I said as one of the dump trucks reversed away from the building in a cloud of dust emitting a loud electronic beeping sound, "I saw a fuel tanker from the air."

"Correct," said Temba. "We use 40,000 litres a week here."

"Amazing," I said as I stared at the dystopian chaos to my left. "To think all of this is happening out here in the middle of nowhere."

"Oh yes," said Temba proudly. "We go to great lengths to do our job. It's not easy but we do it well."

"Indeed," I said. "You do."

"Now then," he said, "where would you like to go now, Mr Green?"

"I think we just continue on a general tour Temba," I said. "I'm in your hands."

We carried on down the road past the gate to the crushing plant. Temba pointed out the conveyor system that moved the ore to the second crusher building and the wash plant and sorting area beyond.

It was clear that security in that particular section was extremely high as there were armed guards stationed everywhere and yet more electric fencing. We took a left turn at the workers' mess hall and skirted the front left of the workers' compound.

"One thing has struck me Temba," I said as we drove on the uneven surface. "I have not seen many women here."

Temba laughed as he engaged third gear.

"You're right Mr Green," he said. "Apart from the nurse at the clinic and my wife, there are no women on the mine at all. Mr Klopp prefers it that way."

"Your wife lives here at the mine?" I said.

"Yes," he replied with a half-smile. "My wife Betty works as a maid for Mr. Klopp and also as the chef in the managers' dining room. She was the one working there at lunchtime today."

"Ah I see," I said nodding. "Oh well. Good for you."

We skirted the workers' compound to the right but my attention was focussed on the second crushing plant and the nearby buildings to the left. It was clear to me that the area was the real business end of the mine and I looked forward to the time when I would be able to take a closer look.

With the workings out of sight, we rounded the base of the hill and passed what Temba told me was the water reticulation plant. Once again, the area and its associated buildings and machinery were fenced off and guarded. A grouping of thick steel pipes protruded from the side of the concrete walls of the pump house before elbowing downwards and going underground to supply the workings and the compounds with water.

"The aquifer can produce 50,000 litres an hour," said Temba as we drove past "The water is crystal clear and pure."

"It seems lucky that you actually *have* water out here in the middle of the desert," I said.

"Yes," he replied "The mine is situated on an ancient watercourse. Without the underground water, our operation would be difficult, if not near impossible."

We continued driving down the dusty track until we reached the power plant for the mine. As usual, the area was fenced off and under armed guard. Three huge stainless steel storage tanks were at the centre of the yard and the fuel truck I had seen from the air was busy off-loading its cargo to the left. Near the front was a small building with a concrete forecourt and two fuel pumps while at the rear stood a factory unit that housed the giant generators that powered the mine. Soon enough we arrived at the mine boundary and yet another security checkpoint. With our details logged, the boom was lifted and we drove out into the flat expanse of desert beyond.

"We are now heading around to the mine dump," said Temba. "From there we will pass the airstrip and we will have done a full circle of the facility."

"Thanks for this tour Temba," I said "I've got a pretty good idea of the layout now"

"My pleasure, Mr Green," he replied.

As we drove I realised my instincts about the young man had been correct. I found him to be friendly, open, frank and dedicated to his job. He was also proud of his work and his position at the mine and I decided at the time not to question him about anything negative. I liked him a lot and I decided it would be best to keep our relationship light and cordial. He reminded me of Danny in many ways. Young, enthusiastic, and with a bright future to look forward to.

Temba stopped the vehicle near the vast mine dump that stretched away to our left into the desert. We stepped out of the vehicle and I lit a cigarette as we watched one of the giant tipper trucks from the mine approach in a cloud of dust to dump its load of processed stone.

"We call it fines," said Temba wiping the sweat from his brow with a cloth.

"Fines?" I asked.

"Yes," he replied. "Basically what is left after the crushing and sorting process. A fine powdery sand. You could also call it quarry dust."

"I see," I said. "And I guess it has no further use out here surrounded by thousands of square miles of nothing."

Temba laughed heartily at my observation.

"Exactly!" he replied. "There is no shortage of fine sand around here."

The huge burning orb of the sun was making its way down towards the east as I crushed out the cigarette and got back into the vehicle. It was a short drive to the airstrip and once again Temba waved at the guard who was stationed there. Before we had reached the perimeter fence and the boom gate at the entrance to the mine, we pulled up to the small shop we had seen when we arrived.

"How about a cold drink Mr Green?" asked Temba.

"Sure," I replied. "You mentioned beer earlier."

"Sorry Mr Green but I'm still officially on duty," he said "But I can pick you up after dinner if you'd like and we can come back for a beer. I'll be off duty by then."

"Sounds good," I said. "I'll just have a Coke for now."

I sat in the cool of the cab while he walked into the darkened gloom of the store. The glare of the setting sun shone through the windscreen and glinted off the razor wire atop the boundary fence ahead of me. The sandy soil outside the store was littered with discarded crisp packets and the dustbins overflowed with empty cans. I pulled the sun visor down to eliminate the glare and took a deep breath as I scanned my surroundings. *Christ Green. You certainly do find yourself in some unusual places.*

Temba returned with ice-cold canned drinks. We drove to the gate and had our passes checked and logged before driving into the mine complex once again.

"I hope this afternoon's drive gave you an idea of how things operate here Mr. Green," said Temba. "I'll take you back to your cottage now."

"Very much so. Thanks, Temba," I said. "What time is dinner?"

"That will be at 6.30 pm.," he replied.

" I'll see you there," I said.

He paused and shifted in his seat uncomfortably.

"Actually Mr Green I only have lunch at the management dining room," he said. "Dinner I eat at my house. But like we arranged I will pick you up after dinner, say 7.30 pm, and we will go for that beer."

I found it unusual that he and Max would eat their lunch at the management compound but not dinner. Sensing his discomfort on the subject I decided not to question it and instead let it ride.

"Perfect," I said cheerfully, "I look forward to it."

It was 4.45 pm. when we finally drove up the hill past the green lawns and sprinklers in the management compound to my cottage. I bade farewell to Temba and walked into the lounge to find Danny working on his computer at the desk near the front window. His hair was still wet from the shower and he had changed his clothes into more casual attire. The television was tuned to a news channel and there was a fresh pot of coffee on the kitchen counter.

"Hey Jason," he said looking up from the screen, "how was the tour?"

"Impressive," I replied as I poured a coffee. "This is quite an operation I must say."

I left him to work and sat on the couch to read some more from the file. The sun came down to the West and sent rich yellow beams of light through the windows.

It had been a lot to take in, especially after the long journey and even with the caffeine I began to feel drowsy.

"I'm going to lie down for a while," I said as I walked to my room. "Wake me up half an hour before dinner will you Danny?"

"Sure thing!" he said turning in his chair.

I lay on the bed and stared at the white ceiling above with my fingers entwined behind my head. The room was completely silent apart from the quiet whisper of the air conditioning.

So, what have you learned today Green? There is a huge hole in the middle of fucking nowhere. The work is hard and hot and there is little room for any comfort here. The people you have met? Mostly pleasant apart from a few obvious bad eggs. Too early to make any assumptions. It's obvious you're not very welcome but who gives a fuck? A job is a job and you're not here to be a congenial guest either. My thoughts drifted as sleep encroached and I saw the faces of the men I had met during the day. Before long I drifted into a deep and comfortable sleep. I was awoken, as promised by Danny at exactly 6.00 pm. It was then I heard the siren Temba had been talking of that afternoon. Feeling groggy I headed straight for the shower and emerged feeling refreshed and energized. After a change of clothes, I joined Danny in the lounge watching the news on television. As I sat down we heard the explosions of the blasting in the mine. They were deep and thunderous and they shook the very foundations of the building. We sat and waited a few seconds for the rumbling to finish.

"What are your plans tonight Danny?" I asked as I sat down.

"No plans at all," he replied. "I guess I'll just come back to the house after dinner and get a good night's rest before the flight tomorrow. I need to be at the airstrip by 6.45 to prepare the plane"

"And tomorrow you are taking Klopp and a shipment of diamonds to Windhoek correct?" I said.

"Yup," he replied. "It's pretty standard. Happens like clockwork and I'll be here the following day to bring Mr. Klopp back. Not sure if I'll see you though. I'll only be here for an hour at most. I have to fly down to Swakopmund afterwards."

"Tourists?" I asked.

"Ya," he said, "a group of Japanese clients. I'm taking them up to Etosha on a safari."

"Nice," I said.

We sat chatting until 6.25 pm. when Danny frowned and looked at his watch.

"Well," he said with a sigh and a resigned look on his face, "I guess we better head down for dinner."

I smiled to myself knowing full well what it was he was dreading.

"Let's do it," I said, standing up.

The air was still and warm as we made our way down the hill on the tarmac. I lit a cigarette as we walked and marvelled at the sunset over the mine workings. The dust from the blasting had risen and created dramatic psychedelic swirls of purples, reds, and yellows on the horizon. Below, the workings were silent and there was an air of peace and tranquillity in the stark twilight of our surroundings. We arrived at the dining room building to the welcoming smile of Betty who ushered us to the same seats we had used at lunch. Danny and I took our places and waited as Betty brought chilled bottles of water to the table.

"Tonight, we are having Eisbein," she said proudly. "One of Mr Klopp's favourites."

"Sounds good Betty," I said. "Thank you."

Heinrich Klopp arrived as I poured my water. I noticed Danny lick his lips nervously and glance at the door upon hearing the crunch of the Mercedes' wheels on the tarmac outside. The big man was still wearing the clothes he had been in at lunch and he strode into the room with purpose and bluster. As it had done earlier, the mood in the room instantly changed upon his arrival.

"Daniel, Mr Green," he said sternly as he pulled his chair out.

"Evening, Mr. Klopp," I said cheerfully as Danny mumbled a greeting.

"I trust your tour of our facility this afternoon was satisfactory, Mr Green?" he said without looking at me as he once again adjusted his cutlery.

"Very impressive," I said. "I had no idea of the scale of the operation."

"You mean to say that you came here without sufficient research, Mr Green?" he replied with a tone of sarcastic malice.

I saw Danny's eyes lift to mine in anticipation of my response to the challenge. I decided it would be best to play dumb and kill him with kindness.

"Well not really Mr Klopp," I said, "It was all a bit rushed I'm afraid."

"Hmm," he replied before turning to look for Betty.

As it happened Betty was making her way to the table carrying a chilled bottle of water. She placed it on the table in front of Klopp and backed away nervously.

"Dankeschon," said Klopp without looking at her, staring ahead into space.

"Daniel," he said suddenly. "Is everything in order for the journey tomorrow?"

"Yes Mr. Klopp," said Danny. "The aircraft is fuelled and we are due to leave at 7.30 am. I believe."

"That is correct," replied Klopp, once again staring ahead into space.

At that moment Betty approached the table once again and spoke in a meek, soft voice.

"Excuse me, Mr. Klopp," she said, "May I serve dinner now?"

"Yes Betty," he replied in a booming arrogant voice. "I am sure our esteemed guests are hungry and I hope they will enjoy our fine German cuisine."

"Thank you," she replied as she backed off and turned towards the kitchen.

The next few minutes were spent in uncomfortable silence as we waited. Klopp, once again, stared blankly ahead towards the windows and drummed the fingers of his right hand impatiently on the crisp white tablecloth. It was a great relief when Betty arrived carrying a silver serving platter with three enormous deep-fried pork knuckles. She placed

THE STAR OF THE DESERT

it in the centre of the table and immediately Klopp reached forward and lifted the biggest one onto his plate using a silver serving fork.

"Ja!" he said to himself in German. "Das ist gut."

Danny and I loaded our plates with the huge chunks of crispy meat as Betty approached carrying a tray with two more serving dishes. It was as she placed them on the table that I noticed her hands trembling. I looked at her face briefly and I could tell immediately that she was afraid. This was confirmed when she accidentally dropped one of the serving spoons which clattered noisily onto the meat tray. She froze with a look of horror on her face and I immediately felt awful for her.

"Dummkopf!" shouted Klopp at sudden volume. "Idiot!"

The outburst was loud and unexpected.

"Thank you, Betty," I said in an attempt to defuse the situation. "This looks lovely."

The poor woman backed away shaking and blinking tears from her eyes as she went. I felt the anger rise inside me but with an effort I managed to calm myself as I waited for Klopp to serve his own mashed potato and sauerkraut. *What a total fucking prick.*

Despite the initial upset, the meal was superb and I managed to finish most of it. Upon finishing his, Klopp placed his knife and fork neatly in the centre of his plate and stood up.

"Gentlemen you will excuse me," he said with a stiff bow. "I shall return home to complete some work. Daniel, I will see you at 7.00 am. Good evening."

The big man left the room without a word to Betty who waited in the wings. I glanced at Danny who sat with a satisfied but resigned look on his face.

"Jesus Christ Danny," I said "What a wanker."

The young man lifted his right hand to his mouth to contain his laughter. "I know," he chuckled as his body shook with mirth, "I did tell you."

Although we were offered dessert both Danny and I refused as we were both too full.

"That was spectacular Betty," I said as she cleared the table. "Thank you very much,"

My words seemed to cheer her up somewhat and I saw the smile return to her face.

"Well Danny," I said. "Shall we hit the road?"

"Ya," he replied. "Let's do that."

On the way back up the hill to the house, I asked the young man if he would like to come for a beer with Temba and me. He declined the invitation graciously saying he wanted to get a good night's sleep before his flight in the morning. I suspected that he would rather chat with his girlfriend but I couldn't hold that against him.

"I'll come with you to the airstrip in the morning," I said as we walked into the cool of the lounge.

"Sure thing," he replied as he turned the television on.

Temba arrived a few minutes later and I saw the lights of the vehicle as it made its way up the hill.

"That's my lift, Danny," I said. "See you in the morning."

The air was warm and still as I walked out to the waiting pickup. Above me, the stars blanketed the sky in a display of clarity I had never seen before. I glanced up the hill to my right and saw Klopp's black Mercedes parked under the shade cloth of the carport next to his house. *Heinrich Klopp. King of the castle.*

"Evening Temba," I said as I climbed in the front seat.

"Hi Mr Green," he said with a grin. "Hope you had a nice dinner?"

"Very good thanks," I replied.

It crossed my mind that I would say something about Klopp's outburst at the table, but I decided against it. It had been, after all, directed at the young man's wife and I saw no point in bringing it up so early in our friendship. *No, you can find where his loyalties lie and his real feelings with time Green. Keep it light for now.*

"There is a small pump house near the top of the back of this hill," said Temba "We could get a few beers and drive up there. It's not actually on the mine grounds and the road is rough but there will be a view even at night."

"Sounds good Temba," I said as we approached the gate. "Let's do that."

The drive to the main gate took five minutes and our exit was once again logged by the guard. Temba pulled up outside the store and parked in a cloud of dust. A small group of men sat outside in the darkness on plastic chairs drinking beer and listening to music. They all stood and greeted Temba warmly as he walked into the dim yellow light of the interior of the shop. It was obvious he was a popular figure on the mine.

He emerged a few minutes later carrying a six-pack of Windhoek Lager which he placed in a cooler box on the back seat.

"It's been a while since I've been up there," he said as he put the vehicle in gear. "We might have to use four wheel drive but I think you'll like it, Mr Green."

"Looking forward to it," I said.

THE STAR OF THE DESERT

The drive up the back of the hill was steep, slow and incredibly rough. On two occasions Temba did have to use the four-by-four to negotiate particularly rocky patches but eventually, we emerged at a flat point near the summit. Temba parked the vehicle near a low concrete block structure that housed a water pump and we both climbed out of the vehicle to take a look around. The millions of stars above shone like glowing silver glitter and cast an ethereal light over the desert below. A steady warm breeze blew in from the South and I marvelled at the spectacle as I took a seat on the concrete wall of the pump house.

"Now that is quite something Temba," I said as he passed me an ice-cold beer from the cooler box.

"Glad you like it, Mr. Green," he said as the pull tab of my beer cracked and the beer hissed.

The young man took a seat on the concrete nearby and we both sat in silence taking in the vast expanse of the Namib Desert in the starlight below. Eventually, we began to chat and, keeping the conversation light, I asked him about his history at the mine. He spoke openly about how he had joined the company soon after getting his degree in engineering from the university in the capital. He told me of his humble background and how his parents had toiled in the fish canning factories of Walvis Bay in order to put him through school. It soon became apparent that although he was humble and easy to talk to, he was completely loyal to the mine, and I knew it would be improper to ask him about the unusual events that had brought me there.

I decided instead, to keep our friendship amiable and light, and to enjoy the moment in the stunning surroundings I had found myself in. It was when he passed me the second beer that he pulled a brown paper bag from his top pocket and offered it to me.

"Would you like some biltong, Mr. Green?" he said.

"I would," I said taking the packet from him. "I haven't had biltong in a while."

The thin strips of dried, cured meat were perfectly spiced with black pepper, coriander, salt and vinegar.

"This biltong is superb Temba," I said as I chewed on a piece "Where did you get it?"

The young man chuckled as he took a sip of beer.

"Glad you like it Mr Green," he said. "I make it myself."

"Really?" I said turning to face him, "What is it, beef?"

"Game biltong," he replied. "Klipspringer. I go hunting on my days off."

I knew he was referring to a small antelope common in the hills of Sub-Saharan Africa.

"Where do you go hunting around here?" I asked.

"Oh, it's about forty kilometres South of here," he said. "There is a canyon and a few rocky hills. I like to go there to get away sometimes. I could take you there if you like. If you have time."

"Sure," I replied, "that would be great. I guess we'll see how things go at the mine."

It was clear that the young man had no idea the real reasons I was actually there and I had no intention of spoiling things by letting on. I was more than happy for the company and the break from the mine premises.

"Man," I said "I've got to have another piece of your biltong Temba. It really is superb."

He obliged happily and we sat in comfortable silence as we finished the beers. It was 9.40 pm. by the time we drove up the hill through the managers' compound to my cottage.

"Thank very much for this evening Temba," I said as I got out of the vehicle. "I really enjoyed it."

"A pleasure Mr Green," he said grinning at me from the driver's seat. "I will bring you a packet of biltong tomorrow morning."

"Now you're talking," I said as I closed the door. "Goodnight."

I watched as the vehicle reversed and made its way down the hill through the lush green lawns. As I turned to walk to the front door of the cottage I glanced up the hill at the house of Heinrich Klopp. The lights were still on and the vehicle parked where it had been when I left. I shook my head briefly and walked towards the door. My entrance startled Danny who had been dozing on the couch in front of the television.

"Jason," he said with a yawn. "You're back."

"Hey Danny," I said closing the door behind me. "It was very pleasant. We had a few beers at a viewpoint on the hill."

"Oh excellent," he said sitting up.

"I think I'm going to sit in my room for a while and do some work," I said grabbing my bag from the opposite couch. "See you in the morning."

"See you then," he replied. "Good night."

I closed the door behind me and plugged my laptop into a socket near the desk at the window. Below me, the lights of the workers' compound twinkled through the row of wattle trees and the ominous dark silhouettes of the crushing plants rose up to block the immediate horizon. I lifted the screen and stared out at the scene as I waited for the laptop to boot up. *Fucking hell Green. You certainly do find yourself in some strange places.* I sat and typed my rough initial impressions of the mine and the people I had met that day. I included my thoughts on Mr Heinrich Klopp although these would obviously be sanitized for my official report. It was half an hour later when the fatigue overtook me and I closed the laptop and lay on the bed. I closed my eyes briefly with the intention of getting up to turn off the light, but I never did. Almost immediately, I fell into a deep dreamless sleep.

6

Chapter Six: Secrets

I woke at 6.00 am. sharp and at first, I had no idea where I was. I lay there and looked around the room for a while as it all came back to me. I sat on the edge of the bed and stretched before heading to the bathroom for a shower and a shave. After dressing I walked into the lounge to find Danny making coffee in the kitchenette. He wore a freshly pressed white cotton short-sleeved shirt with the pilot epaulettes on the shoulders.

"Good morning Jason," he said with a smile. "Did you sleep well?"

"Morning Danny," I replied. "I did thanks, how are you today?"

"I'm doing great," he said. "Would you like some coffee?"

"I would," I said. "Thanks very much."

We both sat down with our coffee mugs and discussed the morning. For him, it would be the short flight with Klopp and the diamonds to Windhoek. I decided that I would accompany him to the airstrip to witness how the transfer took place. There would be no harm in doing so and although I found Klopp to be repulsive, I thought it might at least be interesting to see. I decided that later in the morning I would venture into the mine itself, to the bottom of the big hole, to see exactly how the ore was extracted. Then there would be the initial crushing process to cast an eye over. As far as the rest of the day was concerned there was plenty to keep me busy and already I was forming a plan for a nocturnal excursion later that night. It had been made clear by Klopp that my presence at the mine was not welcome, but I would not let that stop me from doing my job.

I intended to scrutinize every aspect of the operation from the ground up and nobody would stop me from doing so. It was 6:30 am. exactly when we heard the crunch of the vehicle tyres on the tarmac outside. Danny stood up and walked to the window for a look.

"That's our lift," he said as he walked towards the bedroom. "Time to go."

THE STAR OF THE DESERT

After grabbing our hard hats we both walked out to find it was Temba who had come to collect us. I glanced quickly up the hill to see Klopp's Mercedes was still parked under the awning of the carport.

"Klopp's leaving it a bit late," I muttered to Danny as we approached the vehicle.

"Oh, he'll be there," he replied ruefully.

The drive to the airstrip took less than ten minutes and once again I found Temba's company to be refreshing and exuberant. He laid out a few options for me to consider and happily agreed to my suggestion that we venture down the shaft to the base of the workings that morning. Even at that early hour, the heat was oppressive as we all got out of the vehicle beside the hangar. The far horizons had begun shimmering in the haze and I walked over to wait in the shade at the front of the building while Danny began his pre-flight checks on the aircraft. At 7.00 am. precisely I heard the approaching vehicles. There were three of them and they drove at speed in convoy down the dirt road leaving a plume of yellow dust behind them. The first vehicle was a standard white mine pickup with two armed guards stationed in the open load bay. The second vehicle was Heinrich Klopp's black Mercedes driven by the sullen Max, while another pickup took up the rear, again with two armed guards.

All three vehicles drove into the parking area near the hangar and parked parallel to each other at the boundary. Immediately, the armed men jumped from the pickups and glanced around in a show of force and authority. Upon ascertaining all was clear, a signal was given and the two occupants of the Mercedes emerged from behind the tinted windows. Heinrich Klopp made a beeline towards the waiting aircraft while the guards and Max watched from the sidelines. Klopp carried a thick aluminium briefcase attached to his wrist by a long chain.

Staring straight ahead he walked purposefully towards the plane. From where I stood it appeared to be an extremely well-rehearsed process conducted with military precision and all under extremely tight security. Rightly so, given the enormous value of the stones he carried in the briefcase. It was only when I emerged from the shade of the hangar that Klopp saw me.

"Good morning Mr. Green," he said with a look of disgust on his freshly shaven face.

"Morning Klopp!" I said cheerfully as I walked with him towards where Danny was performing the last of his pre-flight checks at the front of the aircraft.

Without greeting Danny, he opened the passenger door of the aircraft and climbed inside, placing the thick silver-coloured briefcase carefully on the floor beside him. I stood near the door with my hands on my hips and a dumb smile on my face. He pulled a pair of expensive sunglasses from the top pocket of his shirt and turned to face me as he put them on.

"You know you really did not need to come down here this morning. Mr. Green," he said looking at me with a scowl on his face.

"Oh, I did Mr Klopp," I said warmly, "I want to see everything."

The man pulled the open door towards himself and slammed it shut. I saw Danny physically wince at the sound. I smiled at the theatre of it all and walked around the front of the aircraft to bid farewell to the young pilot.

"Have a great flight, Danny," I said "and thanks for everything. I guess I might see you tomorrow when you get back."

"Thanks, Jason," he replied as we shook hands, "I'll only be here for an hour at most as I've got to fly down to Swakopmund, but if I don't see you then I'll be back to collect you when your work here is done."

I nodded and walked back to the shade of the hangar while he climbed into the aircraft and began his final pre-flight preparations. The armed men to my right stood silently and watched the proceedings from the apron. Eventually, the engine fired and the propeller spun into a blur. With a final wave, Danny pushed the throttle forward and the small aircraft moved off to the left to make its way down the runway. I was immediately enveloped by a wall of dust from the prop wash. With their work now done, the armed men started making their way back to the vehicles they had arrived in. I walked back to where Temba was waiting and lit a cigarette as the plane turned in the distance to face us. Soon enough there came the distant roar of the engine as the small aircraft began its run for take-off. It was only when it was parallel with the hangar building that it finally left the ground, climbing into the perfectly blue sky above.

I smoked and watched as the plane banked to the left and headed east towards Windhoek. Before long, it was a distant speck in the sky and a great silence descended over the place. I crushed out the cigarette and opened the door of the vehicle.

"Well," I said to Temba. "That was a lot quicker and easier than I thought it would be."

"Yes Mr. Green," he replied, "the same process will be repeated not too long from now. Such is the nature of the mining business. Where can I take you now?"

THE STAR OF THE DESERT

"I think we should start with some breakfast," I said feeling hungry.

"Good idea sir," he said with a smile. "My wife Betty does an excellent breakfast."

I smiled as I closed the door and we drove through the gate and onto the dirt road that led back to the main gate. With Klopp now out of the picture I felt a certain sense of calm and freedom as we took the rough road past the hill where Temba and I had sat the previous night. There were the usual formalities at the security checkpoint but soon enough we entered the mine premises and made our way down the row of wattle trees towards the management complex. After entering we parked the vehicle near the dining room and were greeted by the beaming smile of Betty who opened the door for us. I sensed a certain shyness on her part when she realized that I would be eating breakfast with her husband. I immediately put her at ease by explaining that we had shared a beer the previous night up on the hill. Ever the professional, she led us to our table, set us down, and gave us coffee. Temba and I both decided on the full English breakfast which was served 15 minutes later followed by a fresh pot of coffee.

The atmosphere was relaxed and informal and once again I found myself enjoying talking to the young man. His knowledge of the mining industry in Namibia was second to none and his willingness to share this knowledge with me was welcome given that I had basically been dropped in the middle of the desert with very little preparation. There was, however, a certain naivety to him. It was not that I thought he lacked ambition, but it seemed clear that he was more than happy in his current position at the company with his wife working nearby and would gladly continue to do so. It was 8:15 by the time we were done. Temba told me he would collect me from the cottage once the initial extraction of ore from the previous night's blasting had taken place. It would give me some time to watch the news and check my emails and I made my way up the hill on foot while he drove off to attend to some business. By then the sun was beating down in earnest and it was a relief to step into the air-conditioned interior of the cottage. I flicked the television on and retrieved my laptop from the bedroom. Sitting on the couch I typed out more initial impressions of the mine and the personnel I had met so far. I sent a quick email to the head office of the insurance company to let them know I had arrived safely and my work was progressing as expected. When I was finished I walked to the kitchenette and made a fresh mug of coffee. I stood at the front window and looked down over the manicured lawns at the tall structures of the twin crushing towers below. Both buildings were shrouded in a pall of dust and I could almost feel the grinding of the raw stone vibrating under my feet.

Temba arrived as I finished the coffee and I grabbed my hard hat and headed out into the furnace that was the morning.

"Well Mr. Green," he said as I took my seat in the front of the vehicle, "I have arranged for us to travel down the shaft on my personal quadbike It will be a lot quicker and easier than walking and safer too."

"Sounds fine to me Temba," I said, "let's go."

The drive through the compound to the ore dump and the entrance to the shaft took ten minutes. The security formalities at the boundary fence were thorough and complicated but eventually, we were allowed through. Ahead of us was a confusing, noisy, dust-filled blur of activity as the giant yellow front-end loaders lifted gargantuan loads of raw stone from the ore dump and delivered them to the conveyors and the gaping jaws of the first-stage crushing plant. The giant vehicles never stopped moving and kicked up blinding clouds of thick dust while emitting loud electronic beeping sounds as they reversed and manoeuvred in the space between the dump and crushing plant. At least a hundred men in their familiar blue work suits and yellow helmets rushed from place to place fixing giant water hoses to quell the dust while blowing into silver whistles to direct the controlled chaos of the place. All of them wore filthy brown-coloured dust masks over their noses and mouths. Temba turned left and skirted the boundary fence to avoid the traffic and chaos and drove around the back of the giant pile of raw stone that was the result of the previous night's blasting. Having done so we took a right and drove past the many parked underground trucks, some of which were being attended to by mechanics from the nearby machine shop. Ahead of us was the entrance to the shaft. It was set in rough concrete and painted with bright yellow and black chevrons. At the top of the gaping orifice were a row of spinning yellow lights and large sirens obviously for use during the evening blasting. With the extraction now complete there was a metal barricade blocking the front and a steady stream of workers busy carrying giant hoses and pneumatic drills making their way around it and heading down into the bowels of the earth. The scene was one of ordered chaos. A massive well-oiled machine designed to blow the very earth into jagged chunks and grind those chunks into dust. *Fucking hell. This is quite something.* Temba parked the truck at an area to the left of the shaft entrance.

A group of men had just finished spraying the area with a huge water hose that had left the ground a creamy yellow sludge. We both got out of the vehicle and immediately I was hit once again by a stifling blast of baking air that almost took my breath away.

"My quad bike is parked over here!" shouted Temba over the din.

The thick sodden dust was sticky and squelched underfoot as I followed the young man around to the left of the shaft where another group of men stood taking a break. They greeted us happily as we passed and walked towards the left-hand side of the shaft. Parked in the sun nearby and covered in a thick layer of dust was a powerful-looking Honda quad bike.

"Here she is!" shouted Temba with a wide grin as he straddled the machine. "Jump on Mr. Green!"

I climbed on the back and immediately Temba fired the engine. The machine lurched forward in the muck and we were off. He took a wide left turn and allowed the workers at the mouth of the shaft to remove the metal barricade at the entrance. Once that was done we moved forward into the gaping humid gloom of the shaft and began descending at a steep forty-five-degree angle. All around was a confusing mess of jagged stone walls that dripped with slippery moisture and the cacophony of the compressors and the hundreds of rock drills below came up towards us like a solid wall of noise. Along the jagged walls of the shaft were bright yellow industrial lights to guide the trucks and pedestrians who made the journey up and down every day. To the left of the shaft was a deep trench cut into the rock that housed a massive spaghetti-like mess of pipes and cables that fed power, air, and water to the workings below. I clung to the side rails at the back of the seat as Temba carefully negotiated the uneven, slippery surface. Eventually, we emerged at the base of the hole and Temba parked the quad bike at a foreman's station to the left of the shaft. There were at least two hundred men at work there and they scrambled over giant jagged boulders pulling air hoses and carrying giant pneumatic drills. The noise was almost unbearable and it was a great relief when Temba pulled two new sets of soft foam earplugs from his top pocket and offered me one.

"These will help Mr Green!" he shouted over the clatter.

I ripped the small plastic bag open and there was instant relief when I inserted the plugs into my ears.

"That's better!" I shouted back. "Thanks!"

Although I had seen it from above nothing could have prepared me for the utter bedlam that was the bottom of the big hole. The jagged walls rose 130 metres above us like a perfect cylinder to the sky above. Although I realized that the people who worked there every day were probably used to it, it still came as a shock to me. The heat, the noise, the dust, the water, were all overwhelming at first and I stood for a good five minutes taking it all in.

"Would you like to see a charge hole being drilled?" shouted Temba as he wiped sweat from his face.

I nodded back at him and followed as he scrambled over a pile of rock near the left wall and made his way along a thick air pipe to where three workers were busy drilling. We stopped a few metres short of the men and watched as the dull metal of the crude machine vibrated violently and shook the sweat-soaked body of the operator as he drilled. A steady flow of water pumped from a nozzle near the bit and splashed thick yellow mud on everything and everyone nearby. A few minutes later the men had finished drilling and they marked the completed hole by painting a large 'X' in pink spray paint on the rock. Temba and I walked further along the perimeter wall and stopped by a group of men who were working on a large cavity in the side wall.

It was at least six feet high, about a metre wide and stretched three metres into the solid rock.

"What is this?" I shouted over the din.

"That is an exploratory chamber," he replied. "We blast a few of them out every now and then just to check we're following the line of the diamond pipe correctly."

I nodded back in understanding and we both paused to look back towards the centre of the workings. By then the dust and the heat had gotten to me and I felt I had seen enough.

"Shall we head back up?" shouted Temba.

"Ya, I think so," I replied. "It's thirsty work down here."

He nodded and motioned towards the shaft opening. We both began the arduous task of making our way back over the rough and uneven surface. By the time we arrived at the foreman's station near the mouth of the shaft I was dripping with sweat and my entire body was covered with a film of pale dust. Temba and I both jumped on the quad bike and we drove off into the gloom of the shaft, climbing at the 45-degree angle towards the surface. We emerged into the baking sun and the loading of the ore into the first crushing plant was still in progress. Even so, it was a relief to be out of the pure chaos and the appalling conditions at the bottom of the hole. Temba drove the motorcycle around the metal barricade and made his way to where he had parked the truck. When we arrived, he pulled two chilled bottles of water from a cooler in the back seat.

"I think by now you might need one of these Mr. Green," he said knowingly.

"Jesus Christ, Temba," I replied as I took one of the bottles, "You're right I do."

The iced water was a blessed relief for my parched throat and I downed almost half the bottle.

"Well," I said, "I don't think I've ever seen anything like that in my life. The conditions down there are pretty tough."

He chuckled as he screwed the plastic lid back onto the top of his bottle.

"Ahh," he said. "You get used to it after a while."

It took a good three minutes for the air conditioning to cool the interior of the cab and we sat with the engine running and the windows closed with the constant muffled grind of the mine in the background.

"So," he said. "Where would you like to go now, Mr. Green?"

"I think I'd like to have a look at the first crushing plant if that's okay with you," I replied.

"Sure thing," he said amiably. "We can head over there right now."

Temba reversed and once more drove around the perimeter fence avoiding the huge pile of rocks and other vehicles. We passed the machine shop to our right and eventually parked near the front of the tall building that was Crusher Number One.

"I think you're going to need those earplugs again Mr. Green," he said as he turned the engine off.

"I'm sure I will," I said as I pushed the spongy rubber plugs into my ears. "Right, let's do this."

The scene was similar to the workings at the bottom of the hole as far as the dust and the noise were concerned. The giant front-end loaders came in one after another and dumped their huge loads of raw stone into a giant steel hopper. The huge machine vibrated on massive springs, eventually spitting out a row of rock onto a heavy-duty conveyor belt which travelled up towards the gaping jaws of the crusher. Although the process was mostly automated, there were groups of men on the tall steel walkways monitoring and controlling the flow of material. The noise inside Crusher Number One building was almost unbearable. From the clattering of the hopper to the squeaking of the rollers on the conveyor belt and the terrible mind-numbing din from the crusher, it was as if I'd entered a special kind of hell. Added to that the dust and the appalling, stifling heat, it was a perfect combination for very real discomfort. Regardless, Temba and I walked on under the steel gangway until we reached the base of the giant crusher. There were industrial extractor fans placed all around to protect the machine from the inevitable wear and tear that came from the dust. At the base of the machine on the far side, there came a steady flow of fist-sized rocks. They fell through a thick wall of steel mesh that was perfectly sized to the correct gauge needed for the second stage. The reject rocks that were not of the correct size vibrated down an angled shaft and returned to the main conveyor for crushing once again. The process was continuous and it was clear that the men in charge of the plant were under strict instructions that there were to be no breakdowns or stoppage of work. I stood for a few minutes and marvelled at the scale of the operation. Once again I was amazed by what lengths men would go to for the tiny stones. At the time they seemed so insignificant and miniscule compared to the gargantuan machines that were used to find them.

It was from this point that the security was stepped up for the second stage of the process. The conveyor that carried the fist-sized rocks was shrouded in a steel cage that rose at a 45-degree angle and travelled on up towards the second building not far from where Temba and I stood. From there I could see the electric fence and armed guards that surrounded the tall structure. Beyond that was a series of low concrete buildings none of which had windows. I wanted to question Temba about them, but the noise was becoming unbearable and I signalled to him that I had seen enough. *It can wait till we get out of here Green*. We both walked back through the building under the steel gangway and emerged into the beating sun at the entrance. I took another drink of water and pulled out the foam earplugs when we got back to the vehicle.

"You said you have no access to the second stage of processing?" I said to Temba.

"That's right Mr Green," he replied. "But you will be able to fully inspect it when Mr Klopp gets back tomorrow, I'm sure. There is the second crusher followed by the wash plant and the sorting rooms and the vault."

"Hmm," I said as I drank again from the water bottle. "I look forward to that."

By then it was almost 12.15 pm. and Temba spoke after briefly looking at his watch.

"Now sir," he said. "Lunch will be at 1.00 pm. I suggest I take you back to your accommodation so you can wash up beforehand and then we are free to continue this afternoon."

"That sounds fine Temba," I said. "Let's go."

THE STAR OF THE DESERT

It was 12.45 pm. when I walked out of the shower into my bedroom. I stood at the window with a towel around my waist as I dried my hair. Below at the mine the grind continued unabated and it was a great relief to hear the whisper of the air conditioner above the window. *This is a harsh place, Green. Possibly the harshest you've ever seen. Dangerous too. These men are here to work and that's all they do. So far it looks like a tight ship. You're going to have to dig quite a bit deeper to find out exactly what's going on here.* I ate lunch in the company of Temba at the managers' dining room. The meal of chicken schnitzel was superb and was served by a very happy and relaxed-looking Betty. It was as if Klopp's absence had lifted her mood and she fussed over the two of us like a mother hen ensuring everything was perfect. Afterwards, I spent an hour in the lounge of the cottage reading further from the file on Apex Resources Namibia. There was an interesting chart at the back showing the comparative use of consumables for each Apex mine in Southern Africa. Marked in red, to emphasise the difference between them, were the exact figures for nearly all of the equipment and spares used. The figures plainly showed that the Namibia operation was using almost double what the other, similar mines were using. I stared at the sheet of paper for five minutes as I took it all in. The figures did not lie. For a similar output of product, this mine was using almost twice as much and there had to be a reason for it. This was separate and apart from the outrageous insurance claims that were being made. But from what I had seen so far, the operation was a model of efficiency and order. I had seen nothing to indicate any tardy practices or carelessness. Feeling somewhat confused, I put the file back on the couch and stared at the blank television screen. *There's a reason Green. It's a puzzle. But there must be a reason.* The afternoon was spent touring a large factory building that served as the mine warehouse. Everything from huge electric and diesel motors to hoses and tiny rubber seals was housed in the building and every single item within was present and accounted for using an advanced computerised stock control system.

While I was inspecting the front desk a refrigeration engineer arrived to collect a new compressor for one of the blast freezers that had broken down in the staff mess hall. The faulty unit was offloaded from the open back of his truck using a forklift and a brand-new replacement promptly checked out and replaced by the same forklift. The broken unit was stored in a fenced-off area at the rear of the building along with everything else that had malfunctioned or failed. There was no single bit of machinery or equipment that could not be immediately replaced. Everything was in place to ensure the smooth running and efficiency of the operation. I left the warehouse feeling somewhat perplexed. There seemed to be no loopholes. No glaring reasons why this particular operation was any different to the others. Something was going on, but for the life of me, I couldn't see it. I spent the next two hours back at my cottage planning for the night ahead. In the back of my mind was the possibility that the trip might end up being a failure and that was something I wanted to avoid completely. My brief had included the instruction to take a good look at Mr Heinrich Klopp and with him being absent there was a perfect opportunity to do just that. I unpacked and laid the equipment I intended to use on the bed before going for a shower before dinner. The sun was setting and glowing like a deep orange orb through the headgear of the mine beyond the trees as I made my way down the hill to the dining room. I was disappointed to see the sullen and towering figure of Max shuffle in with Temba for dinner but the meal of braised oxtail and mashed potatoes more than made up for that. Betty, as usual, was helpful and attentive and when we were done I made an arrangement to meet Temba at 8.00 p.m. for another beer on the hill. As I waited for him in the cottage, I continued working on my rough report of what I had seen so far. The process was somewhat frustrating, as so far I had failed to actually see how and why I had been sent there in the first place. I was missing something and felt as if I couldn't see the forest for the trees. Eventually, I sat back on the chair and looked at the equipment I had laid out on the bed earlier. *Perhaps there'll be some answers later Green. All will be revealed.* Temba arrived at 8.00 pm. on the dot and we drove through the darkened mine premises and left through the main gate. After grabbing a six-pack of beer from the store we made our way up the hill to the same viewpoint we had sat at the previous night.

"Oh!" he said taking a brown paper bag from his pocket, "I forgot to give you this earlier."

The packet of biltong was bulging at the seams and tasted amazing with the cold beer.

"You say you hunt this yourself?" I asked.

"Yes," he replied, "mostly if and when I get some free time I take the quad bike and head into the desert. There is a rocky area with a canyon about forty kilometres from here. There is some game there."

"Forty kilometres out into the desert," I said quietly. "Sounds dangerous. Is there a road?"

"No sir," he replied, "I found the spot about a year ago. I keep it to myself. My secret place so to speak. It's peaceful and I get to have a bit of time alone, away from my work. Take a look."

He pulled his phone from his pocket and began showing me a series of pictures of the place. Stark and bone dry, it had a certain beauty and charm to it.

"How do these animals survive out there with no water?" I asked.

"There is water," he replied. "Not very much but at the floor of the canyon, there is some water."

"Well," I said munching on a fresh stick of dried meat. "The biltong is superb. Thanks very much."

The next hour was spent in pleasant conversation with the wide expanse of the constellations twinkling above. The night was quiet and a steady warm breeze blew in from the west. When we were done we took a slow drive back into the mine grounds and up the hill to my cottage. I said goodnight to Temba and told him we would meet for breakfast in the morning. When he had left, I made a beeline for my bedroom and began packing the equipment, I had laid out earlier, into a small black bag. When I was done I glanced at my watch. It was only 10.00 pm. and I needed to kill at least two hours before carrying out my plan. I tried in vain to watch some television but ended up surfing the internet and drinking coffee until eventually, at midnight it was time to move. After changing into some dark clothing, I smeared my face and the backs of my hands with black boot polish and put the bag on my shoulders. Finally, I checked myself one more time at the full-length mirror in the corner of the bedroom.

"Right," I said quietly. "Time to go."

I left the cottage using the back door which led out through the kitchenette. Before opening the door, I turned the dull yellow light off inside. I paused and squatted in the darkness near the drain and waited for my eyes to adjust to the darkness. Gradually it all became visible in the moonlight. Ahead of me, the hill rose steadily towards its summit while fifty metres above to the left stood the house of Mr Heinrich Klopp. My intention was to enter using the back door and take a good look at the inside. I knew for certain that the managers' compound was under armed guard but I also knew that they spent the majority of their time down at the entrance gate. In the event that one of them was to patrol the perimeter fence, I would surely see the light of the torch approaching and would have ample time to lie low and hide. In any case, my intention was to get inside the house as soon as possible where I would have the freedom to move about and the time to do so. I crept up to the corner of the building and poked my head around to look for any signs of movement. There was nothing and all was silent.

Crouching low I made my way up the lawn at the rear of the cottage until I was level with the rear of Klopp's house. I paused and looked behind me then sat for a while to listen, but everything was quiet. Keeping low I moved off to my left in the direction of the house and after a few minutes I arrived at the back corner. Panting lightly, I slipped around the corner into the darkness and stood there silently as I listened. Satisfied I had made the journey undetected, I took the bag from my shoulders and placed it on the ground at my feet. Using a pencil torch I retrieved the global GPS satellite tracking device from the bag. The tiny Japanese device was magnetic and had a battery life of six months once activated. I had debated whether or not to use it earlier that evening but had decided that as the company was covering all my expenses, there was no harm in doing so. Part of my brief was to take a good look at Heinrich Klopp and this was part of that. Squatting in the darkness I pushed the tiny button on the steel casing of the device and it immediately emitted a sharp electronic bleep to indicate it was active. Satisfied it was ready to be installed, I poked my head around the corner to take a look. The coast was clear and seeing a band of clouds drifting past the moon, I walked out along the side of the house towards the Mercedes that was parked under the shade cloth of the nearby carport. The device attached itself to the top of the inside of the front wheel arch with a satisfying clunk. I knew it would go undetected for a very long time and if I was unable to retrieve it, it would more than likely simply drop off the vehicle sometime in the next few years. I crept quickly back along the side of the house to the dark place near the rear where I had left my bag. I withdrew a head torch which I pulled over my head and retrieved the lock pick set. It appeared the layout of the house, albeit bigger than the cottage I was staying in, was similar with a back door and outside scullery to the rear. Leaving the bag in the darkness, I crept up to the back door, switched on the head torch, and got to work on the lock. It turned out to be a standard Yale house lock and it only took me four minutes to get it open. I crept back to retrieve my bag and with a final look around I walked back, entered the kitchen of the house, and closed the door behind me. I sat with my back to the door and turned the head torch off. The darkness was absolute and I closed my eyes as I caught my breath and listened for any movement.

THE STAR OF THE DESERT

The silence was overwhelming and the only sound was that of my heart beating in my chest. *That's it, Green. You're in!* A minute later I switched on the head torch, keeping the beam of light low and away from the curtains. I was acutely aware of the very real possibility that there may have been passive infrared motion detectors installed. Carefully, I moved the beam across the floor to my right and slowly lifted it up to check the corners of the room. There was nothing. I noticed the curtains to the left were thick and dark in colour. This would help prevent me from being seen by any patrolling guards. Keeping the beam low I stood up slowly and moved towards the centre of the kitchen. The silence was deafening and my shoes squeaked on the tiled floor as I went. The kitchen was spotlessly clean and modern but there was nothing there that interested me. I walked towards the door and slowly turned the handle. The front room was an open-plan dining room lounge similar to my own only bigger. Once again, I checked the corners of the room for motion detectors. There were none. Again, the curtains were heavy and dark in colour and this gave me the confidence to move around freely. The decor in the room was distinctly Bavarian with wooden panelling on the walls and stags' heads mounted between the curtains. It was clear he was trying to imitate the medieval half-timbered construction of grand old German houses. There were wooden sculptures of bears and other animals that I imagined had come from the Black Forest area of Germany. On the top of the curtain pelmet were rows of antique beer steins. The dining room table was fashioned from dark heavy wood and reminded me of a table one might find in a beer hall in Munich. To the right of the room was a large bookcase that caught my attention immediately. *You can tell a lot by what a person reads Green, that might be a good place to start.* I walked up to the bookcase and began scanning the titles from left to right. There were a lot of books on aircraft maintenance plus many very much older ones with titles in German that I could not understand. The second row was mainly populated with books about mining, some in English, some in German, but it was the third row down that really received my attention. Positioned in pride of place was a large collection of first-edition books about the Third Reich and the Second World War in Germany. Also present were four first-edition copies of Adolf Hitler's Mein Kampf.

Many of the other books had titles in German but I didn't need a translator. The emblem of the swastika was on many of the spines. *Well, well, well, I see now Mr Klopp. This explains quite a lot. I should have known all along that you're a fucking Nazi.* Positioned at the centre of the bookcase was a glass and wood display cabinet with a collection of medals mounted on green velvet. Using the light of the torch I scanned each one and recognized the Iron Cross First Class in amongst them. Although the bookcase and its contents spoke volumes about Mr Heinrich Klopp it was not what I had come to see. I needed to find his private office, the nerve centre of his operation. With a final glance around the room I made off towards a heavy teak door that I was certain would lead to the main corridor of the house. The hinges on the door squeaked as I opened it and the torch beam revealed a long corridor with a series of doors on either side. Once again, the space was designed to mimic the interior of an old Bavarian mansion with wood beam ceilings and shields and stag heads on the walls. I crept silently down the corridor and opened each door as I went. As expected there appeared to be several spare bedrooms and bathrooms but three of the doors were locked and these were the ones that interested me most. Being in a corridor there was no risk of the beam of the torch being seen from outside. I strapped it to my head and got to work on the lock of the first room. The mechanism was more sophisticated than the simple kitchen door one but after 10 minutes I cracked it and I heard the soft click as the tumblers fell and the lock opened. What lay beyond was clearly an office or a private workspace. The walls were filled with books and files of all descriptions and to the left of the room was an antique desk with a green leather centre. Acutely aware that the room was front-facing I kept the beam of the torch low and walked up to the windows to inspect the curtains. Thankfully they were made from the same heavy, dark material and had thick backing behind them that would enable me to move freely within the room. *Good. Very good. Time to get to work, Green.* With the head torch strapped to my head, I sat at the desk and began looking through the files closest to me. The majority of them appeared to be receipts and documents pertaining to certain properties around Namibia. At first, it was confusing and it took a while for me to realize what I was actually looking at.

Five of these properties were upmarket houses in the capital Windhoek while the other three were beachfront properties in Swakopmund and Walvis Bay. Initially, I was puzzled as to why he would have such files in his personal office, but I soon realized that he must be the owner of said properties. Many of the invoices and receipts were made out to Klopp himself while others were in the name of a company by the name of Coburg Holdings. Coburg Holdings was a name that cropped up in each of the files. It appeared Heinrich Klopp was a very meticulous man who filed anything and everything pertaining to these properties. Most of the invoices and receipts were for improvements and repairs and many had pictures attached of the work in progress and the final results thereof. The properties were large and expensive looking. I found myself wondering if indeed he did own them then how had he found the money to buy them. There was nothing in the file I'd been given to indicate he owned any properties in Namibia so naturally it came as a surprise to see this. Again and again, the name Coburg Holdings cropped up, many times with the name Heinrich Klopp as well. Using my phone, I took several photographs of the various invoices and receipts until I thought I had enough. I replaced the files where I had found them on the shelf at the top of the desk. It was then I noticed a file near the computer tower to the left which was marked in English, 'Rental Agreements'. This piqued my interest greatly and I pulled it out to take a look. In the file, as indicated, were several rental agreements between Coburg Holdings and various tenants. The leases seemed to be for 3 years each and the rentals were substantial when converted to pounds or US dollars. Once again, I took numerous photographs before replacing the file where I had found it. What I had seen was interesting, but in no way did it indicate that Klopp was up to no good. I had no idea that he owned property in Namibia and the file I'd been given had said nothing of the sort but the photographs I had taken and what I'd learned so far was potentially important. I sat back in the chair and looked around the room. To the left, surrounded by wooden bookshelves was a steel filing cabinet. I reached over and tried to open the drawer, but it was locked. I sat forward on the chair and studied the tiny lock mechanism. Using the lock pick set I attempted to open it. It proved fiddly and frustrating at first but eventually, I heard the click and I was in. The interior was a treasure trove of information.

One of the files contained a certificate of incorporation registered in the country of Namibia. The certificate was for a company by the name of Coburg Holdings, registered three years previously in the capital, Windhoek. Listed as directors were two people. Mr Heinrich Klopp and another man by the name of Ivan Cavalera. I placed the certificate on the desk and took a photograph of it. It was becoming clear that Klopp was indeed quite a wealthy man. Another of the files in the cabinet was for a chalet in the mountains of Heidelberg in Germany. The name of the holding company once again, Coburg Holdings. Again, there were numerous photographs of the property, rental agreements, invoices and receipts from various contractors. I sat back in the chair and took it all in before replacing the files and locking the cabinet. If the true extent of Klopp's property portfolio was not known by Apex Resources, it would certainly come as a surprise to them. I stared at the desk and noticed a leather pen holder standing in the corner. Inside were a bunch of sixteen pens. Feeling puzzled I grabbed them all and spread them out on the desk in front of me. All of them were Parkers and there were four sets of four identical pens. My mind went back to the pens I had seen in Heinrich Klopp's pocket in the dining room. *There were four pens, all identical, in his pocket. What the fuck?* I looked around the room and that was when I began to see the pattern. I stood up to look at a set of old German medals that hung in a display case on the wall. Hanging in a neat row were four identical German War Merit Crosses. They had been polished to a bright finish and they hung in perfect symmetry and the swastikas stood proud. *Four of each. Again.* I turned around to take a look at the bookshelf on the wall behind me. It was filled with mining journals and geology handbooks. And once again, there were four of each. Shaking my head, I stood up and walked back into the lounge to take a closer look at the beer steins that decorated the top of the curtain pelmets. By then it came as no surprise that there were four of each standing side by side. With a puzzled frown on my face, I walked back to the office to make sure I was leaving it as I had found it. It was when I was about to re-lock the door that I noticed the painting. It was an old oil depiction of the famous Neuschwanstein Castle, built on a rugged hill in South West Bavaria. The antique frame was ornate and heavy looking and for some reason I felt it warranted further investigation. Sure enough, when I attempted to move it.

I found there were hidden hinges which opened on the left of it and it turned out there was a small wall safe cleverly hidden behind the painting. Unfortunately, it was a heavy-duty combination safe and there was no way my rudimentary lock-picking skills would help me open it. With a fair measure of frustration, I gave the office a final glance to ensure everything was as I had found it and stepped back into the corridor. I looked at my watch to find I had been engrossed in the files for a good hour and a half. The time was 1.45 am. and there were still two locked rooms to investigate. *Better get a move on Green. This will probably be your only opportunity here.* I moved on to the next room. The lock was identical to the one from the office and within a few minutes, I opened it. I stepped into what appeared to be a very plain bedroom. Of course, it was decorated in the same Bavarian style as the rest of the house but there was nothing much of note within. However, it came as no surprise to me when I opened one of the cupboards to find the clothes neatly hanging and piled in identical sets of four each. This was repeated even down to the underwear, socks and shoes. *Four of everything all identical and all neatly stacked and hanging together. This man has a very strange obsession Green. Very strange indeed.* After finding nothing more of interest I stepped into the corridor and closed the door. I glanced at my watch before heading to the final locked door further down the corridor. Once again, the lock was similar and only took a few minutes to open, but it was what I found within the room that really shocked me. Heinrich Klopp had effectively created a private torture chamber for himself. A dungeon of sorts. The room was built without windows and, similar to the rest of the décor, the walls were fashioned from dark wood panelling. On the walls were a series of unnerving oil paintings depicting various acts of sexual torture from bygone ages. In the centre of the room stood a black leather bondage bed complete with ankle and wrist restraints and a stretching bracket. To the left of the room stood a full-length mirror set in a dark wood frame. Nearby hung a full-sized sex swing suspended from a large 'O' ring that was screwed into one of the beams on the ceiling. Standing near that was a large antique artillery shell case that contained all manner of whips, chains, and cat-o'-nine tails. An extensive collection of strap-on dildos, ball gags, masks, rack compactors, whips, and restraints hung from every available space on the walls and the room had a darkly ominous and gloomy atmosphere.

"Christ on a bike," I said to myself under my breath. "Very kinky indeed, Mr. Klopp."

The air was filled with the sickly-sweet aroma of latex and rubber and of the lubricants and moisturisers that stood atop an antique cabinet in the far corner of the room. I was immediately repulsed by the room which had the effect of making my skin crawl and I felt the urge to leave immediately. *Wait Green. The cameras. You need to place the cameras.* I stepped out of the room and squatted down in the corridor to retrieve the tiny devices from my bag. The lenses of the expensive devices were no bigger than two match heads but provided a clear fishbowl view of the room where they were placed. They were activated by either motion or sound and provided infrared vision in the event there was any activity without lights. Added to their impressive capabilities was the option to activate the sound recording on each device. I had tested this on a few occasions and although faint and tinny, it was easy to pick up conversations that were happening nearby. In short, if I placed them correctly and they remained undiscovered, the devices would transmit and record video and sound for the life of their Lithium batteries. Roughly 100 hours each. All that was needed was for me to link my phone or laptop to the pre-set WIFI code for the devices and I could watch and listen to the goings on within the target areas from anywhere in the world. The devices were hugely expensive but that didn't concern me in the slightest at the time. I placed the first pin-hole camera at the top right of the full-length mirror in Heinrich Klopp's torture chamber. The slim Lithium battery fitted snugly on tough double-sided tape behind the heavy wood of the frame. Even with the eerie dull yellow light turned on in the windowless room it would be totally invisible to the naked eye. Satisfied, I moved back to the office where I placed the lens atop one of the mining journals in the bookcase. I ran my finger along the tops of the books and it came back slightly dusty giving me a modicum of assurance that it too would go undiscovered. The third one I placed near the base of one of the beer steins in the centre of the front-facing curtain pelmet in the lounge. The height of it hid the slim battery perfectly and I knew it would take a concerted effort to find it.

I opened the app on my phone for the cameras. It took some seconds for it to find them but eventually an emoji of an eye appeared on the screen. I tapped it with my thumb once and instantly it showed there were three cameras active. I stepped back into Klopp's dungeon and tapped the first camera icon. The device responded by emitting a barely audible electronic bleep. Instantly the screen on my phone showed a clear image of me standing staring at it.

"Testing one two three," I said quietly.

A series of bars to the right of the screen rose up as I spoke to indicate the sound was functioning. I repeated the process with the other two cameras before checking again that I had left the rooms as I had found them. Finally, I returned to the corridor with the lock pick set to ensure all the doors I had opened were once again locked. Feeling satisfied that my work for the night was done I headed back through the kitchen to the rear door. I glanced at my watch before opening it. It was 2.45 am. and I had one final gauntlet to run before I was in safety. I pulled the curtain slightly to one side and glanced out at the hill that rose behind the house. The slope was bathed in moonlight from above and there was no sign of any patrolling guard. Feeling confident I pushed the door open slowly, stepped out into the hot night, and closed it behind me. It took me three minutes of twisting the lock pick set but eventually, the door was locked and as I had found it. With the bag strapped to my back, I moved quietly to the back corner of the building and glanced around at the carport and the road that led down the hill to the guard house. It seemed all was quiet from where I stood. I walked quietly back to the darkness at the rear of the house to prepare to make the crossing down the hill to my cottage. With a final look around I set off into the darkness moving at a diagonal angle down the hill. It was when I reached the halfway point that I heard the whistling and saw the first swing of the torch beam to my left. It was a guard on patrol. He was clearly doing the rounds of the perimeter fence and had decided to make his way back to his station directly in my path.

Instantly I froze where I stood and got down on my haunches. It was more than likely he was so used to his route he hadn't bothered to use the torch on the way up the hill. The quiet whistling grew louder and I moved onto my stomach and lay as flat as I could in the grass. *No fucking way! After all of that, there's no way this can happen, Green.* My limbs tensed up as the man approached totally oblivious of my presence. I held my breath and did my best to sink into the very earth as the swing of the torch beam got closer and closer. I gave a silent sigh of relief as he passed by, not three metres from where I lay. He never had a clue. I watched him as he made his way down the hill towards the tarmac road and only when he was twenty metres away did I dare to breathe once again. *Fuck. That was close.* I waited until he had finally joined the road before getting up and moving quickly to the back door of the cottage. I closed the door quietly behind me and breathed a sigh of relief. After a long shower and a cigarette, I lay on the bed in the cool of the air conditioner and stared at the ceiling. I had learned a lot. Klopp was not a poor man. Certainly, he was odd. His weird obsession with the number 'four' was one of the strangest things I had ever seen. There was no doubt he had Nazi sympathies and was obviously a sexual deviant. But there was nothing to suggest the man was a crook. There were more questions to be answered and I would have to dig a bit deeper for the answers. It would have to wait. It was late and I was totally exhausted. As I drifted off to sleep in the last vestiges of consciousness a scene like a movie played over in my mind. Heinrich Klopp was seated in the office of his house. On the surface of the desk was a glittering pile of diamonds. In his left hand, he held a small black velvet pouch. One after the other he picked up a single diamond with his right hand and dropped it into the bag. As he did so he counted out loud. 'One, two, three, four."

7

CHAPTER SEVEN: BAD PENNY

I woke at 7.00 am. sharp and my eyes stung from the daylight that filtered through the curtains. I felt exhausted but the memories of the strange discoveries I had made the previous night immediately filled my thoughts. I sat on the edge of the bed and yawned before getting up to boil the kettle for coffee. As I waited, I Googled the phenomenon of people being obsessed with numbers or a particular number for that matter. The results were interesting. It turned out that in most cases it was a simple expression of an obsessive-compulsive disorder or OCD. In more severe cases it was known as Arithmomania. A neurological disorder that sometimes develops into a complex system where the sufferer assigns values or numbers to objects or people in order to deduce their coherence. I shook my head as I heard the kettle boil and walked back into the kitchenette to make coffee. After a quick smoke outside the back door, I walked back to the laptop and sent an email to my principals at the insurance company. The main gist of it was simply to let them know my work was progressing steadily, but I did include a question asking them to make enquiries as to whether Apex Resources were in any way aware or had dealings with a company by the name of Coburg Holdings. There was no letting on as to why I was asking, but I knew that they would get straight on to it and would come back to me as soon as they knew. The account was simply too valuable for them to dismiss anything that might pertain to it. Once done I took a shower and a shave before heading down to the dining room at 8.00 am. I glanced up at Klopp's house as I walked through the already stifling morning and once again recalled the rather unsettling memory of his 'secret room'. Breakfast from the smiling Betty was superb and I ate once again with Temba who was anxious to know my plans for the day. Not wanting to be office-bound like I had been the previous afternoon, I suggested that I might want to see the fuel storage facilities before going to meet Klopp at his scheduled arrival time of 11.00 am. It was agreed he would collect me at 9.30 am. and I thanked Betty as we left. After another cigarette, I went back to my laptop to browse the news. I knew it was far too early to get a reply from the insurance company but as I sat at the desk I noticed, through the window, Betty making her way up to Klopp's house. I had been told by Temba that she worked as a maid for him alongside her main duties in the dining room, so it came as no surprise.

I felt a twinge of anxiety as I watched her walking and I knew that as soon as she entered, if the equipment was still operating as I had left it, I would get a notification on both my phone and the computer that the hidden cameras were both recording and streaming live video. I sat drumming my fingers on the dark teak surface of the desk as I waited. Not a minute later my phone pinged in my pocket and the tiny icon for the cameras flashed in the bottom corner of my laptop screen. I clicked on it and immediately it brought up three small screens. Betty had entered through the front door and walked right up to the camera I had placed on the curtain pelmet. The room was suddenly filled with bright daylight as she opened the curtains that had hidden my nocturnal activity only hours beforehand. I clicked on the small screen which then opened up to a full-screen view and watched as she inspected the room to make sure everything was ship shape for the imminent return of her boss. For a moment I worried that she might see something out of place and be alerted to the fact that someone had been in there, but my fears were unfounded and I watched as she made her way into the kitchen and I could hear her humming a tune to herself. *Christ!* I thought *I wonder if she does the same for Klopp's special room?* Thankfully she never once even tried to open the locked doors and after five minutes of rudimentary inspection, she left the house leaving the curtains in the lounge open. I watched as she made her way down the tarmac back towards the dining room where she would no doubt begin the preparations for lunch. Temba arrived a few minutes later and I closed the laptop, grabbed my hard hat, and headed out to meet him. A thick pall of dust shrouded the crushing plants in the distance beyond the row of wattles and I was secretly glad we were heading in the opposite direction. Security at the entrance to the fuel depot was tight and it took a good few minutes before our details were logged and we were granted access. Temba parked the vehicle in the shade of the depot workshop and we both got out to meet the shift boss on duty. The man spoke very little English but was welcoming and gave us free rein to inspect anything we wanted. Just as with the stores warehouse the previous day, each lot of petrol or diesel that was pumped was logged both on a computerised system and a physical delivery note that was signed for at every stage.

Temba and I watched as a dust-covered dump truck was fuelled up and headed back to the crushing plant. At the time it almost felt like I was simply going through the motions and I found it difficult to put the strange events of the previous evening out of my mind. It was 10.30 am. and the heat was becoming unbearable by the time Temba reminded me it was time to head to the airstrip to meet Klopp. He handed me a chilled bottle of water before starting the engine and heading for the gate. Before we arrived at the boom, a large diesel tanker arrived to make a delivery. Pulling 30,000 litres of fuel in the aluminium tank, it looked similar to the one I had seen from the air as we had flown in.

"Where would this have come from Temba?" I asked before taking a swig from the bottle.

"This would have come from the port at Walvis Bay, Mr. Green," he replied as he pulled over to the left to allow the giant truck to enter. "It would have taken the driver maybe eight or ten hours to get here. The road is pretty tough with the shifting sands in the desert."

"I'm sure," I said as the gears of the truck crunched and it began to move into the yard. I watched as the dust-covered cab passed Temba's closed window and it was then I noticed the company name painted in small black letters below the door. It read 'Cavalera Logistics, P.O. 6459 Windhoek', followed by a telephone number. *Interesting*, I thought. *I saw that very name in the files last night. Ivan Cavalera, partner of Mr Heinrich Klopp and co-director of Coburg Holdings.*

"Cavalera Logistics," I said as the huge truck passed and entered the depot. "Do they supply a lot of the fuel to the mine?

"Oh yes," said Temba matter of factly, as he engaged first gear and headed for the gate once again. "Not only fuel but pretty much everything here at the mine. All of our plant and machinery spares from crusher jaws to hosing and seals. And all the foodstuffs as well. A very big company here in Namibia."

"Okay," I said as the vehicle passed and Temba drove forward.

Going to have to look into that Green. Temba took a left turn and we drove out of the mine premises at the exit near the dump site. The sandy soil and rocks of the hill to the right sparkled in the mid-morning sun as we sped towards the airstrip leaving a plume of dust behind us. By the time we arrived and had driven through the gate, there was already a small welcoming crew consisting of Max and another security guard waiting. Totally ignoring our arrival, Max continued polishing the black Mercedes as we parked. Temba and I sat in the cool of the cab with the windows slightly down so we could listen. It was exactly 11.00 am. when I first heard the distant drone of the plane. It appeared as a twinkling speck in the sky, to the east, growing in size as it approached. The sight of the tiny aircraft in the vast emptiness that surrounded us was a stark reminder that we were totally isolated there. As he had done when we had flown in, Danny banked the aircraft to the north on approach and flew around the mine to meet the runway from the south. Temba and I got out of the vehicle and went to stand in the shade of the hangar building as the small plane landed to our left and bounced along the rough surface of the airstrip. We watched as Danny taxied the plane onto the concrete apron and came to a stop in the full glare of the sun in front of us. The passenger door opened before the propeller had stopped turning and I watched as Heinrich Klopp scowled impatiently as he waited for Danny to cut the engine.

A great silence filled the air when the propeller finally stopped with a jerk, and immediately Klopp alighted and started making his way towards the parked Mercedes. Once again, he carried the silver aluminium briefcase but this time the chain was not attached to his wrist.

My first thought was to offer my hand in greeting but it was clear he was in no mood for conviviality.

"Morning Mr Klopp," I said cheerfully as he walked past.

The big man scowled once again and simply grunted in acknowledgement of my presence as he strode towards the vehicle. I decided to put him out of my mind and walked instead towards the aircraft where Danny was still performing his post-flight checks. He opened the door as I approached and greeted me with a warm smile.

"Morning Jason," he said with his hand outstretched. "How's everything here at the big hole?"

"Going well thanks," I replied as I shook his hand. "How was the flight?"

"Smooth today," he said. "I have a short hop down to Swakopmund next. Should be ready to head off in twenty minutes or less."

"How was Klopp?" I asked with a half-smile.

Danny raised his eyebrows behind his Rayban sunglasses and muttered under his breath.

"He's in a foul mood today," he replied. "Didn't say a word to me the whole way."

"I noticed," I said. "Looks like he got out of the wrong side of the bed this morning."

"That's for sure," he said as he stepped out of the plane. "Man! It's a scorcher down here."

"It certainly is," I replied.

We both walked into the shade of the hangar building where we sat for ten minutes and drank a bottle of water each. Danny enquired how my work was going to which I replied that I thought I might be done within a few more days. He told me that as he was on permanent call for the mine he could return to take me back to Windhoek as soon as I was finished. For a brief moment, I wished that I was leaving with him that very day. The thought of spending more time with Heinrich Klopp didn't appeal to me in the slightest but I knew there was more work to do. After he had made a few more checks on the aircraft we bade each other farewell and I retreated to the shade of the hangar to watch him taxi down the runway and take off on a westerly heading towards the coast. I walked back in the sweltering heat to where Temba waited in the vehicle and climbed in.

"Will be lunchtime soon Mr Green," he said looking at his watch. "I'll drop you back at your cottage and we can discuss your plans for the afternoon afterwards."

"Sure," I said. "Let's go."

I opened my laptop as soon as I got back to check my emails. As I had expected, the insurance company had got straight back to me. The message was brief and clear. They had been in touch with the Apex Resources head office and had been told categorically that they had no knowledge of any company or organization by the name of Coburg Holdings. I sat back in the chair, stared out at the workings below, and drummed my fingers on the desk. *No knowledge. No connection to Coburg Holdings.* I sat forward once again, opened Google and typed in the words 'Cavalera Logistics Namibia.' The results came up and filled the page immediately. All directed to the website of the company which turned out to be fairly simple as far as content was concerned. I browsed it for a few minutes, clicking on various links but although it was slick and professional, it seemed there was not a lot to see. I clicked back through to the initial search results and paged down searching for any titbits of information I could find. Apart from a few old newspaper articles further down the search results it seemed as if the company preferred a low-key presence on the internet. My browsing was suddenly disturbed by the sight of the black Mercedes driving through the gate below and I watched as it pulled up to the car park near the dining room. I glanced at the time and watched as Heinrich Klopp alighted from the vehicle and walked stiffly into the building. *Right on time as usual. Time to go Green.* The lunch of fillet steak with mushroom sauce was delicious served with dauphinoise potatoes and green beans. The ambience, however, was ruined by the stony silence and tense atmosphere provided by Heinrich Klopp. I sat at my usual spot, with him at the head of the table and he stared icily into space as he ate, not saying a word as he did so. The only conversation was the muted mumbling from Temba and Max who were also at their usual table across the room. My own knowledge of his secret life as a Nazi sympathizer and a sexual freak further added to my own discomfort making the overall experience of being near him even more unsavoury. Regardless of all this, I kept up my act of cheerful ignorance, occasionally commenting on the food and thanking the very nervous-looking Betty as she served it.

It came as a huge relief when eventually the big man put his cutlery neatly in the centre of his plate stood up and pushed the chair back under the table.

"Good afternoon, Mr. Green," he said curtly. "I have work to attend to. If you find it necessary to inspect the final crushing and sorting facilities, I will be in my office until 5.30."

"Thank you, Mr. Klopp," I said without thinking. "That would be most interesting."

The man winced visibly at my reply but immediately recovered and bowed jerkily before walking off without a word to anyone else. The very fact that he had left the room seemed a relief to everyone who was left there. Immediately the atmosphere lightened and the conversation from Temba's table grew louder.

I sat back and took a drink of chilled water as I watched the Mercedes reverse and head off down the hill towards the gate. It was 1.50 pm. when I stood up, thanked Betty, and made my way over to where Temba and Max sat.

"I think I would like to see the final crushers and sorting process this afternoon Temba," I said. "Mr. Klopp has given me the go-ahead."

"Certainly, Mr Green," he replied as he stood up. "I will collect you at 2.30 if that is okay?"

"Perfect," I replied as I walked towards the sliding door. "See you then."

The walk back up to the cottage was airless and torrid in the blazing sun. Still feeling exhausted from lack of sleep I fought the urge to sprawl myself on the bed and instead returned to the laptop. The Google page was still open on the search results for Cavalera

Logistics. I yawned as I scrolled down through the results and was about to give up when I noticed an obscure website on the fifth page. It turned out to be the website for the Namibia Registrar of Companies in the capital Windhoek. Although it was primitive and looked like it had last been updated in the mid 90's it showed there were details for my search term. It was only after clicking and scrolling for a good three minutes that I had my eureka moment. It appeared that Namibian law required all companies registered in that country to appear on the website along with a list of said companies' directors and holding entities. The brief paragraph of information listed two names that I was familiar with. Mr Ivan Cavalera was listed as the sole director of Cavalera Logistics, while the company itself was owned by another entity by the name of Coburg Holdings. *That's it, Green. Well, I'll be damned, would you look at that.* I sat back in the chair and stared at the screen as I took it all in. Temba had told me that Cavalera Logistics was the main supplier of goods and materials to the mine. I had seen the fuel truck bearing the very name arriving from Walvis Bay. Apex Resources had stated categorically that they had no dealings with any company by the name of Coburg Holdings. A company that I knew full well was owned by Mr Heinrich Klopp and the mysterious Ivan Cavalera. So. in effect Klopp was hiding his involvement from his primary employers and milking the system for huge profit along with his partner. This would explain the inflated running costs of the Namibia operation in comparison to the other mines and would also explain the source of funding for the huge property portfolio they had built up. *Very clever Mr. Klopp. Very clever.* With my tiredness now forgotten I opened a new window on the screen and Googled the name 'Ivan Cavalera'. The results came back quickly and I clicked on one that looked promising. The website was for a newspaper in Brazil by the name of 'Estado De Sao Paulo'. Although the page was in Portuguese, there was the option to translate it near the top. It took two attempts but eventually, it showed in English. The article had been written four years previously and recounted a botched diamond deal involving a businessman from The United Arab Emirates and local mining magnate Ivan Cavalera.

    The deal had been for a consignment of industrial diamonds and was due to be worth over $50 million U.S. Dollars. The deal had failed to go through and both players were said to have been aggrieved and a subsequent criminal case had been opened in Brazil against Cavalera. At the top of the article was a grainy picture of a man standing on a beach with curly black hair, a beard, and dark sunglasses. The man looked like a caricature of a South American playboy. His shirt was unbuttoned to reveal a thick gold chain around his neck.

THE STAR OF THE DESERT

The caption beneath the photograph read 'Ivan Cavalera pictured in Rio De Janeiro in happier times'. The case had fizzled out without resolution as several crucial dockets had 'disappeared' from court offices and police stations. It had been suspected at the time that payoffs had been made to investigating officers and it was common knowledge that the courts in Brazil were notoriously corrupt. Cavalera himself had been said to have travelled to Switzerland soon afterwards where he was concentrating on building another mining venture. *Well well. It seems he has done just that. And very successfully too with his partner Heinrich Klopp.* There were a few other articles all with the same picture of the man, but it seemed that after the debacle with the Emirati, Cavalera had gone underground and was keeping a very low profile. *Until now.* I stared out of the window at the shroud of dust that hung over the mine workings below as I thought. *It'll be easy enough Green. Request the accounts for the mine for the last three years and it'll speak for itself. A simple price comparison and costing analysis can be done by an auditor in a matter of days. The proof will be easy to uncover and the evidence will be there in black and white. You've cracked it Green! Klopp is a crook and you have the evidence to prove it. The work here is done.* With my mind made up, I sat forward and began typing an email to my head office. I kept it brief but informed them that I believed that I had made a breakthrough in the investigation and requested that arrangements for my extraction and return to London be made as soon as possible. I knew full well that my request would be acted on immediately due to how important the Apex account was to them. Danny had told me that he was on call for mine business at any time and head office would be awaiting my report anxiously. After sending the email I closed the laptop and walked outside to smoke a cigarette in the shade of the carport to the side of the cottage.

There was a steady breeze blowing in from the east that felt like a giant silent hair dryer. I knew then that any further inspection or viewing of the mine or its processes would be simply an exercise of 'going through the motions.' The thought of spending any more time with Mr Heinrich Klopp was repulsive but I knew it had to be done. *You just carry on with the act Green. Play dumb for another day and then get the fuck out of here. Perhaps spend a day or two in a hotel in Windhoek while you write up the report? Might be pleasant.* Temba's vehicle drove through the security gate below as I crushed the cigarette out and I walked back inside the cottage to retrieve my hard hat.

8

Chapter Eight: Lucy In The Sky

Although my mind was preoccupied with my recent discovery, I knew it was important for me to go through the motions and I had a genuine interest in seeing the final processing. It felt as if I had been purposely excluded from it until then, but I put it down to Klopp simply demonstrating his authority and control. The young man greeted me with a smile as he handed me a new laminated clearance identity card.

"I've been given one as well," he said. "The security at that section of the mine is very tight."

"I can imagine," I replied as I pocketed it. "How often do you go in there?"

"Maybe once a month Mr. Green," he replied as he reversed the vehicle, "I spend most of my time supervising the blasting and excavation of the Kimberlite."

"Tell me about the final process as we drive please Temba," I said. "I'd like to have a basic idea of what I'm looking at before we arrive."

"Certainly!" he replied with his usual enthusiasm.

As we drove down the hill Temba explained the history of diamond mining in Namibia. He told me that the initial processing of the Kimberlite rock had not changed since the precious stones were first discovered. The giant rocks were blasted, extracted, and screened and then the crushing process began using giant jaw crushers and a series of ball mills.

Pools of silicon mud were used to float off any material with a specific gravity of less than 2.5 and then once again, after drying, the material was passed through another set of ball mills.

The long, steel-lined cylinders would revolve constantly and the fist-sized steel balls would tumble and crush to fine dust any material softer than 4 on the Moh hardness scale.

"And that process is the same today?" I asked.

"Exactly the same Mr. Green," he replied. "There's really no easy way to do it."

"And what happens next?" I asked. "How did the old timers do it?"

Temba went on to explain how, years ago, a series of angled steel tables were covered with thick grease and vibrated using motors and shafts with offset weights. The processed gravel was mixed with water and then run across the tables at a steady and controlled rate.

"Grease," I said. "Why grease?"

"To catch the diamonds," he replied. "The wet gravel will flow over the grease but a diamond can never get wet. Neither can the grease. So, in effect, any diamonds that are present in that gravel will stick to the greased surface of the tables like chewing gum on a blanket."

"I see," I said as we turned to drive through the worker's compound, "and I assume this old method, this process of vibrating greased tables is no longer used?"

"Correct," he replied with a smile, "No, now it is all computerised. Very high-tech. I will walk you through the entire process."

"I look forward to it," I said as we approached the boom at the initial crushing plant.

The first security check was done in a matter of minutes and we drove across the dusty ground with the towering structure of the first crushing plant to our left. As usual, there was a constant and steady flow of rock being delivered by the giant dump trucks. I could feel the earth rumbling below the vehicle as we approached the heavily guarded entrance to the second-stage processing area. Both Temba and I had to produce our new identity cards and once again our details were logged before the boom was lifted and we were able to proceed. We passed a tall electric fence beyond which was a separate fence made from razor wire. The mine had made certain that it would be extremely difficult to enter by any means other than the official entrance. On each post of the fence, a closed-circuit camera was mounted above clearly marked motion detectors. Temba parked the vehicle in the shade of a wattle tree and we both disembarked wearing our hard hats. Ahead of us was a modern, brick-faced single-storey building with tinted windows set in grey aluminium frames. There were cameras mounted on each corner and another at the entrance door. Temba and I walked up to the door where he pushed a green button, set above a small screen in the wall. The electronic buzzing sound was immediately answered by a human voice from within the building.

"Yes?" said the voice.

"Temba Zulu and Mr Jason Green," said Temba. "We are here to inspect the crushing and sorting facilities."

"Please look into the camera and hold up your identity passes," said the voice.

We did so and our photographs were taken before there was a loud buzzing sound from the door.

"Step inside please," said the voice from the speaker.

Temba pushed the door open and we entered the building.

The interior was bright, modern, and spotlessly clean. I could only assume that the building had been soundproofed as the only noise was the whisper of the air conditioning. At the back of the room was a reception area with a wide black granite counter and a uniformed guard sitting behind a computer screen. He greeted us formally and asked to inspect our passes which he did individually. Once satisfied he motioned to his left at a series of doors. Above each door were two lights. One red and one green. A sign written in red letters between them read 'Changing Area.'

"Please go ahead into the changing rooms gentlemen," he said.

Temba and I both walked towards the doors.

"Mr. Green, in the room you will find a pair of white overalls, a hard hat and a set of brand-new gumboots," said Temba as we approached. "There will also be a large cardboard box. Please remove all clothing down to your underwear and re-dress in the clothes provided. Please place your clothes and shoes in the box and bring them out with you. I will meet you back at the reception."

"Everything off down to the underwear?" I said.

"I'm afraid so Mr Green," he replied, "mine regulations."

"No problem," I said as I opened the door. "See you shortly."

The small room was windowless and as promised, sitting on a pine bench near a full-length mirror was a large cardboard box. Neatly packed in the inside of the box was a new hard hat, a pair of gumboots, with a spotlessly clean set of overalls underneath. I looked around the room briefly to see a camera discreetly placed in the far corner near the ceiling. As instructed, I began removing my clothes until I had stripped down to my underwear. Whoever had chosen the boots and the overalls had picked the right size and I stood in front of the mirror and zipped up once I was done. With my clothes and original hard hat packed into the box, I stepped out of the room and walked back towards the reception. The soles of the new boots squeaked on the tiled floor as I walked carrying the box which I handed to the guard. Temba was waiting already dressed in his overalls.

"All set?" he asked as I handed the box to the guard.

"Yep," I replied.

The guard placed the box under the counter, stood up and spoke.

"Follow me please gentlemen," he said making his way to another door to the left of the reception.

He entered a code on a keypad near the door and I heard the clunk of the locking mechanism as it unlocked. To the centre of the room stood a full body scanner similar to the ones found in airports. The guard motioned for me to stand inside the unit while he took a seat at the control screen. I placed my feet on the rubber surface on the inside of the unit and lifted my hands up as the diagram in front of me indicated. The scan took less than ten seconds and once done I was told to step through by the guard. I waited while Temba went through the same process and eventually joined me at the far side of the room. The guard keyed in another code and I heard the lock of the nearby door open.

"Thank you, gentlemen," he said. "Have a pleasant afternoon."

Temba and I stepped out the back of the building and walked in the burning sun towards the secondary crushing plant that stood a hundred metres ahead.

"That is some serious security," I said quietly.

"Oh yes," said Temba with a laugh. "Has to be that way, Mr Green. When we leave, the guard will even examine the treads on the bottom of these boots. Just to make sure there are no stones wedged in there. Before the body scanner arrived they would even check inside people's mouths."

"All for good reason I expect," I said.

"Yes," he replied. "Very few people get to see what we are about to see."

"What are we about to see?" I asked as we walked.

"Well first of all we will see the second crusher building. It's much like the first, only more sophisticated and automated. Then we will take a look at the silicon pools and finally the cyclone and X-Ray building. Then I believe Mr Klopp will be showing you the vaults."

"Sounds fine," I said. "Let's do it."

As Temba had described, the second crushing plant building was almost eerily deserted but there was an armed guard to escort us through the works. A series of closed conveyors with multiple sensors ensured a constant flow of material to the four ball mills which looked like 1950's science fiction style rockets lying on their sides. All four of them spun slowly and continuously and they fed each other through a complex series of belts and hoppers. Compared to the first crushing plant there was a lot less noise and dust and it was clear this was a highly automated and controlled space with only a few engineers wearing work suits patrolling and monitoring from the raised walkways. Wherever Temba and I walked we were constantly scrutinized by the guard and the many cameras that were placed throughout the building. It was a relief to finally take off the earmuffs we had been given and walk outside once again to stand in the shade of the building. We moved off towards the silicon pools after picking up some bottled water from the guard station nearby. The brief lapse in the noise allowed Temba to tell me more about the history of the diamonds of Africa. He told me of the freak stones. Diamonds that were so large or unusual that they had attained legendary status and been given their own names.

The Jonker and the Jubilee diamonds, and then of course the two most famous being the Cullinan diamond and the great Star of Africa which form part of the crown jewels of England. Although the young man spoke with a level of naivety, there was no mistaking the passion and knowledge he had for his work. His vivid descriptions were fascinating and swayed my thoughts from my recent discoveries. Had it not been for the almost unbearable heat I could have listened to him talk all afternoon. The silicon pools were comprised of four shallow ponds each the size of a tennis court. They were situated at the rear of the second crushing plant and I had been unable to see them from the ground. The entire space was surrounded by a tall concrete wall and two thick barriers of razor wire with security cameras placed at intervals of every ten metres. Temba and I climbed up twenty feet at one of the guard towers to see inside. Giant tangles of pipework emerged from the ground on either end like spaghetti and there was a constant dull drone of the water pumps in the air. Mechanised agitators moved slowly back and forth along the length of each pool leaving swirling bubbling wakes behind them.

"Everything with a gravity of less than 2.5 is floated off at this stage," said Temba, "that way when the material gets to the Cyclone it has less work to do."

"I see, and what exactly is the Cyclone?" I asked. "How does it work?"

"You know a cream separator?" he replied.

"I do," I said as I stared at the swirling mud below.

"Well the principle is the same," he replied. "Material of a certain gravity is spun away in a giant cylinder and what is left moves on to the final stage."

THE STAR OF THE DESERT

"And the final stage is what?" I said taking a drink from the bottle of water.

"The final stage is the X-Ray process," he replied. "What comes out of the Cyclone is dried and spread and then travels under an X-ray machine. Every diamond will fluoresce under that machine and its location is pinpointed by the computer. The computer then removes each and every diamond using a complex system of compressed air blasts and suction tubes. Once that is done the section of material travels through the X-ray once again to ensure every diamond has been removed. The system is accurate enough to extract stones as tiny as a grain of sugar."

"Amazing," I said shaking my head. "I had no idea it was such a complicated process."

"It is," he replied. "In fact from here onwards there is very little, if any human contact with the material until it reaches the vaults. The entire process is automated and 100% secure."

"Well I think we should move on Mr Green," he said wiping sweat from his forehead "We are about to enter the most secure area in the entire mine apart from the vaults."

"Fine," I said. "Let's go."

The walk to the hidden facility took a full ten minutes. Once again it was an area that was completely invisible unless seen from the air. Screened by rows of wattle trees and multiple fences, the exterior reminded me of pictures I had seen of Fort Knox. The wide and low, grey concrete building was surrounded by sharp palisade stake walling and I was certain the earth on the inside would be armed with underground sensors. The entry process took another ten minutes until finally, we walked into the cool and surprisingly bleak concrete interior of the reception. We were greeted by an armed guard who instructed us both to take a seat on a wooden bench to the right of the room.

"Mr Klopp will be with you shortly," he said.

Running through the centre of the room was a low steel-clad concrete section of wall. It stood four feet high and was roughly three feet wide.

"That is the conveyor that leads to the Cyclone," said Temba quietly. "As you can see there is little or no human involvement at this stage"

I nodded as the door to my right opened silently. Heinrich Klopp strode out of his office and towards us with a bitter scowl on his face. Temba and I both stood to greet him. Before we could say a word, he stopped in his tracks and spoke.

"Temba, I don't think there is any reason for you to accompany Mr Green and me on what will be a very short inspection of the facility," he said with genuine malice.

"No sir Mr Klopp, Temba replied "I can wait here."

"Mr Green," said Klopp with a sweet sarcastic smile, "if you would like to follow me please."

He turned on his heels and headed towards a large sliding steel door at the far side of the room. The big man entered a code on a keypad and the heavy door slid open with a hissing sound. The room beyond was cavernous and brightly lit with a huge white cylindrical structure in the centre. The steel-clad conveyor that ran through the reception room behind us ended at the base of the structure and a 20 cm. pipe rose from the concrete and was attached to the base. Numerous other pipes and fittings were attached to the strange-looking machine up its length until near the top of its upper conical shape there was one single steel pipe. On the right of the room was a control centre situated behind a soundproofed glass wall. Klopp spoke over the hum of the giant machine.

"Step this way, Mr Green," he said.

Two men in white coats were seated behind a series of screens and controls. Once the door was closed I was better able to hear what Klopp had to say.

"Mr. Green although I am very busy I have been compelled to allow you to see this part of the operation," he said with obvious disdain. "I would be grateful if this can be done as quickly as possible."

It was more of a statement than a question. I decided to play along once again.

"Certainly Mr. Klopp," I said. "I have no wish to disturb your work. A brief tour will suffice."

He set his jaw and continued.

"You are now looking at the controls for the final extraction of product from this mine. In front of you is what we call the Cyclone. From here, the material we need is transported through a series of blast furnaces for drying and then it travels into an X-ray room. Of course, that room is clad in lead sheeting to protect from radiation and we will not be able to enter but you can see the process on this screen here."

I leaned forward to see a view of the X-Ray room on the screen. There was a large rotating metal table with a series of honeycomb shapes on the surface. It moved constantly and I saw rapid puffs of air being blown from beneath it. I recalled Temba's description of the process and the feeling of being rushed by Klopp was overwhelming. I saw no need to dwell on it further.

"Where is this room, Mr. Klopp?" I asked.

"This room is beyond the blast furnaces Mr. Green," he replied impatiently. "From there stones are automatically transported to the vaults once there is a specific weight. Not one human hand is involved until the stones reach the vaults. The system logs every single activity constantly. The process is foolproof and incapable of error."

There was a definite note of pride in his voice as he spoke. It was as if he was trying to prove something. Once again, I played along.

"Is there any chance of seeing the vaults Mr. Klopp?" I said.

The man sighed deeply.

"If you insist Mr Green," he replied.

I followed him out of the control room and back into the din of the Cyclone area. From there we exited the room on the far side and walked along a corridor with steel doors on the left. Klopp stopped briefly and opened one of them. Beyond was a small viewing platform with a thick glass wall. The blast furnaces were set out in a row below and I could feel the residual heat from the process. Klopp closed the door and we walked further down the corridor past an alcove which had a large leaden door, set within which multiple signs read 'Warning Radiation'. There was no doubt it was the X-Ray room. we arrived at the entrance to the vault. The door was similar to the ones seen in banks and financial institutions. It was circular in shape with a chrome wheel in the centre. Above were a series of lights and to the left a keypad and screen were set into the heavily armoured wall. Heinrich Klopp casually keyed in a code and the wheel began to silently spin slowly to the left. Heinrich Klopp rocked on the balls of his feet and glanced at his watch in a theatrical display of impatience. Eventually, there was a heavy clang of metal and a hiss of compressed air and Klopp pulled the thick chrome handle at the right-hand side of the door. It was a physical effort and I guessed the door alone must have weighed at least a tonne.

Beyond was a surprisingly small room with a polished floor and ceiling of marble. Subtle lighting glowed from inset panels on the ceiling and we both stepped inside. The air was cool and crisp and the space was completely silent. The walls on either side were made up of a series of grey rectangular boxes with two simple keyholes in the centre of each. The guard stepped in behind us and both Klopp and he proceeded to unlock one of the boxes on the left-hand side. As soon as I heard the locks click, the box slid out slowly and a light in the centre of the chamber was illuminated.

"This is our product, Mr Green," said Klopp with a sigh. "I'm sure you would like to see."

I stepped forward and looked down into the box. Initially, the sight was underwhelming and seemingly insignificant. A small pile of dully glittering stones lay at the rear of the box. All in all, there were perhaps 200 of them. Their sizes ranged from around 2 millimetres to roughly the size of a small pea.

Their shapes were varied but I noticed a lot of octahedrons as well as other amorphous stones without defined shapes. Some were silvery-looking while others appeared dull and soapy, and it was at first a shock that such gargantuan efforts were actually made to extract them.

"Is that it?" I asked, incredulous.

"No Mr Green," said Klopp impatiently. "The process will deposit stones of varying sizes into separate boxes. I have chosen some of the larger ones to show you. A lot of the stones are of industrial grade and are no bigger than a grain of sand."

Of course, I knew full well that the sheer scale of the operation fully justified the final value of the product. That once cut and polished they would glitter and sparkle and gain value a hundredfold, but the sight paled into insignificance given what I had seen. *It seems so small! Miniscule even. All of that heat, blood, sweat and tears for this! Incredible.* I nodded and stepped back from the box.

"Thank you, Mr. Klopp," I said. "I will let you get back to your work now."

Without a word, the big man slid the box closed and he and the guard locked it once again. We stepped out of the vault, and I watched as Klopp swung the heavy round door closed and keyed in a code on the nearby keypad. The shiny wheel on the great door began spinning slowly until I heard the clunk of the heavy bolts hitting the strike plate. The guard accompanied Klopp and me on our walk back to the reception where we found Temba waiting as promised. He stood up as we walked through.

"I will now get back to my work," said Klopp. "Good afternoon gentlemen."

Twenty minutes later Temba and I emerged from the face brick building where we had changed our clothes. The meticulous security had ended with another full body scan and the guard examining the treads of our once-used boots.

"Well Temba," I said as we walked towards the parked vehicle in the late afternoon sunshine. "That was an education."

"A pleasure Mr Green," he replied. "I think you've seen most of the mine now."

THE STAR OF THE DESERT

"Yes," I replied as I climbed in and closed the door. "I think I have."

9

Chapter Nine: Strange Days

On the way back to the cottage I arranged to meet Temba after dinner for another beer up the hill behind the mine. He would collect me at 7.30 pm. and we would stop as usual at the mine store and pick up a few cans on the way. The afternoon had been a huge eye-opener and I realized then that the true scale and worth of the operation was staggering. Heinrich Klopp's ingenious malfeasance and milking of the system was established beyond doubt and there was a spring in my step as I walked into the bedroom and opened my laptop. As I had expected there was an email from head office. In short, they expressed their gratitude that my investigation was complete and went on to inform me that I was to be flown from the mine to Windhoek the following morning and to expect the plane at 11.00 am. The email went on to ask when I might have a report ready for them and also when I would like them to book my flight back to London. I knew full well that the actual date of my return to London was relatively unimportant to them - it was my report they were awaiting anxiously. I typed a quick reply thanking them for the information and informing them that I would have compiled a full report within 48 hours. I sat back in my chair briefly to consider when I should return to London. After a few seconds of contemplation, I sat forward and added that I would only request the London booking to be made once I had sent the report. *Good idea Green. London is miserable this time of year. Take a break. Do some sightseeing.* It was as I clicked the 'Send' button that I heard and felt the explosions from the blasting in the big hole below. I glanced at my watch before looking out of the window. The setting sun had once again caught the dust from the workings below the hill and turned the horizon into a massive bursting swirl of purple and orange. *6.00 pm. Right on time.* I closed the laptop and headed into the bathroom for a shower before dinner. There was very little conversation during the excellent meal of Rinderroulade and Kartoffelkloesse but it was a consolation to know that it would be one of the last times I would have to sit with Mr Heinrich Klopp. By then he too had learned that I was to be extracted from the mine the following day and I wondered if I had picked up a certain sense of relief in his manner. It might just have simply been his usual blunt and surly attitude.

Klopp had left the dining room early and I spent twenty minutes chatting to Betty after I had finished my dessert. It was only a few minutes after I had returned to the cottage that Temba arrived and we took a slow drive through the mine grounds to the store beyond the main gate. The beers were ice cold and there was a strong and constant breeze coming in from the east that made the warm evening even more pleasant as we sat under the swathe of stars on the rock at the viewpoint.

"I will be leaving the mine tomorrow Temba," I said between sips from my beer. "I wanted to thank you for your hospitality. I appreciate it."

"A pleasure Mr Green," he replied. "That reminds me, I have something for you in the vehicle."

Leaving his beer on the concrete he walked to the vehicle and returned with another packet of biltong.

"Ahh, fantastic," I said as he handed it to me. "Thank you very much, Temba."

"I will be going hunting at my secret spot this weekend," he said as he took his seat. "It's a pity you are leaving, you could have come with me."

"Hmm," I said thinking of the miserable London weather. "Sadly, I have to get back to work."

The next few hours were spent in light conversation interspersed with extended lengths of comfortable silence.

I had a lingering feeling of unease about the fact that I would be leaving both the tracking device on Klopp's vehicle and the pinhole cameras in his house. There would be no opportunity to retrieve them but I consoled myself with the fact that Heinrich Klopp would very soon be fired from his position as mine manager and I would inform head office to instruct Apex to retrieve them once he was gone. Whether or not they actually would do this was immaterial as they would go down to expenses if not. It was at 9.45 pm. when Temba and I took the slow drive back to the managers' compound and he stopped the vehicle at the cottage.

"Thank you, Temba," I said. "I'll see you in the morning. I believe Mr Meyer will be flying in at around 11.00 am. to collect me."

"Have a good night Mr Green," he said as he engaged reverse.

I stood outside for five minutes after he had left and smoked a final cigarette before heading in. All around was silent and I was feeling pleasantly full and tired. *Job done Green. Time to hit the road.* I glanced up the hill at the house of Mr Heinrich Klopp as I crushed out the cigarette. *Very clever, Mr. Klopp. Just not clever enough.* I opened the laptop and left it booting up as I took a quick shower. It was afterwards when I returned and sat down to check my emails that I saw the tiny camera icon flashing in the bottom right of the screen. After the pleasant evening I had spent on the hill it was the last thing I expected or wanted to see. I debated whether or not I should click on the icon for a good ten seconds until curiosity got the better of me and I succumbed. Three small screens popped up but only one showed any movement at the time. I leaned forward to look but it was too small, so I clicked on it to bring it up to full screen. Suddenly the sound came on and the screen expanded to full size to reveal an astonishing live stream. Heinrich Klopp stood rigidly in the centre of his 'dungeon' room wearing nothing but a studded black leather open-front thong.

His semi-erect penis protruded from the hole at the front of the thong and he stood facing the full-length mirror. In his right hand, he held a cat 'o' nine tails bondage flogging whip which he swished over alternate shoulders every four seconds. He did so with considerable force and it was abundantly clear he was inflicting a significant amount of pain on himself. His pale skin seemed to glow in the gloomy light of the room and it was only upon closer inspection that I realized he had smeared his entire body with some kind of lubricant. The initial shock of witnessing this extraordinary performance was amplified when I realized his lips were moving as he lashed himself. Mesmerized, I moved my finger on the touchpad of the laptop until I found the volume slider. Although slightly tinny, the sound grew in volume and I was immediately witness to a spectacle more bizarre than anything I could have possibly imagined. Heinrich Klopp was counting from one to four in German repeatedly. His voice was loud, strained, and high-pitched from the pain and his very obvious arousal. Upon counting to number four he replaced the German word 'Vier' with the word 'Klopp'. As he did so he brought the glistening whip with great force over one of his shoulders and I could clearly hear the sting and crack as the thin leather strips connected with bare skin.

"Eins, Zwei, Drei, Klopp!" he shouted as he brought the whip over his shoulder.

"Eins, Zwei, Drei, Klopp!" again he whipped himself, but now over the other shoulder.

He had a maniacal look in his eyes and his brow was furrowed with avid concentration. With every repeated blow his body shuddered and his semi-erect penis wobbled and bobbed.

"Eins, Zwei, Drei, Klopp!" he repeated.

"Eins, Zwei, Drei, Klopp!"

I sat back in the chair and tried to look away from this grotesque display of self-flagellation but it was simply too strange and given the circumstances, somewhat compelling.

What the fuck? What the actual fuck.

It was a full minute later that I was unable to control myself any longer. The laughter started as a silent body-shaking chuckle and steadily grew into great wheezing gasps of mirth. At one stage I counted out loud and slapped my own knee in time with the shout of "Klopp!" and I almost fell off my seat as the tears literally rolled down my cheeks. Eventually, I sat back in the chair and stared at the ceiling as I fought to control the convulsions of laughter. I forced myself to look away from the screen and wiped my eyes once again as I decided to walk outside for a cigarette. *Thank God you're getting out of here Green. Jesus Christ.* It was then that Heinrich Klopp's repeated chanting stopped suddenly and I turned once again to look at the screen. The scene in the 'dungeon' room that was streaming on my computer had suddenly taken a very chilling and sinister turn. The man appeared to be talking to someone out of the scope of vision of the hidden camera. I sat forward and cocked my head to hear who he was talking to. The female voice was faint but familiar, and my worst fears were confirmed when I saw the figure of Betty walk into the room. Heinrich Klopp placed the cat 'o' nine tails on the nearby cabinet and pointed towards the antique artillery shell in the corner.

"Take the stinger, Betty," he said in a strained voice.

I watched as she silently walked over to the tall brass shell and removed a long thin tapered cane. As she did so Heinrich Klopp lay down on the waist-high black leather bondage bed and made himself comfortable. It seemed that what I was witnessing was well-practised and almost routine for Klopp although I could not say the same for Betty. Still dressed in her uniform from the dining room she appeared fearful and reluctant for her part in it.

What the fuck?

With his head resting on the bulbous hump in the leather at the top of the bondage bed, Heinrich Klopp began masturbating slowly with his right hand.

"You may begin now Betty," he said.

I watched in horror as Betty took her position at the foot of the bed and began counting with the cane raised in her right hand.

"One, two, three, four!" she said quietly.

It was on the count of 'four' that she brought the cane across swiftly and the tip connected with the soles of Heinrich Klopp's bare feet with a high-pitched cracking sound. Klopp's body shook with pain and he began to masturbate faster.

"One, two, three, four!" counted Betty with another stroke from the cane.

"Harder!" cried Klopp as his body shook and trembled.

"One, two, three, four!" said Betty as she delivered another swishing blow.

By then all memories of my laughter had faded and I felt the nausea rising in my throat. I felt an overwhelming urge to close the laptop and block the vision from my mind but it was so completely outrageous and shocking that I found myself glued to it.

"Ja!" shouted Klopp. "Again...Harder!"

"One, two, three, four!" said Betty as the cane found its mark but this time with a loud crack.

Heinrich Klopp's body shuddered and his right hand became a blur of motion as he climaxed.

"Yaaaaa," he cried out loudly. "Yaaaaaa!"

Realising it was over, Betty walked silently back to the artillery shell and replaced the cane before leaving the room immediately. Heinrich Klopp lay convulsing and writhing on the now greasy surface of the bondage bed. Feeling completely gobsmacked and totally disgusted, I minimised the screen and clicked on the window that would show the lounge view. I watched as Betty walked towards the kitchenette and it was clear that she was sobbing quietly. She walked up to the sink and began to scrub her hands vigorously under the tap. It was as if she was trying to wash away the very memory of what had just transpired.

When she was finished she dried her hands and stood silently staring into space in the kitchenette. Two minutes later Heinrich Klopp emerged from the corridor and walked into the lounge wearing a silk dressing gown and slippers. He walked straight into the kitchen and approached Betty who stood motionless with her head bowed.

THE STAR OF THE DESERT

"Thank you, Betty," he said as he pulled a white envelope from his pocket. "As usual here is your tip."

Betty accepted the envelope with a brief curtsey. I knew that this was a common tradition for females of certain Southern African tribes and was commonly a gesture of thanks. At that time, however, it made me sick to my stomach.

"I hope we will keep our little secret?" said Klopp quietly.

With her eyes lowered Betty nodded and left the house quickly through the back door. I got up immediately and walked to the front room where I parted the curtains slightly and waited. I watched as she walked quickly down the hill to my right in the lights of the road. As she walked her body shook slightly and she dabbed her face periodically with a handkerchief. Betty Zulu was sobbing. Feeling profoundly shocked, I waited for her to walk out of sight and then retrieved my cigarettes from the room. I stood, still wrapped in just a towel, in the warm breeze outside and smoked. *This man is a monster, Green. Not only is he a thief, but he is also a deeply disturbed masochistic freak.* I turned to my right and looked up the hill towards the house at the top. *But you're not here to judge his private life, Green. Focus. Focus man! You came to do a job and that job is done. This is not your business. In any case, he will be gone soon.* I sighed deeply and thought of Temba.

This is his wife! Does he know about this? Probably not. The exchange of money would indicate that. That and the tears. Jesus. What a thing to witness! What a shame. That night I lay awake for a long time and tried to force the images I had seen, from my mind. In the end, it was only the knowledge that I would be leaving the next day that allowed me to sleep. I awoke at 6.30 am. and took a shower before opening my laptop to check my emails. The tiny flashing icon of the cameras distracted me and it was only when I had poured a cup of coffee that I clicked on it. Thankfully Heinrich Klopp was performing similar normal morning routines and I quickly minimised the screen as I saw no use in watching him further. I knew there would be one final meeting before Danny arrived to fly me out and given what I had seen I was dreading it. I watched some news on the television until it was time to head down for breakfast. As I walked I thought about poor Betty and the appalling scene from the previous evening. *Game face Green. It never happened. Just be normal.* It was as I was on the driveway near the dining room that the black Mercedes pulled up at speed and parked near me. Heinrich Klopp stepped out of the vehicle with a smugly satisfied and arrogant look on his face. He wore a full sleeve light cotton chequered shirt and he strode past me on his way to the sliding door. I have no idea what came over me but the very sight of him flicked a switch in my brain. It was completely spontaneous and unplanned but as he passed me I gave him a friendly but firm clap on his back which I knew would be painful from the previous night.

"Morning, Klopp!" I said smiling cheerfully as I walked. "Lovely day isn't it?"

The big man suddenly stopped in his tracks and turned to look at me. His face turned bright purple with rage and his left eye twitched uncontrollably.

"Never touch me," he hissed through gritted teeth.

"What's up, Klopp?" I said loudly. "You look a bit unsteady on your feet today. Are you okay?"

The big man leant forward and brought his face close to mine. I saw the veins in his neck and temple swell as he fought to control his fury.

"Mr Green," he growled, "whatever you came to see here, I sincerely hope this is the last time we meet. Get off my mine!"

"I share your sentiment Mr Klopp and I saw a lot," I said quietly holding my ground and holding his stare. "I saw a lot more than you think."

The man's eyes narrowed slightly as I said the words. His cold blue eyes searched my own. It was as if, for a brief moment, there had been a slight suspicion or realisation that perhaps there was some truth in what I had just said. That maybe, just maybe, I wasn't simply the cheerful, happy-go-lucky employee of the insurance firm I had portrayed myself to be. In a split second, the doubt in his face was gone and he sneered, spun around and walked towards the door. That morning I ate breakfast alone. Although Betty was concerned by this fact, I was polite and thankful as usual and as I left, I thanked her for everything she had done during my stay at the mine and wished her well for the future. I spent the rest of the morning packing and preparing for the flight to Windhoek at 11.00 am. There was an email from the insurance company enquiring when they should book my return flight to London. I sent them a reply informing them that I wished to spend a few days in Namibia upon my return to Windhoek but also told them that as promised, I would have a report sent to them within 48 hours. *That'll keep them happy*. It was at 10.40 am. whilst I was pacing the front room impatiently that I saw Temba's vehicle driving up the hill to collect me.

I walked out the front door with my bags before he turned the motor off.

"Ready to go Mr Green?" he said cheerfully.

"Yup," I replied as I climbed into the cool of the cab. "Let's go."

It took ten minutes to reach the airstrip and Temba parked in the shade of the hangar and left the motor running as we waited alone for the first sight of the aircraft. It was then that I first noticed the blurry white band on the horizon to the east. It continued as far as the eye could see and seemed to block out the point where the earth met the sky. I took my sunglasses from my face and screwed my eyes to get a better look.

"What is that Temba?" I asked. "On the horizon."

The young man opened the door, got out of the vehicle, and brought his hand up above his eyes to shield them from the sun.

"Looks like a dust storm." he said "I've seen a few but not as big as that. But Mr Meyer must be on his way or I would have been informed by now."

"Hmm," I said feeling somewhat perturbed.

It was a minute later when he pointed up to his left and spoke.

"There he is Mr Green!" he said. "Coming in from the northeast."

I craned my neck and saw the tiny glint in the sky to my left. Feeling somewhat relieved I placed my hard hat on the back seat and got out of the vehicle to smoke a final cigarette before Danny landed. The blazing heat of the day was made worse by a steady wind blowing in from the east and as I smoked, I could see the band of white on the horizon growing larger. I crushed out the cigarette as I watched the shiny new aircraft bank to land. The wind was stronger by then and I watched while the wings rocked as Danny struggled to level the plane for landing. Temba and I retrieved my bags from the back seat of the vehicle and we both walked onto the concrete apron as the plane trundled up and came to a stop in front of the hangar. From where I stood, I could clearly see that Danny's forehead was furrowed with worry as he cut the engine and completed his post-flight checks. He opened the door and removed his headphones as I walked up to the plane.

"Morning Jason," he said. "Looks like we have a bit of a gust front back there. It's blowing up a huge cloud."

"I've been watching it for a while," I said "Is it a problem? Are we able to leave?"

"I'm not sure," he replied. "I need to contact the tower at Windhoek."

"We have WIFI here at the hangar Mr Meyer," said Temba.

"Ah great thanks Temba," said Danny as he got out of the plane and closed the door "Let's get in there quickly and I'll call them."

We followed Danny as he walked swiftly into the shade of the hangar. He paced the front impatiently as he made the call all the while looking at his watch and out at the growing sandstorm on the horizon. Eventually, he hung up and turned towards us to speak.

"Jason I'm afraid we will have to sit out this weather front," he said resignedly. "The good news is it's moving fast and with a bit of luck we should be able to leave later this afternoon."

"That's fine Danny," I replied. "Can we do anything?"

"I'd like to get the aircraft into the hangar before the dust arrives," he replied. "The three of us should be able to manage."

By the time we had pushed the plane into the hangar and sealed the sliding door, we were all dripping with sweat. By then the band of dust to the east had grown into what looked like a giant tsunami of yellow and white that threatened to swallow everything in its path.

"I guess we should head to the cottage and sit this out," said Danny. "I can track the weather front on my laptop and stay in touch with Windhoek tower from there. Will be cooler as well."

"Certainly Mr Meyer," said Temba. "Shall we go?"

Danny and I spent the next four hours back at the cottage in the management compound. Temba had requested a plate of sandwiches to be sent up from the dining room and had told us to contact him as soon as we had been given the all-clear from Windhoek to depart. Outside the front windows, the wattles thrashed in the howling wind and even the green blades of grass were covered in a fine coating of grey dust. It was 3.30 pm. when Danny put down the phone and delivered the news I had been dreading.

"Well Jason," he said "It looks like it'll be too late by the time this duster passes us. The tower has just told me to wait for the morning before we depart. This was unexpected and I apologize. I informed them that we intend to leave at 6.00 am. tomorrow. By then this storm will have blown out to sea."

"Hey, it's not your fault mate," I said. "Now I haven't told you, but I had a bit of a run-in with Klopp this morning."

"Oh really?" he replied with a half-smile.

I had no intention of telling the young man the reason. My business with the mine was strictly confidential and it would have been unprofessional and more than improper to tell him any of my findings.

"Ya," I said. "It was nothing serious, but I had hoped not to see him again."

"That's not an issue," he said with a knowing grin. "We can arrange a braai here at the cottage for dinner this evening. I'm sure Betty will send up a feast for us to cook."

"Fine," I said. "Well, that's settled. We'll do that."

Danny immediately picked up his phone and came good with his promise. Within an hour a pick-up truck arrived with a barbecue and a small load of charcoal. The men who delivered it set it up on a bricked area to the right of the cottage and soon after a cooler box of steaks, boerewors, and assorted cold meats and salads arrived from the kitchens. By 5.00 pm. the dust storm had passed leaving everything in its path covered with a fine film of grey powder. The unusual weather phenomenon had resulted in what had become a spectacular sunset that looked like a physically painted splatter of purples, reds, and orange on the horizon above the mine workings. Danny and I lit the fire at 6.00 pm. by which time it had cooled down and we sat nearby on folding chairs as we waited for Temba who was to join us for dinner. I had noticed during the day that he seemed to be in a particularly upbeat and chipper mood and I decided to press him for the reason as we waited.

"You seem very upbeat today Danny," I said. "What's going on?"

He looked at me and I saw the twinkle in his eyes as he pulled an envelope from his pocket and handed it to me.

"What's this?" I asked as I opened the envelope.

"The title deeds for my place in Stellenbosch," he said. "They finally came through."

"Nice!" I said as I glanced at the document.

"But there's more," he said as he pulled a small black box from another pocket.

Danny opened the box to reveal a small but perfectly formed diamond engagement ring.

"I'm gonna ask Charmaine to marry me."

"Really?" I said with a smile. "Congratulations mate."

"Hmm," he replied. "Hope she says yes." "Well," I said, "The way you two are constantly calling and messaging each other I'm sure she will!"

Temba arrived at 6.30 with a six-pack of cold beers and the three of us spent the next two hours grilling the meat and talking quietly in the relative cool of the night. After Temba had left Danny installed himself on the couch in front of the television while I began compiling and typing my report to the insurance company. We had spent the entire evening without even a mention of Mr Heinrich Klopp and I was feeling pleasantly full and content by the time Danny stood up, stretched and announced that he was retiring to bed.

"Good night Jason," he said. "Thanks for a pleasant evening. I'll see you at 5.00 am. sharp in the morning."

"See you then Danny," I said as I closed the laptop. "I'm gonna shower and hit the sack as well."

That night I had absolutely no reason nor wish to see what was going on at Klopp's house. As far as I was concerned my work at the mine was done and had it not been for the freak dust storm, I would have been hundreds of miles away happily ensconced in a top Windhoek hotel. It was for that reason that I had purposely avoided clicking on the tiny flashing camera icon on the screen of my phone and laptop. The evening had been congenial and I was feeling sleepy by the time I stepped into the shower. It was as I was drying myself off in the bedroom that, through the curtains, I saw the lights of the vehicle coming up the hill. The night was dead quiet apart from the hushed whisper of the air conditioning and I heard the crunch of tyres on the tarmac nearby. A few seconds later there came a loud knock on the front door. I glanced at my watch. *11.30 pm, what now?* I walked through the lounge with the towel wrapped around my waist and opened the door to find Temba standing there. His face was shiny with sweat and his eyes were wide with alarm.

"Temba," I said. "What's wrong?"

"Sorry Mr. Green," he said. "I really didn't want to disturb you."

At that moment Danny walked out wearing nothing but boxer shorts.

"What's going on?" he said rubbing sleep from his eyes. "Oh, it's you Temba. What's up?"

"I'm really sorry for disturbing you," he said, "but I just came from the clinic."

"Yes," said Danny, "and..?"

"It's one of my shift bosses," he replied. "He only came back from leave ten days ago. The nurse says he has cerebral malaria. He's in a coma. The nurse said unless he gets to a hospital in the next 24 hours he will die. He's only 21 years old. I know I shouldn't have come to ask but I had to try."

"You're asking if we can take him with us to Windhoek?" I said looking at Danny.

"Well," he replied, "I know it's strictly against regulations but I had to try."

Danny put his hands on his hips and sighed deeply.

"Look Jason," he said, "I don't mind. This is an Apex charter but it's for you specifically. There's plenty of room in the aircraft. He can be put on the back seat and I can have an ambulance waiting at the airport. Temba is right though. If Klopp were to find out."

"Oh, fuck Klopp!" I said. "It's no skin off my nose. I don't mind at all. If it might save his life why not? That's fine by me Danny."

Temba sighed and dropped his head in relief.

"What about the guard at the airstrip?" he said quietly.

"The aircraft is in the hangar," said Danny. "The guard will remain at his post at the gate. We can drive round the front, put him in the plane and leave without anyone being any the wiser."

"Yes," said Temba as his eyes lit up with hope. "Yes, that will work."

"You be here as arranged at 5.00 am," said Danny. "You and the nurse put the patient in the back of your vehicle. Not a word to anyone. The windows are tinted and the guard will be expecting us. He won't see anything. We'll get through easily and I will fly him to Windhoek, no problem."

Temba dropped his head in gratitude and wiped the sweat from his forehead with the back of his hand.

"Thank you," he said quietly, "I'll be here at 5.00 am. sharp."

10

CHAPTER TEN: NIGHT MOVES

Heinrich Klopp lay on his bed staring at the ceiling and glancing at his watch periodically. The confrontation with Green in the morning at the dining room had infuriated him initially but soon afterwards feelings of worry and fear had begun to creep into his consciousness. All morning he had been unable to concentrate on his work and spent the time pacing his office and fighting these feelings. *What had he meant? He said he had seen a lot more than I think. There had been a look in his eyes that indicated there was an element of truth in that statement.* Until that moment in the morning, Heinrich Klopp had dismissed the annoying man from London and simply tolerated his stupid questions and wide-eyed enthusiasm. But the niggling paranoia and worry had set in and by 9.00 am. he had become distracted to the point of despair. Time after time he had told himself to concentrate and focus on the job at hand. *There is no way he knows anything. The system is bulletproof. Everything will continue as normal.* It was only at 12.15 pm. when he learned of the dust storm and the fact that their return flight had been delayed because of it. This twist of fate had sparked an idea in Heinrich Klopp's mind and he had spent the afternoon glued to his computer studying the weather patterns for the area and willing the storm to intensify. Finally, at 5.00 pm. the message he had hoped for came through. The flight had been cancelled by the Windhoek tower and would only leave the following morning. *Ya.* He thought. *Now I will fix him properly.* It was 1.00 am. when he finally rose and walked through to the lounge where he collected his toolbox. Wearing a dark tracksuit, he slipped out of the front door and paused to check the lights on the nearby guest cottage were out. They were. *Sleep tight, my friends.* He thought as he quietly opened the door of the Mercedes. Heinrich Klopp reversed the vehicle quietly and glided down the slope towards the gate with the lights out. As he passed the guest cottage, he glanced at the front of the building to check the lights were out. Feeling satisfied that Green and the pilot were asleep, he turned on his headlights and after passing through the security gate he turned left and headed around the base of the hill towards the main entrance to the mine.

The guard at the main gate stood up sleepily as he saw the lights of the vehicle approaching and upon recognizing the Mercedes he saluted stiffly and quickly lifted the boom without a word. It took only minutes to reach the gate to the airstrip and once again the guard opened up without question. Heinrich Klopp parked the Mercedes on the concrete apron at the front of the hangar and walked into the hangar using the side door. The interior was illuminated by rows of neon lights that were bright enough to be similar to daylight. The sudden brightness caused his eyes to ache for a few seconds, but they soon adjusted and he focused on the shiny new aircraft that stood in the centre of the hangar. Klopp walked up to the right-hand side of the aircraft, placed the toolbox on the floor, and opened the cowling of the engine bay. The space was immaculately clean and it was clear that both the pilot and the mechanics had taken great pride in the servicing and maintenance of the aircraft. He craned his neck as he followed the copper fuel line as it came down from above the firewall and entered the engine bay. He gripped the thin copper tube with his right hand and brought it down under the engine until he felt the heat shield near the exhaust manifold. It had been many years since Heinrich Klopp had worked on an aircraft, but he found the small metal plate exactly where he expected to find it. *Good*. He thought. Crouching down on his haunches he found the mini ratchet in the toolbox and attached the correct sized socket to it. With both arms in the engine bay, Heinrich Klopp felt for the bolt on the right-hand side of the heat shield. He found it with the index finger of his left hand and quickly brought the socket around it. It was a tight and perfect fit. It was with considerable effort that finally the bolt loosened with a metallic cracking sound and Klopp worked the threads loose with a back-and-forth movement of the ratchet in his right hand. After what seemed an eternity the bolt came free and he carefully brought both the ratchet and the bolt out through the side of the engine cowling. The second bolt proved more difficult to loosen given the awkward angle and he was sweating profusely and cursing in German by the time he had freed it. Both the heat shield and the bolt fell and clattered noisily onto the sheet metal below the engine and he had to sit underneath with his arm up under the nose to retrieve them. While in that position he removed the hammer from the toolbox and using the base of the rubber handle, he knocked the copper tubing of the fuel line repeatedly until it had been permanently shifted to a new position closer to the exhaust manifold.

Heinrich Klopp knew full well that without the heat shield protecting it, the copper fuel pipe would get hotter and hotter until the precious liquid it carried to the carburettor would start to evaporate and cause what is commonly known as a vapour lock. The very fact that the aircraft would be flying in a naturally hot environment plus the obvious effect of the missing heat shield and the shifted position of the fuel line would be enough. But Heinrich Klopp knew there was more work to be done. When the engine failure happened, as he knew it would, the pilot would almost certainly switch on the emergency fuel pump. This would physically force the fuel to its intended destination regardless of the vapour lock. There was only one way to prevent this from happening and that was to install a hidden fuse in the 28volt electrical system. The 25-volt fuse would ensure that during the pre-flight checks, all electrical systems would appear to be working as expected, but when the emergency fuel pump was switched on the fuse would burn out within a minute, rendering it completely useless. The job was complicated and took more than half an hour of tracing wires and soldering but eventually, it was done. The fuse sat in amongst the wiring loom and Heinrich Klopp hid his work by wrapping the job with black insulation tape ensuring it would not be spotted even by the keenest of eyes. It was 2.15 am. when Heinrich Klopp finally closed and secured the cowling on the engine of the aircraft and stood back to wipe the shiny surface with a cloth. He walked slowly around the aircraft looking for anything he might have left on the shiny concrete floor and then finally, feeling satisfied, he dropped the small heat shield and the two bolts into his toolbox. He closed the side door of the hangar on his way out, leaving everything exactly as he had found it, and briefly stopped to speak to the guard at the gate on the way.

"I am very happy with your work," he said to the wide-eyed young man. "What time does your shift end?"

"My replacement arrives at 5.00 am." he replied.

"Okay," said Klopp. "I have decided to give you a bonus and some home leave. Please come to my office at 9.00 am. and bring your logbook so we can process it."

The young man broke into a wide grin and saluted stiffly.

"Yes, sir!" he said happily.

Fifteen minutes later Heinrich Klopp lay back on his bed once again and stared at the ceiling. He had driven up the hill to his house with the lights off and the guest cottage had been shrouded in darkness as it had been when he had left. The mission had been a success and although he was tired, he had a smug half smile on his face as he reached for the glass of water on the bedside table.

Ya. He thought. *That'll fix him.*

11

Chapter Eleven: Icarus Rising

I awoke at 4.20 am. and took a quick shower before going through to the kitchenette to make coffee. Danny had beaten me to it and was already fully dressed in his pilot's uniform.

"Morning Jason," he said. "Kettle's boiled can I make you a coffee?"

"Thanks, Danny," I replied. "Are we all set to go?"

"Yup," he replied as he filled the mug, "just a few pre-flight checks and we'll be off."

I spent the next twenty minutes packing while Danny watched the news on television. Temba arrived early and stood at the front door anxiously when I opened it.

"Morning gentlemen," he said quietly. "The patient is stable in the back of the vehicle."

"Fine," said Danny, "I think we're ready to go then."

Danny and I carried our bags to the vehicle and placed them on the back seat. The patient lay on a thin mattress on the load tray at the rear. Hanging from the roof of the canopy was a drip that the nurse had fitted to his arm with a cannula insert. He was a small man, already emaciated by the malaria, and he lay motionless covered in a white sheet.

"I hope the drip will be okay in the plane?" said Temba as we looked at the unconscious man.

"It's fine," said Danny. "We will hang it on one of the hooks above the rear window. No problem."

The drive to the airstrip took ten minutes and we cleared all the security checkpoints easily. The tinted windows on the canopy at the rear of the vehicle ensured our patient went undiscovered and Temba parked the vehicle out of sight at the front of the hangar. Danny quickly opened the hangar doors followed by the right-hand side door of the aircraft.

"Let's get him in right away," he said as he walked swiftly back to the vehicle. "I'll do my pre-flight checks after we push the plane out."

Temba and I carried the man using the corners of the thin mattress while Danny held the drip. It only took a few minutes to get him into the back seat of the plane and the entire operation went unseen by the guard who was still at his station near the gate. Danny hung the drip that was attached to the man's arm on a clothes hook above the left window and we were done.

"Right," said Danny. "Let's get the plane out on the apron."

It was easy enough for the three of us to push the aircraft out of the hangar. Even at that early hour of the morning, the heat was intense and I was sweating by the time we had got it into position. Temba and I stood back as Danny began his pre-flight checks. He started by removing the gust lock from behind the yoke and ensured the ignition and avionics switches were off.

Next, he flicked the master switch and checked electrical and fuel gauges before turning it off once again and removing the fuel cup. He moved along the outside of the aircraft carefully checking doors, rivets, and antennas high and low. Next, he checked the flaps and the lower surfaces of the wings following the ailerons. Danny took a fuel sample from the underside of the wing and held the small clear bottle up to the sky to check for water or sediment. After checking the landing gear, he opened the inspection hatch on the engine cowling and removed the dipstick to check the oil levels. After pulling the fuel strainer knob for four seconds he moved around to check the propeller, the spinner, and the air intakes. Finally, he turned to us and spoke.

"Right gentlemen," he said. "We are good to go."

Danny and I said our goodbyes to Temba who thanked us both once again for helping the sick man. He walked back towards the hangar and stood watching as we climbed into the aircraft and strapped ourselves in. The engine fired on the first attempt and the propeller blurred in front of us. With a final wave to Temba, Danny pushed the throttle forward and the small plane began trundling along the apron towards the runway. The interior of the cabin was stuffy and there was a strong smell of body odour from the comatose man behind us. Danny and I opened the windows to allow air to flow in, and both of us donned our headphones as we taxied away from the hangar. With a final view of the mine dumps ahead to our left, Danny turned the plane to face south and the long sandy stretch of the runway lay ahead of us. After a final glance at the instruments, he pushed the throttle forward and the cabin was filled with the solid roar of the engine as the aircraft lurched forward. The ride was bumpy and I watched the wing to my right shake and bob as we gained speed but eventually, after what seemed an eternity, we left the ground and gained altitude slowly. Below me, to the right, the rocky hill and the mine complex beyond it grew smaller and smaller as we climbed. Danny banked the aircraft sharply to the left and the mine went out of sight.

The bright morning sun glinted off the endless cream-coloured expanse of the desert and the air in the cabin began to cool noticeably. Danny turned to look at me and smiled from behind his Rayban sunglasses. He lifted his right hand and gave me the thumbs up which I returned. Once again, I was astounded by how isolated the mine actually was. I looked around and turned in the seat to marvel at the sheer scale of the flat, featureless landscape. I felt a tangible sense of relief to be leaving the confines of the mine and there was an added feeling of accomplishment at having finished the job and being 100% confident that my report would expose Klopp and his crooked ways. The forensic auditors would get to work and the insurance company would be grateful to keep their account with Apex Resources. *It wasn't easy Green. But it was a success. Now get back to civilization and some R 'n R in Windhoek while you prepare your report.* Danny levelled the plane out at 9000 feet and turned to speak. "How about some water Jason?" he said reaching behind the seat to retrieve some plastic bottles.

"Sure, thanks," I replied.

"You glad to be leaving the big hole?" he asked.

"I am," I replied as I opened the bottle. "I think I'll take a few days off in Windhoek and see some sights before heading back to London."

"Great," he said. "We'll stay in touch and if I'm in town we could meet for a drink or some dinner."

"Sure," I replied. "Can do."

The next fifteen minutes were spent in casual conversation. Danny told me of his plans for the smallholding he had bought and described the house he would eventually build. The young man knew not to ask too much about the reason I had come to the mine in the first place and he seemed happy enough to skip the subject. In the distance ahead I noticed a blue haze on the horizon. I lifted my sunglasses and screwed up my eyes to get a better look.

"That's the Boshua Pass and the mountains beyond," he said. "We'll be leaving the desert soon."

The landscape below began to change and random rocky outcrops and scrubby bush began to appear in the featureless desert. The foothills of the mountains ahead became clearer and before I knew it, we had left the desert behind us and were surrounded by the dry and rugged mountains with their grey and ochre-coloured rock formations and jagged peaks. The change of scenery was a tonic and the contrast between the earthy colours of the rough terrain below and the clear blue morning sky was breathtaking.

It was exactly two minutes later that I first heard the engine sputter. It was brief and only lasted for a split second, but it was noticeable. Upon hearing it Danny immediately placed his water bottle behind the seat, sat forward, and studied the gauges. Thinking nothing of it I sat back and stared out at the mountains to my right but within fifteen seconds it happened again.

"Damn," said Danny quietly. "Vapour lock."

The engine sputtered once again but this time for a full two seconds and I felt the sudden drop in altitude.

"Everything alright?" I asked quietly.

"Will be fine," he replied. "I'm just going to enrich the fuel mixture."

He reached forward towards a red knob on the control panel and slowly depressed it.

As soon as he did this the engine rallied again and the sound returned to normal. I glanced at him briefly as he did this and instantly noticed the frown lines on his forehead. It was three seconds later when the engine stuttered again and I saw him shake his head in frustration.

"Fuck," he murmured to himself. "Emergency fuel pump."

Danny flicked a switch but still the engine only fired in brief spurts and I felt my ears pop from the drop in altitude. Suddenly the engine stopped completely and there was only the sound of the air rushing past the body of the aircraft. Danny's breathing became fast and heavy and I realized he was now panicking. The propeller was now only spinning due to our own forward motion and the rushing sound of the air was growing louder by the second.

"We have a serious problem Jason!" he said in a loud strained voice.

"Can you get back to the desert Danny?" I said. "Like glide there?"

"No way!" he shouted as he frantically worked the fuel mixture knob "We're losing altitude fast!"

I felt a cold sliding sensation in my stomach as I watched the young man desperately try to restart the engine. But it was to no avail. The only sound was the rushing of the air and Danny's frantic, terrified breathing.

"Strap yourself in as tight as you can!" he shouted, his voice distorted in my headphones. "I'm going to make an emergency landing!"

Suddenly my whole world changed as the true terror of our situation sank in. The rugged mountains below were steep, jagged, and covered with boulders and small trees and they were getting closer by the second. Danny turned his head frantically from side to side looking for a space to put us down as he battled to control the plane in the blasting heat of the thermals that rushed up from the burnt earth.

"Fucking hell!" he shouted once again. "There's nowhere to land!"

He was right. Ahead of us, a jagged peak of rocks jutted out of a mountain and I could tell, given our current downward trajectory, that we would hit it at full speed if no action was taken. I reached down on either side of my seat and tightened the seatbelts as I had been instructed. My mouth was dry with fear as events then seemed to start happening in slow motion. At the very last moment, Danny banked the stricken aircraft to the right and I saw the living burnt orange lichen on the rocks of the peak as they passed metres below us with an almighty whooshing sound. Ahead of us was a low hill covered with rocks and small trees. The earth was the colour of milky coffee and furry in places with tufts of dried grass.

To the left of that was a valley which was relatively flat but it was full of trees and it wound around the foot of the hills with no straight lines. It was as if the world around me had gone silent and I felt like I was floating quietly through the beautiful landscape as if in a dream.

"Brace!" shouted Danny as we approached. "We're going down!"

Once again events seemed to be in slow-motion and I felt somehow detached from the horrifying reality we were in. The ground came up faster than I had expected and suddenly we were at the valley floor just above tree level. The last thing I heard was Danny's voice as he spoke quietly into the microphone.

"God help us," he said quietly.

The impact, when it came, was preceded by the violent whipping of branches on the undercarriage of the aircraft. Although it was only for a second or two, it felt like it lasted for an eternity. I turned to my left, put my arm around the back of the seat, and pulled as hard as I could to save myself from being flung forward into the instrument panel. Suddenly my world was transformed into a confusing blur of motion and an appalling cacophony of wrenching, twisting metal and smashing glass. The right wing of the aircraft clipped a boulder on a ledge in the canyon and was instantly ripped clean off. This sent the fuselage tumbling sideways and upside down as we crashed repeatedly into the trees that lined the valley floor. My body was repeatedly slammed into the door at my back and again into the seat. The force wrenched the tendons in my arm and cracked my ribs where the seat belt restrained me. The final blow came as the aircraft scraped and screeched over rocks and sand and slammed into a pile of boulders in a dry riverbed. The blow of the sudden stoppage whipped my neck sideways and my vision filled with the stars of concussion.

The battered aircraft sat upright in the bright morning sun, its landing gear ripped off a hundred metres back. I became aware of a loud hissing sound and an overpowering smell of aviation fuel. I opened my eyes to see the windscreen was gone and the mangled interior was full of glass and dust that was still settling. My vision began to fade until I finally caught my breath and realized I had been winded by the brutal force of the crash. The air came in great wheezing sobs as I fumbled with the quick-release mechanism on the seatbelt. It came free on the first attempt and I glanced at Danny as I worked my right hand until it found the latch for the door. The young man appeared confused and sat blinking repeatedly in his seat, his face was deathly pale. At that moment the latch on the crumpled door gave way and I fell out of the plane backwards onto the sand. *Danny*. I thought. *Danny. You have to get him out now Green*. Even at that time in the morning, the hot sand burnt my hands as I crawled around the ruined front of the plane and eventually got to my feet. I staggered around until I arrived to find Danny's door had been half ripped away. I gripped the jagged metal and pulled it with all of my strength until it gave and swung open with a loud creak. Whilst still inside the plane I had not noticed the true extent of the terrible mutilation the young man had suffered. The tough plastic grips of the yoke had broken away and the steel shaft they surrounded had travelled through his stomach and shattered his spine. A huge pool of blood had formed between his ruined legs and the thick, sweet smell of it mixed with the sharp tang of the aviation fuel. Still, he sat there in silence with the same bewildered look on his ghostly white face.

"Someone must have messed with the plane," he said quietly. "It's most unusual."

"Danny," I said still breathless. "We've got to get you out of here mate."

The young man turned and looked at me and for a brief moment his thinking cleared and his faculties returned.

With his left hand, he reached into his chest pocket and pulled out the khaki envelope and the small black velvet-covered box containing the ring he had bought for his girlfriend.

"Jason," he said softly as he held the items out towards me "Jason, please promise me you'll give this to Charmaine? Tell her I love her. Please, Jason."

"You will give it to her yourself Danny!" I shouted angrily as I took the items and shoved them into my pocket. "I'm going to get you out of here."

The explosion came as I reached in to grip the yoke shaft near his stomach. It was sudden and all-encompassing, and it blew me back a full five metres from where I stood. The blazing white heat singed the hair off my arms and peeled a layer of skin from the right-hand side of my forehead. I will never know how long I was out for, but I awoke briefly and lifted my head to witness the inferno and the macabre dance of death as Danny's body twisted and convulsed in the raging flames. After that, there was only darkness.

12

Chapter Twelve: Oom Piet

My consciousness returned slowly. I was aware of the skin on my forehead stinging in the full glare of the midday sun. My limbs felt heavy and I felt like I had been drugged. The next thing I became aware of was voices. They were men's voices and they were nearby, but I couldn't understand a word that was said. They spoke in the soft clicking dialect of the San Bushmen. I had seen films and documentaries about them in the past. Next, I felt my body being lifted by the armpits and ankles. Their hands were powerful and I groaned as my cracked and bruised ribs shifted from the movement and I kept my eyes closed from the glare of the sun overhead. The two men carried me thirty metres from where I lay and placed me in the shade of an acacia tree at the foot of the valley. One of the men placed a bag under my head and held the open top of a plastic bottle to my mouth. The water was warm and brackish but deliciously wet and I opened my eyes after the first gulp. The blackened wreck of the plane was still smouldering and creaking as the aluminium body cooled. One of the men held the grubby bottle in front of me once again and I grabbed it and drank a full litre of the precious liquid. I forced myself up onto my right elbow and then carefully into a sitting position. It was only then that I took a look at the men. Their skin was the colour of milk chocolate and their bodies were small and lithe. They wore nothing but tattered shorts and both had necklaces of tiny white beads around their skinny necks. Both men squatted on either side of me on bare flat feet and they hummed and clicked and fussed between themselves as they studied me. Their heads were covered in tiny tight curls of black hair that resembled peppercorns, and their faces were wrinkled with creases and laughter lines. The man on my left spoke and as he did so I noticed that both of his front teeth were missing. I didn't understand a word he said and simply shook my head as I handed him the water bottle. The man on my right lifted his hand into the air and simulated an aeroplane coming down. As he did so he added childish sound effects that culminated with an explosion as he brought his hand down. I nodded and pointed at the smoking shell of the plane to which they both whistled and cooed with amazement. I glanced behind me to the gnarled trunk of the tree nearby and I groaned quietly as I shifted my body back towards it in the sand so I could lean on it.

The two men followed and squatted nearby as they had been before. We sat in silence for the next five minutes, both men waiting patiently as I stared at the plane and took it all in. *Someone must have messed with the plane. Those were Danny's words. Someone must have messed with the plane.* It was then I felt my pockets. My cell phone was there along with my wallet. In my back pocket was the envelope and the small box containing the ring that Danny had given me right before the explosion. I pulled out the cell phone and checked it. It was still fully charged but there was no signal. *Jesus Green. What the fuck?* It was only then that I remembered the sick man we had put in the back of the plane. Until then I had not given him a second thought. The surrounding trees were alive with insects that hissed and clicked in the mid-day sun and the heat was appalling but it seemed to have little effect on the two bushmen who hadn't even broken a sweat. Both of them still squatted nearby patiently watching me as I thought. *There are two dead men in that plane Green. Both of them burnt beyond recognition. This could work to your advantage especially if Danny was right and the plane was deliberately sabotaged. Think and think fast. It could be days, even weeks until the wreckage is found. There was no time to report an emergency. Danny never had the time to get on the radio. You are out here in the middle of nowhere with these two men. What now?* I fumbled in my top pocket and found the cigarettes and lighter. Both of the men accepted one with wide toothless grins and hums of gratitude. *You need to get out of here Green. You need to get far away. The authorities, when they finally get here, will assume you're dead. Get away, get to civilization and lie low. That is the number one priority right now. If Danny was right and someone did fuck with that plane it can only be one person. Klopp. No one else on this planet would have reason to do that but him, and it'll be better for you if he believes you are dead. Get away Green. Now.* With my mind made up I attempted to speak to the men in the hope that one of them would understand.

"Anyone speak English?" I asked. "English?"

Both of the men looked at me with bemused expressions then muttered something between themselves. There was no understanding at all. I needed to get it through to them that I was looking for a road. Just as the man who had simulated the plane had done, I held up both hands as if I were holding a steering wheel and made the sound of a car. This was a charade they understood immediately and both of them spoke in unison.

"Oom Piet," they said happily.

"Oom Piet," I said feeling puzzled.

"Oom Piet," said the man on my right before copying my simulation of the car with his hands and accompanying sound effects.

It was then I realized that they must be referring to a person. The word 'Oom' was Afrikaans for 'Uncle' and 'Piet' was a common Afrikaans name.

"Where is Oom Piet?" I said holding my hands in an open gesture.

Both of the men immediately pointed north and spoke in unison once again.

"Oom Piet!" they both said with absolute certainty.

Once again, I had to use rudimentary sign language and after a few attempts both men understood that I was trying to ask them 'how far?'

The one on the right indicated with his arm that 'Oom Piet' was in fact in the North and over the hills. I pointed at the two of them and myself and simulated a man walking with my index and middle finger in the sand in front of me. Both men smiled toothless grins and nodded vigorously as they copied my simulation.

"Okay," I said as I slowly got to my feet. "Oom Piet, let's go."

The two men stood up as well and signalled for me to follow them. The older of the two picked up the tatty old bag I had been leaning on and placed the water bottle inside it. He slung it on his bony bare shoulder and we all began walking. Our path took us close to the still-smouldering aircraft and I could both see and smell the charred bodies inside it and for a moment I felt the bile rising in my throat. The path took us down the valley following the long-dried riverbed of sand. Several riverine trees afforded us some shade as we wound our way in the blazing sun. Clad in nothing but their tatty shorts, the men walked swiftly and effortlessly often glancing behind them to check on me. My body ached and there was a constant thumping in my head, but I kept the pace and followed as instructed. It was a full hour later when I stopped and slumped down on a rock in the shade of an acacia tree, panting and sweating profusely. I rested my hands on my knees and hung my head as I caught my breath. Both of the men stood there studying me with concerned looks on their faces. The man with the bag took out the water bottle and offered it to me. I drank the cloudy water gratefully before replacing the top and handing it back to him. Neither of the men showed any fatigue or perspiration. It was clear to me that they were totally adapted to their environment and fully able to walk long miles at the drop of a hat.

"Oom Piet," I said wiping my mouth.

"Oom Piet!" they both said in unison, once again pointing North.

And so the slog continued. The one saving grace was the fact that we stayed on the valley floor and the ground we covered was mainly flat. The hills and mountains that surrounded us were all similar and there were no recognizable landmarks. My fate was squarely in the hands of the two small bushmen who walked swiftly and consistently in front of me. It appeared to me that there had been few, if any, humans in this particular area. The feeling of complete and total isolation was overwhelming and more than a little unsettling. It must have been 3.00 pm. when finally, at a shady bend in the dry riverbed, the men stopped and squatted in the sand under a camel thorn tree. My body ached as I lowered myself to sit near them. The man with the bag opened it and pulled out three long sticks of biltong. He handed me a piece along with the seriously depleted water bottle. The dried meat was salty and chewy but I was ravenous and my body was desperate for the protein. One of them began to dig in the sand near a rock in the dried riverbed. He used a stick to start with and then later scooped it out using his hands. The other man sat happily chewing on his biltong and humming a repetitive tune. Eventually, the sand the man was removing began to change colour and I saw there was moisture in it. He mumbled something to the seated man who casually tossed him the near-empty water bottle. I stood up to take a look at what he was doing. In the bottom of the hole, a pool of muddy yellow water was forming and more of it was seeping in. The man opened the bottle and held it down sideways in the hole to allow it to fill. I, personally, would never have imagined that there would be water in that parched and torrid environment, but these were bushmen and they were well-versed in the ways of the land. Ten minutes later, and somewhat replenished from the food and water, we left the confines of the valley and climbed to our right up a steep hill that was covered in tufts of dried grass and ochre-coloured boulders. The ground was rocky and the going difficult, but the two men maintained the pace and carried on as if it was perfectly normal. On two occasions my shoes slipped and I fell onto my hands which burned on the rocks beneath them. When, at last, we reached the summit, I was disconcerted and frustrated by the sight that greeted me.

Endless miles of similar hills and mountains stretched away to the horizon. Once again there were no landmarks and nothing to indicate the presence of humans, let alone the mysterious 'Oom Piet.'

I sat down on a rock to catch my breath. The sun had started making its way down in the west leaving the surrounding countryside bathed in an unusual orange glow.

"Oom Piet," I said. "Where is he?"

Both men repeated his name and pointed north.

"How far?" I said exasperated.

The two men smiled and signalled it was just over the next hill. By then I had come to know that their idea of distance was completely different to my own. We had been walking for close to five hours and must have covered at least twenty-five kilometres since leaving the crash site. Once again, the two men simply smiled and pointed. The journey down the hill was treacherous and three times I slid on the broken stones and scree. Ahead of us was another climb although of a slightly less punishing gradient. It was twenty minutes later when I had resigned myself to the fact that the journey might not end that day, that we arrived at the peak. The two men stopped and laughed as I climbed the last few metres and looked down.

"Oom Piet!" they said happily pointing down the hill.

Below us, at the foot of the hill, was a flat piece of ground roughly the size of a football pitch. The right-hand side of the area was comprised of a large paddock that was fenced off with rough-hewn poles and barbed wire. There was a dilapidated wooden barn at the far side and a long concrete water trough in the centre.

From where I stood I could see at least fifty cows and numerous goats grazing on bales of hay that had been placed near the barn. To the left was a small house that looked like it must have been built in the 1930s. It was a bungalow built with pale orange bricks with a low verandah that jutted out of the front. The old tin roof of the building had been burnt to a rusty orange colour by countless years of baking sun. Thin tendrils of smoke rose from the small chimney. To the left of the house was an ancient windmill constructed from corroded lengths of angle iron. Its blades were made from cut pieces of sheet metal which had rusted to the same burnt orange as the roof. There was a patch of overgrown green grass in front of the verandah and what looked like a very old Ford pickup truck parked near an outbuilding at the rear of the house.

"Oom Piet," I said breathlessly.

"Oom Piet!" the two men repeated.

The simple sight of some actual civilization was an enormous relief to me and I nodded and smiled at the two men before we started our descent down the hill. We arrived at the flat ground ten minutes later and the three of us walked towards the front of the old house.

It was as we got to within twenty metres of the gloomy, shaded verandah that I heard the repetitive creaking of the old wooden rocking chair. The two bushmen stopped a few metres short of the steps at the front and I followed suit.

"Hoe gaan dit?" came a deep booming voice from within.

I recognized the language as Afrikaans immediately. The man had said 'How are you?'

I stepped forward and saw an old man sitting on the rocking chair near the door at the rear of the verandah. His great belly was almost bursting out of the faded chequered cotton shirt he wore and there were no shoes on his feet. His powerful legs were bronzed to the colour of honey and his long tangled grey hair was wild and in disarray. His long grey beard was stained yellow around the ancient pipe that he held between his teeth. The old man studied me with suspicious eyes and the pipe made a gurgling sound as he inhaled the pungent tobacco.

"Good afternoon," I said. "Are you Oom Piet?"

"Who's asking?" he replied in his booming voice.

"My name is Green," I said. "There was a plane crash, these two men brought me here."

The old man turned his head to look at the two bushmen who stood patiently in the background. He took the old pipe from his mouth with his massive hand and broke into a speech of perfectly fluent Khoisan. The two men behind me laughed and replied to the old man, obviously describing the circumstances in which they had found me.

With a wave of his hand, he dismissed them both and they walked off around the house and out of sight.

"It seems you are a lucky man, Mr. Green," said the old man in his thick Afrikaans accent.

"Yes, Oom Piet," I said. "Very lucky indeed."

"The bathroom is down the corridor!" he boomed pointing behind him with his thumb "Go and clean yourself up then you can join me for a brandy. You look like you need one."

The fact that I had found myself in an extremely strange situation was not lost on me as I walked across the verandah and into the darkened building. I knew I was in shock and certainly exhausted but I followed his instructions. The old wooden floors creaked underfoot and the rooms were filled with a musty smell and furniture that looked like it was bought a hundred years ago. I found the bathroom, as promised, down the corridor on the left. I removed my clothes, shook the dust from them, and stood under a single open pipe that served as a shower. When I was finished I dried off using an old towel that I found in a cupboard. It was stiff and felt like sandpaper on my skin. I emerged from the house feeling somewhat revived and saw that the old man had set up a chair and a small table near where I had found him.

"The traveller returns!" he said in a deep voice as he appraised me.

"Thank you for that Oom Piet," I said as I took a seat. "It's been quite a day."

The old man reached down into a wooden crate on his right and brought out a bottle of Klipdrift brandy. He opened it and tossed the top into a bin on his left then proceeded to pour two large tots into a pair of antique glass tumblers he had placed on the table. He scrutinized me for a few seconds from dark hazel eyes, set behind bushy eyebrows.

"You look like a man who has a story to tell Mr. Green," he said as he lit his pipe with a match. "Why not start at the beginning?"

By then I had gauged that the old man, although fearsome looking, was actually kindly and probably more than a little lonely. I took a sip of the rich fruity spirit and it burned my throat as it went down. The sun had passed beyond the mountain range behind me leaving the verandah even darker than when I had found it. I sat back, took another sip of the strong liquor, and then pulled the pack of cigarettes from my pocket. The sight of the flame from the lighter brought back the horrific images from that morning. I exhaled a plume of smoke into the still, evening air and spoke.

"I guess I'll start from the beginning then," I said quietly.

The old man sat stony-faced for the next two hours. His only response being grunts of understanding, and I only paused when he reached forward to top up our glasses with the fiery dark spirit. I told him of my history in Africa and my current life in London. I explained, in detail, the brief I had been given by the insurance company and the discoveries I had made at the mine. I told him about the confrontation with Heinrich Klopp and the final words Danny had spoken before he died. I explained my reasons for leaving the crash site and expressed my gratitude for his unexpected hospitality. The old man told me the two men who had rescued me were actually well known to him and would occasionally carry out casual work at his smallholding.

I explained that very soon there would be search and rescue efforts and stressed the importance of the authorities believing me to be dead. The old man understood the reasoning behind this and summoned the two men from the nearby compound using a hand-held bell he kept near his chair. They came within minutes and the old man spoke to them in Khoisan for a full five minutes before they left once again.

"I have told them that they must not go back there," he said. "I explained that there are bad men who will return and there is great danger. You can be sure they will stay away and in any case, I have work for them to do for the next few weeks."

"Thank you, Oom Piet," I said gratefully. "My priority now is to get to Windhoek and sort myself out."

"Of course," he said. "I will drive you to the main road in the morning. It is only sixty kilometres from here and you will be able to get a lift from there."

"Dankie Meneer," I replied in Afrikaans. "Much appreciated."

"I don't want any trouble!" he warned in his deep voice.

"Of course not," I replied. "No, I'll be long gone and no one will know I was ever here."

That night we sat and drank brandy by the light of a paraffin lamp. There was no electricity, internet, or phone signal at the old man's remote farm. He told me that his wife had died ten years previously and that he had lived alone ever since.

At around 8.00 pm. a maid appeared and set the table with cutlery. We dined on Bobotie, a well-known South African dish consisting of spiced minced meat baked with an egg-based topping. Before we ate the old man insisted on saying grace which he did in Afrikaans. It was 9.45 pm. when the bottle was almost empty and Oom Piet stood up and announced he was retiring for the night.

"We will leave at 6.00 am. sharp," he said as we walked through the door. "Be ready. You can take the second room on the right."

"Thank you, Oom Piet," I replied.

Even with the brandy, that night I slept fitfully and was plagued by confusing, random nightmares and visions of the plane crash. The mattress was ancient and I felt like I was sleeping on a bag of potatoes. Still, I was grateful for the understanding and hospitality from the old man after what had been a truly astonishing series of events. At 5.00 am. sharp I heard Oom Piet's footsteps on the wooden floors of the corridor. There were three loud knocks on the door followed by the familiar booming Afrikaans accent.

"Wake up, Jason!" he said. "Time for breakfast."

13

Chapter Thirteen: Search and Rescue

"Time to get up Jason!" came the booming voice of the old man as he knocked loudly from behind the door. "I've left you a fresh shirt in the bathroom. Should fit you."

My eyes stung with fatigue as I blinked and glanced at my watch. It was 5.00 am. and I had barely slept. My entire body ached as I lifted from the uneven bed and made my way to the bathroom. I stood under the blasting cold water for five minutes before drying myself off with the same coarse towel I had used the previous day. I found the old man sitting where I had found him on the verandah. He nodded in approval at the ill-fitting white shirt he had given me. The early morning was still pleasantly cool and as I took my seat, a breakfast of eggs and bacon was served piled high on antique silver platters. The old man had an appetite like a horse and he wolfed down at least five eggs before sitting back with a black coffee and lighting the first pipe of the day.

"We will leave at 6.00," he said. "There'll be a bus along at 8.00 which will get you to Windhoek."

"I appreciate everything you've done Oom Piet," I said as I lit a cigarette. "I expect there will be a fair bit of air traffic around here today."

"Well," he grunted. "No one will ever know you were here. On that, you have my word."

At that moment the two bushmen who had found me at the crash site appeared.

They began cutting the long grass at the front of the homestead with crude slashers and they glanced at me periodically with toothless grins on their faces. We sat in silence drinking the bitter black coffee until the old man heaved himself up and shuffled off towards the door.

THE STAR OF THE DESERT

"See you at the back of the house in five minutes," he said.

I waited until he had disappeared into the house before getting up and walking over to the two bushmen. I pulled out my wallet and handed them a couple of notes each to thank them for their efforts the previous day. Both men showed immense gratitude and spoke in Afrikaans.

"Dankie meneer!" they said in unison.

I walked back through the house and stepped out of the back door to find the old man waiting in an old 1968 Ford F100 pickup. The original baby blue paintwork had worn away in places to reveal the red undercoat. The engine groaned and started as I approached and a cloud of blue smoke exploded from the exhaust at the rear.

"All set?" said the old man as I took my seat and closed the door.

"Yup," I replied over the clatter of the motor. "Let's go."

The old pickup rattled along the narrow dirt road as it wound its way through the rocky and barren hills.

Oom Piet's giant belly almost touched the steering wheel and the pipe remained firmly clamped between his teeth as he pulled at the wheel with his huge sun-bronzed arms. On occasions, we passed rusted signs placed near other dirt roads. The faded names on the signs were all Afrikaans and I was told there were a few other ranchers and cattlemen in the area. It took a full hour and a half to reach the main C28 road and by the time the old pickup stopped in a cloud of dust, the heat had set in.

"There'll be a bus along at 8.00 Jason," said the old man. "Have you got some money?"

"I have Oom Piet," I replied as I offered him my hand. "Thank you again."

"Not a problem," he grumbled as his hand enveloped mine and gripped with enormous strength. "I wish you luck, Jason. Totsiens."

I watched as he spun the old pickup around and headed back down the road towards the homestead. As the sound of the engine faded I realized that we hadn't seen a single human being since leaving. Once again there was an overwhelming feeling of isolation as the silence and heat enveloped me. I crossed the rough dirt road and sat on a rock in the shade of a camel-thorn tree. I pulled my phone from my pocket but as expected there was no signal. I looked around me at the stark landscape and the contrast of colour between the perfectly blue sky and the dry African hues of the hills. *Relax Green. This is gonna be a long haul.* It was half an hour later when, as promised, I first heard the distant rumble of the bus approaching from the west. The rickety vehicle came into sight eventually as it trundled around the base of a hill leaving a thick trail of dust behind it as it approached. I stood up and waited in the sun as it arrived. There was a live goat tied to the roof rack near a crude wire cage full of chickens. The driver pulled up and I climbed aboard.

Clearly surprised to see a white man in the middle of nowhere, he simply nodded as he took the money and motioned for me to take a seat at the rear. The interior of the bus was hot and smelled of body odour and animal dung and I took a seat near the open door to ensure some fresh air. After much grating of gears, the engine wheezed and the bus lurched forward. It was then that I noticed the first of many light aircraft flying above. It flew at low altitude and travelled slowly across the sky above. *They're looking for the crash site. No doubt about that Green. They'll find it and once they get a pin on the location they'll send in the choppers. Good thing you're out and away.* The heat and the broken motion of the old bus as it traversed the hills and valleys made me drowsy and before long, I fell asleep. My body was exhausted and I was still in shock from the crash. On the few occasions I awoke I checked my phone for a signal but there was none. It was a full six hours later when I saw the first sign of civilization. Ahead of us, to the right was a large abandoned house. Set on a hill and resplendent in faded blue, it must have been at least a hundred years old and was built in classic German colonial style. It stood like a beacon to a bygone era as it baked in the early afternoon sun. I checked my phone to see that finally, there was a signal. Immediately I searched the local news sites for any news on the missing plane. There was nothing so instead I did an accommodation search. I settled on a boutique hotel by the name of The Old Fort. Situated in the leafy Windhoek suburb of Suiderhof, it boasted luxury rooms, tranquil gardens, a private bar, and a swimming pool. I called them immediately and booked a room for the night.

"How long till Windhoek?" I asked the driver over the noise of the engine.

"One hour from now," he replied.

As I sat back to wait out the remainder of the journey I saw yet another light aircraft in the sky above. I glanced at my watch and saw it had just gone 2.00 pm.

It'll be soon Green. If they haven't found it already it'll be soon. A plan was beginning to form in my mind. It was a long shot, but if Danny had been right, and there had been foul play with the aircraft, there might be a way I could help to prove it. If so, Heinrich Klopp would almost certainly face a murder charge. *You need a computer Green. And a vehicle. And some new clothes.* I drummed my fingers on my leg impatiently as I stared out of the dusty window. The small city of Windhoek appeared suddenly an hour later.

THE STAR OF THE DESERT

The bus stopped near a local market and I quickly hailed a taxi and told the driver to take me to a shopping mall in the posh suburb of Olympia. I told the driver to wait as I went inside to buy some clothes, luggage, and a laptop computer. I emerged forty minutes later and after throwing my bags in the back seat I urged the driver through the building traffic to the nearby branch of Okavango Car Hire. The company specialized in desert and bush-equipped 4x4 vehicles. I made it to their offices just after 4.45 pm. and rushed in after paying the taxi driver. The interior was cool and modern and there was soft music playing in the background.

"Good afternoon," I said to the young lady behind the reception. "I need a good vehicle. Something fully kitted out for the bush and the desert."

"Certainly sir," she replied cheerfully. "We can sort something out for you."

It was 5.45 pm. when the tyres of the Toyota Land Cruiser finally crunched on the stones in the car park of The Old Fort Boutique Hotel. The sun was setting as I stepped into the reception to check in for the night and the receptionist raised his eyes slightly at the sight of Oom Piet's ill-fitting old shirt.

"My name is Green," I said. "Checking in."

The process took twenty minutes and finally, I was led to my air-conditioned second-floor room by a porter who carried some of my bags. After tipping him I walked through to the bathroom to run a shower. My body ached and I felt gritty and dirty from the journey. I walked up to the basin and rested my hands on it as I stared into the mirror. The face that looked back at me was gaunt, unshaven and desiccated. The burn on my forehead was starting to heal but there were dark purple smears of exhaustion under my eyes. *Jesus...Look at the state of you Green.* After showering I dressed in new clothes and ate a steak dinner in the courtyard restaurant downstairs. It was as I was sitting in the bar scrolling on my phone afterwards that I saw the newsflash on a South African website that the wreckage of the plane had been spotted. It was obvious that there would be helicopters sent in the following day and I felt pleased I had been able to get away safely. As I read the article my vision began to swim from exhaustion and I knew I had to lie down. I pushed the beer away, nodded at the barman, and walked upstairs to my room. I knew there was much to do and I desperately needed to get online but my body would simply not comply. I laid my aching body slowly on the bed and stared at the stucco plaster on the ceiling above. *Rest Green. Just rest for a few hours and then you can begin.* I closed my eyes and within seconds I had fallen into a deep dreamless sleep.

14

Chapter Fourteen: Temba Zulu

It was at 2.30 pm. on the same day that the desperately ill man had been secretly flown to Windhoek that the young mine foreman, Temba Zulu, heard that the plane had gone missing. The message had come from the nurse at the clinic who had sent him a text using the Apex WIFI system. He frowned with concern for the three men he knew were aboard the aircraft, but quickly put it out of his mind as he was busy supervising a shift change of the drilling crew at the mouth of the tunnel. When the changeover was complete, he removed his phone from his pocket and replied to the nurse.

'Don't worry,' he typed in his vernacular language. 'I will pass through the clinic after my shift. Say nothing to anyone.'

Temba Zulu put the message out of his mind and continued with his schedule of tasks for the remainder of the afternoon. It had been a long two weeks and although his routine had been punctuated by the arrival of Mr. Green, his short stay, and his subsequent departure, he was looking forward to his two days off which started the following day. Temba Zulu enjoyed the lone hunting trips he made into the desert. His senior position as foreman allowed him the privilege of using the quad bike for these regular outings. They represented a break from the stifling confines of the mine and afforded him some much-needed solitude and time for reflection. Of course, there was also the delicious biltong that he would prepare the day after the hunt. In the year since he had started making it, demand had been consistent, and he enjoyed gifting the succulent dried meat to his friends. At 4.30 pm, when his shift was over, Temba drove back to his humble one-bedroom house on the outskirts of the workers' compound. He stopped the vehicle outside the dusty walls of the clinic and walked in to speak to the nurse who had messaged him earlier in the day. The news that the aircraft had disappeared had played on his mind and in any event, he and the nurse would have to have their story planned in case the fact that they had put the sick man aboard was discovered.

The middle-aged black Botswana national looked up from his small desk as Temba walked in.

"Thank God you came, Zulu," he said standing up. "I am worried about my job. I knew it was a bad thing asking the whites to take that man to Windhoek."

"They are good men, my brother," said Temba. "In any case, it was I who asked them to do that. Try not to worry. Your job is safe."

With the nurse placated, Temba Zulu took the short bumpy drive to his house. He sat back in the stifling heat of the small sitting room and turned on the television. As he waited for his wife, Betty, to return from her job at the management dining room, he cleaned the old Remington .22 rifle he would use on the hunt the following day. Although it was battered and worn, he had fine-tuned the sights and he could blow the head off a pigeon at a hundred yards. But it was not birds he would be hunting. He was after the elusive Steenbok. His secret hunting grounds had produced many over time, and the meat was superb when dried and cured. His beloved wife Betty had returned later and cooked a meal of pap and stew after which they both retired to bed. They awoke as usual at 6.00 am. and before leaving for work, Betty had prepared a packed lunch for Temba for his hunting trip.

"Be careful on that bike," she warned him in Khoisan as she kissed him goodbye "See you later."

It was with a feeling of excitement that Temba Zulu packed his thick canvas rucksack with the bottled water, a pair of binoculars, the ammunition, and the sandwiches. He glanced at his watch to see it had just gone 7.00 am. He figured that if he rode the quad bike at a steady 40 km. per hour he would reach the familiar rocky outcrop by 8.00 am. and then the hunt would begin.

He stepped out of the small house, locked the door and used bungee cords to strap the rucksack and rifle to the rack on the rear of the powerful quad bike. The trip to the gate near the mine dump only took ten minutes and then finally, he turned west and headed out into the vast flat emptiness of the Namib desert.

Temba Zulu revved the machine and brought it up to speed. Instinctively he used the sun to gauge his direction and his spirits lifted with that familiar sense of freedom and the anticipation of the hunt. Forty-five minutes later the familiar outline of the rocky outcrop, that marked the hunting grounds, appeared through the early morning heat mirage on the horizon. On arrival, he killed the engine, unstrapped the rucksack and rifle and took a seat with his back against a rock. The silence was complete and all-encompassing, and he savoured the moment as he retrieved the water bottle from the rucksack and drank from it. It was an hour later when he first saw the flitter of movement on the horizon. He lifted the binoculars to his eyes and slowly turned the focus wheel until the image was clear.

"Ya," he whispered as he saw the small group of antelope. "There you are."

Temba Zulu weighed his options. The animals were far away. Further than he had ever had to go to make a shot. He knew he could take the bike but in doing that he risked spooking the skittish creatures and losing out. *No.* He thought. *I'll go on foot.* He set out making sure that he was upwind of the steady hot breeze that blew in from the west. After what seemed an eternity he squatted down on the blinding, sun-baked sand and brought the binoculars to his eyes. The small group of animals were still there but it was the distance that confused him. He turned back to take a look at the rocky outcrop where he had left the bike and saw that he had travelled at least 800 metres. *You'll need to travel further, Zulu.* He thought. It was a full ten minutes later when Temba Zulu decided he was close enough to make the shot. Any closer and he would risk alerting and scattering the animals. Slowly, he lay down on the burning sand and lifted the binoculars to his eyes. It seemed to him that the animals were lingering around what appeared to be a knoll of grassy sand. He assumed it was some geographical feature he had been unaware of until then. Quietly, and with great patience, he pulled a single bullet from his pocket and pushed it carefully into the chamber of the weapon. Temba Zulu studied his prey through the simple sights of the old rifle.

He chose the larger of the group, closed his left eye and tightened his grip on the trigger as he trained the sights on the head of the animal. The shot rang out with a loud crack and instantly the other animals fled in panic. Temba was certain he had made a good clean headshot, but his chosen animal was nowhere to be seen. Feeling somewhat confused, he brought the binoculars to his eyes where he lay and scanned the area. There was no sign of the carcass or indeed anything. He got to his feet and dusted himself off before heading to where the small animals had been gathered. It was only when he arrived at the spot that he saw the deep ravine that stretched out below him. He scanned the floor of the canyon and saw there were green shoots of grass on the sandy floor below. *That's why they were here*, he thought to himself. It was then he saw the animal he had shot. It lay at the foot of the ravine near a curve in the ancient riverbed. There was a small, neat hole in its skull just below the large ear. Temba Zulu smiled to himself. It had been a clean shot and the animal had died instantly. *Good.* He walked along the side of the canyon until he identified a spot where he felt he could climb down safely. Although steep, there were numerous footholds in the walls and dried camel thorn trees to grip with his hands. Once during his descent, he slipped and fell back onto his rucksack, but he soon got his footing again and he arrived at the floor of the gulley and turned right to find the dead animal. The air was cooler down there and when he finally reached the spot where the Steenbok had fallen, he sat in the shade and leant his back on the canyon wall to catch his breath. With his right hand, he felt the smooth hair on the animal's side. It was a good fat specimen and its flesh was still warm from the kill.

Temba Zulu looked up and considered how he would carry the dead animal out of the ravine. He decided he would simply carry it on his shoulder and exit the same way he had come in. He realized then that he was desperately thirsty. Pulling the rucksack from his back, he removed the water bottle and drank deeply from it. Feeling satisfied he replaced the top and placed the bottle on the hard sand near the head of the animal. It was then that he saw the stone. It lay half covered in fine caked sand and dust but immediately he knew it was different from the others.

The exposed parts of it had a distinctive blueish hue and soapy appearance. Temba Zulu reached down and prised the stone from the ground with his right hand. It came free after some effort and he lifted it up to study it further. The stone was nearly as large as a tennis ball and he knew immediately that it was particularly heavy. Using the fingers of both hands he began pushing away countless years of dust and caked earth from its surface and as he did so his excitement grew.

"This cannot be real," he whispered to himself in Khoisan. "Surely I am dreaming."

Frantically he opened the water bottle again and began to pour the liquid over the stone while rubbing it with his fingers and the bottom of his shirt. As he did so, more of its colour became visible and the true scale of his discovery was revealed. Temba Zulu's breathing quickened and he held the stone up to the sky with trembling hands. The rare pale blue colour was spectacular even in its rough, uncut form and from what he could see there was astonishing clarity as well. He brought it down and held it tightly with both hands while he thought. His mind was alive with possibilities, but these thoughts conflicted with his dedication to his job and the company. *What am I to do with this discovery?* He thought. *I must keep this a secret. No one should know a thing. Not even Betty. I must show it to my boss. Yes, Mr Klopp, he will know what to do. And I will be rewarded well...*

15

CHAPTER FIFTEEN: TRIGGERED

I awoke at 6.00 am. Sharp and sat bolt upright on the bed. I was still dressed and hadn't even pulled the duvet over myself during the night. Cursing quietly I put the kettle on and plugged in the new laptop I had purchased. The initial boot-up process was tedious so I turned on the television and took a hot shower while it started. I closed my eyes as the steaming water ran over my body and in my mind I heard Danny's words over and over.

"Someone must have messed with the plane," he had said with his shocked, deathly pale face. "It's most unusual."

I knew that if he was right, there was a chance that I could prove it. The tracking device I had placed in the black Mercedes of Mr Heinrich Klopp was the key. It was a long shot but certainly worth a try. I called room service as I dried off and ordered breakfast. After I had dressed I took a cup of coffee outside and climbed up a stairway to one of the turrets in the corner of the old castle-like building. The morning was fresh and clear and the sky above was perfectly blue. As I lit my first cigarette I stared out at the hills and mountains to the west to where the Apex mine was situated and the plane had come down. I realized that I had been in a state of profound shock since the crash and had been acting purely on instinct ever since. *Time to get your act together Green. There is much to do.* I met the waiter pushing a trolley with my breakfast as I made my way back to the room. I tipped him as he left and sat down to eat in front of the laptop. By then the machine had booted up properly and I was able to get online easily. There was an article on the front page of the website of a local newspaper saying that a rescue mission was planned for the crashed aircraft that morning. The reporter added that because of the remote location, helicopters would be used but warned that from the initial sightings, there was little hope that anyone had survived. More importantly, the article clearly stated that there had been two people on board.

Good. This works for you right now Green. Next, I went to the website of the tracking device and logged in. The site security was tight and before I could download the app, a code was sent to my phone. Once I had keyed it in I was finally able to download it. I drummed my fingers impatiently on the desk as I waited for it to open and load. My mind went back to the day Danny had arrived to take me to Windhoek from the mine. It had been around midday when he, Temba and I had pushed the aircraft into the hangar to protect it from the approaching dust storm. If Klopp had indeed tampered with the plane, there would have been a window of fewer than eighteen hours for him to do so. I knew from my recollection of the file from the insurance company that Klopp had worked as an aircraft mechanic in the German Air Force before he had started his career in mining. It was certainly possible that he had and if so perhaps the tracking device would prove it. With that in mind, I entered the date we had been due to leave the Apex facility. It took some seconds for the tracking program to gather the information and lay it out on the initially heavily pixelated screen, but once done, I had a detailed log of the movements of the black Mercedes for that entire day. I sat forward in my seat and studied the screen. The familiar landmarks of the crushing plants and the big hole were clear. The movements of the vehicle were mapped in squiggly thin blue lines on the screen. To the left was a time log showing how long the vehicle was parked at each location. The log showed the movements of the vehicle from 12.00 pm on the day to midnight. As I zoomed in, I recognized all of the various locations. There was the main house in the managers' compound, the dining room, the crushing plant and the vaults. Klopp had visited all of them but not once had he ventured anywhere near the airstrip or the hangar. Feeling somewhat disappointed I sat back in my seat and stared at the screen as I zoomed out. Danny, Temba and I had eaten together that night and I clearly remembered seeing Klopp's car parked outside his house in the evening. I sat forward once again and typed in the date of the following day. Once again the screen became pixelated and there was a long wait for the information to load. It was only when it finally cleared that I saw it. The information before me was as clear as day and the thin blue lines confirmed it. Heinrich Klopp had left his house in the darkness at 1.02 am. on the day we had departed the mine.

He had driven straight to the hangar at the airstrip and had remained there until 2.15 am. when he had left and driven back to his house. He had driven right past the cottage where Danny and I had been sleeping.

"No way," I whispered to myself as I took it all in. "Oh, I've got you now."

I paged down the log for the rest of the day, but the movements of the vehicle were normal and as they had been the previous day. *Danny was right, Green. Klopp had absolutely no reason to go to that hangar at that time other than to fuck with that plane. No reason on earth. What now?* With my mind spinning I grabbed the pack of cigarettes, left the room, and walked back up to the turret to smoke. The time was 8.30 am. and the day was beginning to heat up. Once again, I stared out at the mountains to the West as I smoked. *Assuming they recover the bodies from the plane today, there will still be a long delay until the air crash investigators complete their work. Even then it might not be obvious or proven that anything was tampered with. There's no harm in lying low for the moment. It'll give you the time to complete your report and this new evidence can be presented at a later date. Give yourself some time to think things over. When Klopp is finally nailed you can make sure he's nailed properly. Patience is a virtue, Green. Lie low for now.* I walked back to the room, packed my bags, and checked out of the hotel. My plan was to head to the small coastal town of Swakopmund. Once there I would find a quiet hotel, type up my report, and await the news from the crash site. I would decide, once there, when and how to present the fact that I had survived the crash to my principals at the insurance company. The news would no doubt come as a massive shock but there was nothing I could do about that. *All you need is time Green.* I knew Swakopmund was roughly three and a half hours drive from the capital Windhoek and I typed the destination into my phone as I got into the large 4x4 vehicle. By then the heat was stifling and I flicked the switch for the air-conditioning as the big diesel engine rumbled under the bonnet in front of me. The huge, all-terrain tyres of the vehicle crunched on the stones of the car park as I drove out into the pleasant suburbs of the capital in the blazing morning sun.

The directions from my phone led me past a shopping centre and eventually to a circular road that passed the turn-off to the grim C28 road I had travelled the previous day. I glanced at it with dread as I drove past on the tarred surface. Eventually, I emerged onto a highway that led past the university and then left the city heading north. The dual carriageway was modern and there was very little traffic as I sped past the stark dry hills and mountains on either side. The hilly terrain continued for the next forty minutes until I had to slow the vehicle to pass through the tiny town of Okahandja. Once clear, I picked up the speed again until I reached the crossroads at Karibib. It was from there that the surrounding countryside began to change noticeably and became flatter and dryer. I stopped at a lonely service station, bought a coffee, and smoked a cigarette near the vehicle as I drank. There was a different kind of heat in comparison to that of the capital, Windhoek. It reminded me of the mine. There the wind was like the blast of a hair dryer and it was a relief to climb back into the vehicle. The drive continued until I reached the small gemstone mining town of Usakos. This remote outpost marked the end of the tree line and the beginning of the desert. Although somewhat run down, the small town was clean and the signpost that marked the right-hand turn to Swakopmund was clear. The road was long and straight; the flat sands sparkled in the sunlight and quivered in the mirages on the horizon. Eventually, I passed the lone Spitzkop mountain to the right. Its sharp granite peaks jutted out of the surrounding desert and the tattered canvas and plastic-covered stalls of the semi-precious stone dealers rippled in the dusty wind at the turn-off. From there on it was desert and nothing else. The road was quiet apart from the odd heavy vehicle carrying freight from the port at Walvis Bay. The flat featureless landscape was stark and brutal in its emptiness and for a while I felt a similar sense of isolation as I had experienced at the mine. But my mind was preoccupied with the memory of the screen of the laptop with the blue lines that showed the path Klopp had taken that night when he had visited the hangar. My thoughts stayed on him as I drove the long straight road seemingly to nowhere. It was an hour later when I first saw the dunes on the horizon in front of me. At first, I was unsure of what I was looking at but as I drove closer their true scale was revealed. I learned later that they are some of the largest in the world. Spectacular in their sheer size and windswept beauty, the yellow behemoths stretched away as far as the eye could see and marked the point where the Namib desert met the Atlantic Ocean. Soon after, I arrived at the outskirts of the tiny coastal town of Swakopmund.

The main road led straight into the town and I was immediately astounded by what appeared to be a perfectly preserved Bavarian hamlet that seemed to have been physically lifted from Germany and plonked in the middle of the desert. The town was a surreal colonial remnant complete with half-timbered German buildings and it was clear that the architects had decided that it should resemble the German homeland as much as possible. I drove on slowly through the quaint little town until I reached the end of the road at the ocean. The cold green waters of the Atlantic crashed in waves on the sandy beach below and I parked the vehicle in front of the long pier that stretched out into the sea. Flocks of seagulls hovered in the sea breeze above and I was relieved to feel the temperature had cooled significantly from the heat of the desert. To my right was a large wooden building raised on concrete stilts that looked like a restaurant. To the left, a band of green grass with palm trees ran along the seafront to the end of the town where the dunes met the ocean. I got out of the vehicle and stretched as I breathed in the salty sea air. Below me, on the beach, children were playing and groups of tourists were wandering the beach picking up shells. I lit a cigarette and searched on my phone for some decent accommodation. There were several hotels, some modern and expensive, but I settled on a guest house by the name of Keystone Lodge. Set in an old house a couple of streets back from the seafront, it looked clean and comfortable. I called the phone number and it was picked up immediately by an English-speaking lady who spoke with an Afrikaans accent. With the room booked, I got back in the vehicle and entered the address on my phone. I needn't have bothered as I found the place a couple of hundred metres away from where I had parked. The building was an old colonial house that had been renovated and had rooms added. The gardens were green and pleasant and there was a courtyard with a rockery and fountain at the front. I parked the vehicle outside the front gate and walked into the reception. The lady who had answered the call met me and I filled in the booking form. When that was done she led me to my room which had a private verandah to the front. The space was light and airy and fitted with all the modern amenities one would expect. The lady handed me a glossy map of the town and asked if I would like to park inside the property at the back.

"It's such a small town," she said. "You can walk everywhere and the vehicle will be secure."

I agreed and drove the vehicle around the back of the property where a security guard opened a sliding gate for me. The guard helped me unpack and carry my bags to my room where I turned on the overhead fan and set up the laptop at the desk near the window. Finally, I sat back in the chair and stared out at the quiet secluded garden with the trickling waterfall outside. *This is perfect Green. You'll have the peace and quiet you need to get the report done and no one will be the wiser.* I logged on to the internet and searched for any news from the crash site. There were no updates available, so I turned the television on to see if there was any mention of it on the local news. Again, there was nothing. I drummed my fingers on the desk impatiently and glanced at my watch. It was 2.30 pm. and I was ravenous. I picked up the glossy map the receptionist had given me and took a look. There were several hotels, tourist shops and restaurants listed on it and as the lady had said, they were all within walking distance nearby. With my mind made up I closed the laptop, locked the door and headed out on foot.

The afternoon had begun to cloud over and there was a constant cool breeze coming in from the ocean. With the map in hand, I wandered up the street past the rows of old buildings and houses. Eventually, I came to the main street and passed the ancient wood beam facades of the Lutheran church and the Woermannhaus. To the left, down the hill, I could see the lighthouse with its distinctive bright red and white bands and domed top. The wide streets were spotless and there was an air of tranquillity about the place. I found myself relaxing for the first time in ages. Soon enough I came across an old pub by the name of Cookie's on the right-hand side of the street. I walked in and the worn wooden floorboards creaked under my feet. The place was almost empty but a young barman was scrolling on his phone behind the bar. He stood up as soon as I walked in.

"Good afternoon sir," he said.

"Hi," I replied. "I was hoping to get some food. Is the kitchen open?"

"Certainly sir," he replied. "Please take a seat anywhere."

I walked through to look at the restaurant area. It was a large darkened hall with high wood beam ceilings and bench tables. It had clearly been designed to resemble a Bavarian beer house. I settled for a small table at the bar near the front windows and sat down. The barman asked if I would like a drink to which I replied I would have a pint of beer. It was delivered in a stein along with a menu. I settled on the roast beef and placed my order with the young man who walked off to the kitchen to tell the chef. I found the free Wi-Fi on my phone and searched again for any news from the crash site. Still, there was nothing, and I sipped the beer as I stared out of the window at the street beyond while the sun began to make its way down over the ocean. *Relax Green. There'll be some news by tonight no doubt. You're here safe and sound and no one knows it. Relax.*

The roast beef was excellent served with vegetables, gravy, and a powerful horseradish sauce. The serving was massive and I had ordered a second beer by the time I had finished. It was 4.00 pm. when I finally left the pub and stepped out into the cool afternoon air for a cigarette. Instead of heading straight back to the guest house, I decided to take a short walk around the town. I ended up turning right and walking past the grand old railway station which had been converted into a luxury hotel. Resplendent in white and green it stood as possibly the grandest of all the old buildings surrounded by green lawns and palm trees. I carried on walking down the street until I reached the beachfront road where I turned left. I passed the museum and the lighthouse and then crossed the breakwater down to the sand and continued towards the pier. The last of the craft vendors were packing up for the day as I made my way up and underneath the raised restaurant at the head of the pier.

It was almost 5.00 pm. when I arrived back at the guest house and set up the laptop on the desk to type up my report. Before I began I checked the news sites and immediately saw there were updates. The lead story on the main Namibian news website detailed a botched tender process for a Chinese road-building project but the crash was featured directly below. The article read:

'The bodies of two men were recovered from the site of a light aircraft crash late this afternoon. The plane had come down two days ago in a remote mountainous area between Windhoek and Walvis Bay. Both bodies were burnt beyond recognition. Air crash investigators had begun preliminary checks but due to the remote location of the site, it will be some time before their work is finalized. However initial findings indicate engine failure as the reason for the accident.'

I sat back after reading the brief article once again. *It's as you expected Green. It's as everyone will have expected. This is good. Now get on with your work.*

I began typing my report outlining my activities from the moment I arrived in Namibia. I knew full well that the company would expect it to be thorough. My findings would have to prove, beyond doubt, that there were indeed shady dealings going on with the Namibia operation of Apex Resources. The report would be minutely scrutinized by many, if not all, of the top people in the upper echelons of several organizations, and there would be no room for error. The process would involve forensic auditors and accountants, so whatever I produced would need to be completely watertight. It was 5.56 pm. when I saw the tiny icon in the bottom right corner of my screen flash. There was movement in Heinrich Klopp's house. Although my instinct was to ignore it, my curiosity got the better of me and I clicked it. As expected, the small windows that showed the view from each hidden camera expanded and I clicked once again on the one that showed movement. Heinrich Klopp stood in the kitchen near the lounge of his house.

I watched as he poured a glass of water from a bottle he had taken from the fridge. The big man was dressed in his usual attire and stood at the counter facing the camera as he drank. Finishing the water, he placed the glass carefully on the counter, then leaning on both hands, he stood staring out at what I imagined were the open curtains of his front windows. He seemed somewhat melancholy or perhaps deep in thought. *You've read the same news report as I have haven't you Klopp? About the crash and the two bodies. Doesn't seem to have worried you too much though. Just another day isn't it? Well, you can relax for now. But rest assured you will be exposed.* At that moment Klopp lifted his left wrist and looked at his watch. *Just before 6.00 pm. Dinner time for Heinrich. Don't be late now.* Right on cue he lifted the empty glass from the counter and turned to place it in the sink behind him. After that, he walked through the lounge and out of sight of the camera as he left the building. I watched as the vehicle tracking icon flashed. As usual, Klopp had decided to drive to the dining room instead of taking the short walk down the hill. *That's what I like about you Klopp. You're predictable. Apart from that you don't really have too many other redeeming qualities.* I minimised the screens from the now dormant house cameras and continued with my report.

At 6.30 pm. I sat back and looked at what I had written. I gauged I was perhaps a quarter of the way through and I was feeling stiff and tired. I got up and stepped outside into the cool dusk to smoke a cigarette near the rockery in the garden. The sun had disappeared behind the buildings across the street and the moon was rising in the east. The sleepy town of Swakopmund was silent and there was no traffic on the road. I listened to the trickle of the water from the fountain and as I smoked my thoughts turned to Danny, his family and his girlfriend. I sighed deeply as I imagined their anguish at the news from the crash site. I thought of the title deeds and the engagement ring he had shown me so proudly and then given me right before the explosion. *You can hand them over personally as promised Green. All in good time.* The sun had set completely by the time I walked back into my room. The last thing I felt like doing was continuing with the report, but I forced myself and worked for a solid hour until the icon for the cameras flashed once again in the bottom right corner of the screen. I fought the urge to click on it but succumbed after a few seconds. Heinrich Klopp had returned from dinner and was seated at his desk in the study attending to business.

There was a faint noise coming from the tiny microphone on the camera so I adjusted the volume on my own machine so I could hear better. Once I had done that it became clear what the sound was. The man was whistling softly to himself as he worked on his private computer, but I had no idea what the tune was. *That's right, Klopp. You and I both. We're catching up on some important work. Enjoy your evening.* I minimised the camera view screen, turned the volume down a couple of notches so the sound would not annoy me, and carried on with my own work. It was exactly ten minutes later that I heard the faint but clear chime of the doorbell. The sound had come from the front room of Klopp's house and I immediately stopped what I was doing and clicked on the camera icon to bring up the screen array. Initially, I was curious as to who had arrived at Klopp's house but then the memories of the sadistic events I had witnessed in his 'dungeon' came back to haunt me. I had no wish to witness anything like that ever again but I watched as Klopp left the office and walked through the lounge to open the front door. I turned the volume up once again as he stepped out of my line of vision to greet whoever was at the door. There were two muffled voices, both male, and I leant forward to listen. After a while, the two men walked into my line of vision and then I saw who the visitor was. There was no mistaking him. It was my friend, the young foreman, Temba Zulu. He stood there, still in his work suit, with a small rucksack slung over his right shoulder. Finally, the two men were close enough to the hidden camera for me to hear them talking clearly.

"I am not happy at all, this is most unusual Temba," said Klopp, clearly annoyed "Could it not have waited until tomorrow?"

"I apologize but it's important sir. Very important," said Temba evenly. "If you will just give me five minutes of your time, I will show you."

"You say it has to do with our work here at the mine?" asked Klopp.

"Yes sir," replied Temba. "I have made a discovery."

"Very well," said Klopp with a dramatic sigh. "Take a seat at the table."

He motioned towards the dining room table situated behind the seating area. Temba walked over and took a seat on the left-hand side of the table while Klopp sat opposite the camera. The light above the table afforded me a perfect view of the meeting.

My interest piqued, I sat forward and waited. Temba took the small rucksack from his shoulder and placed it on the table in front of him.

"Mr Klopp I'm not sure if you are aware that on my days off, I occasionally go hunting in the desert," said Temba.

"No," replied Klopp impatiently. "I was not aware of that but please go on."

"Well sir," said Temba, "two days ago I went out hunting on the quad bike. I went to my usual spot about forty kilometres from here. My hunt led me further than usual and eventually, I had to climb down a canyon. But it was whilst I was down in that canyon that I found this."

Temba unzipped the rucksack and brought out something round and heavy-looking wrapped in a tea towel. He placed the item in the centre of the table and began unwrapping it methodically. Klopp watched with a raised eyebrow as he did this but sat forward as soon as it was revealed. I did exactly the same, but to me, it simply looked like a lump of rock. Heinrich Klopp lifted the object up to the light and turned it in his hand.

"Ich glaube es nicht," he said quietly. "I don't believe it."

The silence in the room was deafening as the big man turned the stone again and again in the light. Eventually, he placed it back on the tea towel in the centre of the table and spoke.

"Please sit here for a moment Temba," he said calmly. "I need to get some equipment."

"Certainly sir," replied Temba.

Klopp stood up and I heard the chair scrape on the tiles as he did so. He turned and walked down the corridor and I saw the flash of the camera to indicate he had entered his office. With a simple click on the mouse pad, my view changed to the office and I watched as Klopp rummaged in the drawer of his desk. He retrieved two items and quickly left the room. I clicked on the icon for the lounge camera and watched as he took his seat at the table once again and placed the two items in front of himself. He picked up the larger of the two and spoke.

"This is a diamond tester Temba," said Klopp calmly. "It will test the thermal properties along with several other factors. I will now test this stone."

"Yes sir," said Temba. "Please go ahead."

Heinrich Klopp pushed a button on the small hand-held machine. It beeped once and I clearly saw the tiny red light illuminate on the side of it. Once again he picked up the stone and held it to the light. Using his right hand, he held the point of the instrument to the surface of the stone. A row of red, yellow, and green lights lit up on the side of the device and it emitted a single high-pitched beep. After a second the green light showed again and there was another beep. Heinrich Klopp repeated this process on various surfaces of the stone until he was satisfied. He placed the tester back on the table and picked up the second smaller object. It turned out to be a jeweller's loupe which he placed in the socket of his right eye. He brought the stone close to his face and studied it minutely, turning it in his hand as he did so. Finally, he removed the jeweller's loupe and placed the stone back on the tea towel. Heinrich Klopp placed both of his hands on the edge of the table and sat in silence staring at the stone in front of him.

By then I was totally mesmerized as I sat glued to the screen.

"Temba," said Klopp.

"Yes sir."

"This is indeed a diamond and I would like to congratulate you on this discovery," he said quietly in his German accent. "It may well prove to be amongst the most significant in the history of Southern Africa."

"Thank you, Mr Klopp," said Temba. "I knew I had to bring it directly to you."

Heinrich Klopp shifted nervously in his seat, but his eyes never left the stone on the table in front of him.

"Temba," he said quietly. "Have you told anyone about this?"

"No sir," came the reply. "You are the first to know."

"Not even your wife Betty?" asked Klopp.

"I have told no one, sir," replied Temba, "not even my wife."

"I see," said Klopp scratching his chin thoughtfully. "And you say you made this discovery in the desert not far from here?"

"Yes sir," Temba replied. "Roughly forty or fifty kilometres from here."

"And you would be able to take me there, or perhaps show me on a computer?" asked Klopp.

"Yes sir," replied Temba diligently. "I can show you."

It was clear to me that Klopp's demeanour had changed. He was no longer brisk and impatient in his treatment of Temba. Since seeing the stone, it was as if he had almost become sickly sweet. This was slightly alarming as I knew full well what he was capable of when it came to money. The two men sat for another few minutes discussing the location of the discovery. Klopp asked another three times if Temba had told anyone. Once again, he was completely resolute and insisted that he had told no one. This seemed to have a calming effect on Klopp but I, for one, was worried. There I was, sitting hundreds of kilometres away from the very events I was witnessing live on camera, and I could do nothing. It was both fascinating and alarming at the same time. At one stage Temba was even offered a drink. He refused politely and the conversation went on. One of the questions Klopp asked was if Temba had seen any evidence of other diamonds at the site. He replied saying he had not, and that upon finding the one he had presented, he had returned to the mine immediately. Klopp seemed to find this statement plausible given the sheer size of the stone. I felt a desperate urge for a cigarette, but I simply could not stop watching the screen. The conversation steered once again to the location of the find. It was blatantly apparent that Klopp was doing his best to put Temba at ease. Time and time again he lifted the stone and held it to the light.

"Tolle!" he repeated in German as if in awe. "Amazing."

Eventually, it was decided that a computer would be brought through and Temba would pinpoint the exact location of the find on Google Maps.

"It is important that this is properly logged before any exploration work can proceed," explained Klopp.

Temba consented to this with his usual polite professionalism and remained seated at the table while Klopp walked back to the office. I immediately clicked on the relevant camera to watch. It was what happened next that sent an icy shiver down my spine and caused my body to stiffen with fear. Upon arriving in the office Heinrich Klopp immediately opened the cabinet and removed the Luger pistol I had seen. He glanced over his shoulder then pulled out the magazine and checked the breach before placing it on the shelf.

"Oh, Jesus Christ no," I whispered to myself. "No, no, no. Please no."

Next, he unplugged his own laptop and carried it back to the lounge where Temba was waiting. I glanced around the room where I sat feeling there must be something I should be doing. But there was nothing I *could* do. Nothing except watch and wait. Heinrich Klopp placed the computer in front of Temba and stood behind him, leaning over his left shoulder as he began working.

"Now Temba," he said. "I am going to bring up our current location here at the mine on Google Maps and then we can both try to pinpoint the spot where you found this stone,"

"Yes sir," said Temba as he leant forward and studied the screen.

The screen cast a bluish hue on their faces as they began. Temba sat patiently as Klopp worked the mouse pad mumbling from time to time. What Temba could not see was Klopp's eyes. They darted constantly from the screen to the large round stone that still lay on the tea towel in front of them.

THE STAR OF THE DESERT

It was clear to me that the man was now obsessed. Despite the cool conditions at the coast, I found myself sweating profusely and my hands shook slightly as I watched. The scene that was unfolding before me was completely surreal and on more than one occasion I had to fight the urge to pinch myself. The two men remained in their position as they stared at the screen mumbling quietly. After what seemed an age both men pointed at the screen and Klopp stood upright.

"How can you be so sure this is the place Temba?" he asked.

"I know this place very well sir," he replied. "I have spent many days there hunting and I know this outcrop of rocks like the back of my hand."

"And the ravine where you found this stone?" asked Klopp.

"That is it, sir," said Temba pointing at the screen once again. "One hundred per cent."

"Okay, good," said Klopp. "Before we log these coordinates I need to get something from my office. Wait here please."

"Yes sir," said Temba cheerfully.

I watched in horror as Klopp walked out of the line of sight of the camera and my hand shook as I clicked on the flashing icon of the office cam. My breathing became fast and heavy as I watched him pick up the pistol from the shelf and jam it behind his back in his belt.

"Dear God, no!" I said out loud as I raised my hands and ran them through my hair. "Please, no!"

At that moment my mouth went dry and things began to appear in slow motion. I watched as he left the room and turned back towards the lounge. He went calmly and silently and my hand shook violently as I clicked on the lounge cam. The view showed Temba sitting calmly where I had last seen him at the table staring at the computer screen. Heinrich Klopp entered the room and spoke without breaking his stride.

"I have one more question Temba," he said as he arrived behind the seated man and pointed at the screen. "This rocky outcrop."

At the exact moment Temba sat forward to look at the screen, Heinrich Klopp pulled the gun from the belt behind his back with his right hand. With perfectly calm precision he brought it up and held it to the back of the young man's head. The shot was sudden and the sound of it was distorted on my speaker. I half expected the young man's head to flick forward violently but it did not. The bullet travelled through the back of his head and came to rest somewhere in his cranial cavity. His body immediately slumped forward and a thick river of dark blood gushed from the neat hole in the back of his head. Immediately Klopp brought his left hand back and caught his forehead as it fell forward. He gently brought the body back to allow the stream of blood to fall onto the tiles below. Temba's head hung backwards draining the thick mixture of blood and brains steadily. My own emotions were stunned at the sudden tranquillity and silence of the scene that had just played live on the screen in front of me. With my eyes glued to the spectacle, I sighed deeply and brought my right hand to my mouth to stifle myself. I was no stranger to violent death, but this was somehow different and quite unusual in its calmness. Heinrich Klopp walked swiftly towards the curtains below the camera and went out of sight briefly as he looked outside. Apparently satisfied, he walked back to the table and placed the gun next to the laptop.

Completely ignoring the dead man right next to him, he sat down and reached for the stone from the centre of the table. Once again, he held it up to the light and studied it for a good minute. I sat in mesmerized silence watching him. It was only then that my breathing began to calm and I looked around the room briefly and blinked. *What the fuck?* Eventually, Heinrich Klopp turned and regarded the dead man sitting next to him. He studied the body for a moment as if deciding what to do next. His face was completely devoid of emotion. Then, with a final look at the stone, he stood and walked quietly back down the corridor. I clicked on the flashing icon of the office cam and watched as he calmly swung the painting away from the wall to expose the hidden safe. With a few deft turns of the combination, the thick door swung open and he carefully placed the stone inside. Heinrich Klopp left the office and walked back down the corridor towards the lounge. I watched him walk past the dining room table and into the kitchenette. He emerged a minute later with a plastic bag and a bungee cord in hand. He swiftly placed the bag over Temba's head and then wrapped the bungee cord tightly around his neck to effectively stem any further blood and brain matter from escaping. Next, he disappeared into his bedroom only to emerge a few minutes later wearing a dark blue work suit. In a clear demonstration of his strength, he lifted the limp body from the chair holding it under the arms. He dragged it through the kitchen and out the back door. The dragging shoes left a dark smear of blood on the tiles. Heinrich Klopp returned through the back door a minute later. In his hands, he carried a bucket and a mop. With his back to the camera, he turned on the sink tap and waited for the water to fill. I watched as he slowly moved the chair Temba had been sitting on and began mopping the floor. He did this slowly and carefully along the trail of blood, regularly rinsing the mop, until finally the floor was clean. After rinsing the mop and the bucket once again he calmly collected his laptop and returned to his office as if absolutely nothing had happened. I glanced at my watch to see that it had just gone 11.30 pm. I looked back at my screen to see Klopp was busy working on his computer, just as he had been earlier in the evening. There was not a trace of strain or worry on his face. The bluish glow from the screen accentuated his brutal angular features and his cruel lips appeared even thinner. Suddenly the reality of what I had just witnessed hit me and I felt the bile rising in my throat.

I closed my eyes, shook my head and walked out of the room into the garden. With my mind spinning I paced the garden in the moonlight feeling confused and sick to my stomach. The fresh air was a tonic so I decided to take a walk. I locked the room and left the guest house through the front gate. The streets were bathed in a steamy yellow glow from the mist that rolled in from the ocean. At the crossroads I turned and headed towards the jetty, the smell of salt filling my nostrils. I crossed the deserted seafront road and made my way onto the pier. The three-hundred-metre walk to the end was lit by antique iron streetlights on either side and the wooden railings were whitened with seagull droppings. Beneath me, in the darkness, the waves crashed repeatedly, and on more than one occasion I heard the barking and honking of seals in the water. The wind coming in from the ocean was crisp and laden with moisture, but it helped to clear my mind. I arrived at the end of the pier and pulled the pack of cigarettes from my pocket. Shielding the lighter from the wind I lit up and stared out at the heaving, foaming grey swells. *This man is a psychopath, Green. A crook, a sadist, a psychopath, and a cold-blooded murderer. On your watch, he has taken the lives of two bright young men who had great futures ahead of them. He tried to kill you. He's a megalomaniac and he will stop at nothing. Because of him there has been, and will be a great deal of pain and suffering. He must be stopped.* I pondered my next move as I smoked, then finally pulled the phone from my pocket. I scrolled down until I found the saved number of Heinrich Klopp and began typing a text message.

'Klopp, this is Green. I'm alive. I know everything. I'm coming for you...'

16

Chapter Sixteen: Green

It was 1.00 am. by the time I got back to the guest house and I was seething with anger. Immediately I opened the laptop and clicked on the app for the camera array at Klopp's house. All of them were live but there was no movement at all. *In bed perhaps? Surely not.* Next, I opened the vehicle tracking app and sat impatiently as the screen loaded from a pixelated mess to show the location and travel history of the black Mercedes. I drummed my fingers on the surface of the desk as I waited. Eventually, the information was processed and the screen cleared. The map showed the terrain in daylight for ease of use although in reality, it was the middle of the night. It was clear the vehicle had moved and had travelled a good distance from the mine. I zoomed in on the map and saw the thin blue line indicating that Klopp had left the mine using the North exit near the dumps and had headed out into the desert for roughly twenty kilometres. *He's dumping the body, Green. Getting rid of it where he thinks it'll never be found. No doubt about that.* I sat staring at the image for a few minutes wondering exactly what it was he was doing at that very moment. Eventually, I realized that I was simply wasting my own time. The exact coordinates of Klopp's journey would be logged and stored in the cloud and would certainly be used when the time came to prosecute him. There was also the possibility that the body of the missing diamond sorter would be there as well. *A dog always returns to his vomit.* Next, I opened Google Maps to find directions to the Apex mine. It turned out the road I would be taking was the same C28 dirt road I had used to get back to Windhoek from the crash site. The very thought of it brought back a slew of bad memories. On the screen, the road was shown as being an unpaved gravel track that led east through the flat wastelands of the desert until finally reaching the mountains at the Boshua Pass. From there it climbed up steeply and wound its way through the hills until finally reaching the capital. A quick Google search confirmed it as being one of the least travelled roads in the world, classified as 'dangerous' with endless stretches of desert, sand pools, big dips and steep gradients. *You better be sure the vehicle is in good shape for this Green.* I stood up, closed the door behind me, and walked around the front of the guest house until I reached the parking area.

The security guard was surprised to see me arriving at that early hour and stood up immediately to ask if everything was okay. I told him that everything was fine but that I would be leaving early and wanted to look over the vehicle before I departed. He immediately flicked a switch on the back wall which illuminated the parking area. I opened the large 4x4 vehicle and began a thorough check with assistance from the guard who held his torch for me. Thankfully everything that had been promised by the car hire company was there and in good working order. There was even a power supply for a laptop, a mini air compressor and repair kit for flat tyres, and a fully stocked toolbox. In case of sticky or sandy situations there was a set of aluminium sand tracks on the roof rack and a heavy-duty electric winch bolted to the front bull bar.

"Ahh," said the guard quietly as I stood back. "This car can go anywhere boss."

"Looks like it" I replied.

I thanked the man and asked where the manager's quarters were. He pointed me towards a small cottage to the rear of the premises. I walked over and knocked quietly on the door. The same woman who had checked me in came to the door rubbing her eyes with an alarmed look on her face. I apologized for waking her but explained I had been called away on urgent business and had to leave immediately. She said that was fine and that I should leave the room with the key on the bed. I thanked her and walked with the security guard back to my room. It only took a few minutes to pack and the guard helped me with my luggage back to the car park. I thanked the man and tipped him generously before climbing into the vehicle and starting the engine. He slid the gate open on its wheels and I reversed out onto the dark street.

The sand that had blown in from the ocean crunched on the tarmac under the tyres as I pulled away and made a right turn towards the main street. The steamy mist obscured the moon overhead and there was not a single soul to be seen. It took ten minutes of driving around until I finally found a 24-hour service station. I told the sleepy attendant to fill the tank and the four jerry cans on the roof rack with diesel while I walked into the convenience shop. The bright neon lights stung my eyes and I blinked repeatedly as

I walked the aisles. I emerged ten minutes later carrying two shopping bags of supplies. I placed the six litres of bottled water, ten cans of Red Bull, a kilogram of game biltong, and sandwiches in the foot well of the passenger seat. Before paying for the fuel I checked the oil and water levels in the engine bay. It was 3.45 am. when I finally left the small town of Swakopmund and headed east in search of the C14 road that linked the small town to the port at Walvis Bay. According to the maps, this fifty-kilometre stretch was usually only used by heavy vehicles. There was no link from the scenic ocean road to the notorious C28 that led to the mine. As I drove I remembered Temba telling me that the giant fuel tankers that supplied the mine would often spend eight to fifteen hours getting there from the port. The time factor would obviously depend on the condition of the road and the ever-shifting dunes. I figured, given the fact that I was in a much lighter and faster vehicle, that I could make it to the mine in six hours or less. I found the turn-off for the C14 roughly ten kilometres from the outskirts of town. As I made the right turn, the sun began to rise over the horizon of the desert to the east. To my right, the colossal wind-sculpted shapes of the dunes began to glow yellow and pink. The image resembled a Martian landscape from a science fiction movie. I pushed the accelerator and the powerful turbo diesel engine growled under the hood in front of me. As the sun continued to rise the true scale of the stark emptiness that was the Namib was revealed. There was not a living thing as far as the eye could see. Not even a single stalk of dried grass. I found the turn-off for the remote C28 road fifteen minutes later.

It was marked by a rusted green sign that was peppered with bullet holes. I stopped in a cloud of dust in front of it and turned to look at the desolate stretch of gravel that blurred into the horizon to my left. *If you make this turn here, you're committed to this Green. Better to be sure.* I hung my head briefly and closed my stinging bloodshot eyes. In my mind, I saw the smiling youthful faces of Danny Meyer and Temba Zulu. I opened my eyes and looked once again down the road as I lit a cigarette.

"Fuck it," I said to myself. "Let's go."

17

CHAPTER SEVENTEEN: KLOPP

Heinrich Klopp stopped dead in his tracks in the corridor.

"Schweinhund!" he shrieked in total disbelief as he stared at his phone.

For a second he told himself he must be dreaming but he read the message three times over.

'Klopp this is Green. I'm alive. I know everything. I'm coming for you.' it read.

On top of his fatigue, the message had come as a huge shock. *This man is dead. I know he's dead. What is happening?* He walked back into the office and Googled the news once again to reassure himself. It was there for all to see.

'The bodies of two men were recovered,' it read.

"Fuck!" he shouted as he began pacing the office glancing at his phone repeatedly "Bastard! How is this possible?"

Heinrich Klopp sat at his computer once again but his eyes were drawn to the built-in web camera at the top of the screen. The sight of it brought on an immense wave of fear and paranoia.

With a sharp intake of breath, he turned suddenly and looked at the curtains at the window to his right. *Someone is watching me!* He thought in wide-eyed panic. Heinrich Klopp stood up suddenly and the chair he had been sitting on fell over behind him. The noise startled him further and once again he looked around the room in fear. With his phone in hand, he began pacing the corridor and the lounge frantically, only stopping to read the terrifying message again and again. *How, how, how is this possible? Why am I being tormented like this?* By then his body was literally buzzing with alarm. He was exhausted and extremely thirsty but he could think of nothing else. *I must lie down.* He thought. *I must rest. Everything must continue as normal. I must rest.* Heinrich Klopp walked into his bedroom, placed the phone on the bedside drawer, and lay down on the mattress. He closed his eyes and tried to relax, but it was completely futile. The paranoia and fear were eating him alive and it began to dawn on him that he may well be in very serious danger. 'I know everything...' the message had said. *Everything*. He opened his bloodshot eyes and stared at the ceiling above. *If this bastard is alive, and he does indeed know everything, I am in trouble.* He turned his head and noticed, through the gap in the curtains, that the sun was beginning to rise outside. As he did so he let out a long forlorn wail of despair. He realized he was witnessing the fruits of his life's work slip away right before his eyes. The thought of an African prison began to play on his mind and this spurred him into action. Despite his fatigue, he sprang to his feet and walked shakily into the office. With trembling hands, he turned the combination on the safe until the small door swung open.

"Ahh yes," he whispered to himself as he brought the heavy stone out from within "There you are my beauty."

Heinrich Klopp cradled the stone against his bare midriff and stared at it as he turned it in his hands. In his world of confusion and fear, he saw it as his only consolation.

His escape from the terror he felt and his only guarantee of a secure and prosperous future. He closed his eyes and tried to imagine his life beyond the mine. But his vision was soon replaced by the image of a face. A sneering, knowing face. The face of the Englishman. Jason Green.

"Bastard!" he shrieked with furious exasperation.

Heinrich Klopp's sense of fear was beginning to alternate with a seething anger. He walked up to the window and parted the curtains to look out at the dawn. His red eyes flicked around searching for a clue. Any sign as to how this nightmare was actually happening. He stormed into the lounge cursing loudly and stood there searching for anything that seemed out of place. He scanned the perimeter of the room, scrutinizing every square inch of it until his eyes settled on the curtain pelmet above the main windows. There was something there near one of the antique beer steins. A minuscule black dot. A tiny, inconsequential anomaly that may well have been simply a dead insect.

"Was is das?" he whispered to himself. What is that?

He walked up to the pelmet, stood on the tips of his toes and reached for the strange object near the beer stein. It felt hard in his hand and as he pulled it forward the slimline lithium battery came out with it. Heinrich Klopp's face bulged and turned bright purple with rage.

"Bastard!" he screamed as he held the tiny camera in his shaking hands.

Bristling with rage he stomped across the lounge, into the kitchen, and smashed the tiny device into pieces using a heavy wooden rolling pin. But it was then that the real fear set in. With wide eyes, his head began to jerk from left to right as he scrutinized everything in sight.

In a state of blind panic, he ran down the corridor into his office and dialled the number for the only person he truly trusted at the mine facility. The foreman, Max Chawora answered immediately.

"Yes sir," he said.

"Max!" shouted Klopp "I need you to pack a bag and get to my house immediately"

"Is there a problem Sir?"

"Yes!" came the bellowed reply "Did you not hear me? I'll give you ten minutes! Come immediately!"

Heinrich Klopp hung up and stared around once. By then his paranoia was so extreme he saw hidden eyes watching from everywhere. With trembling hands, he lifted the aluminium diamond transport case from the floor next to his desk. The sturdy chain and single handcuff attached to the handle rattled as he placed it on the wooden surface in front of him. After some fumbling with the combination locks it opened and he carefully placed the giant stone inside. Next, he turned to the wall safe and removed a thin brown paper bag of smaller stones he had pilfered from previous extractions.

He placed it in the case near the large stone and closed it firmly. Next, he walked through to his bedroom and dressed while going through a mental checklist of items he would take with him. He placed two large bags on his bed and filled one with clothes and toiletries. The other he carried through to his office and filled it with his files and laptop computer. Finally, he placed the freshly used Luger pistol into an antique leather holster and attached it to his belt. Heinrich Klopp stood panting heavily with his hands on his hips and stared around the room at his treasured belongings.

The books, the German militaria, the paintings, the antiques. They were the products of a lifetime's collecting. To him, priceless artefacts and objects of desire. *And because of one man, I might lose it all*. Tears of rage welled in Heinrich Klopp's bloodshot eyes.

"But I have the stone," he whispered to himself. "I have the stone."

At that moment there was a loud knock on the front door. It startled him briefly but he quickly realized it was the foreman Max Chawora. He pocketed his set of keys and walked to the front door carrying the two heavy bags. He swung the door open violently and looked at the startled, portly black man standing outside.

"Open the Mercedes," he barked, handing the keys to the man. "Put your bag and these two in the back of the vehicle and wait for me in the driver's seat."

"Yes sir," said Max in a shaky voice.

Heinrich Klopp stormed back to his office and gathered up the chain and handcuff on the aluminium diamond transport case. Realizing it would probably be the last time he saw his house, he marched back down the corridor, through the lounge and out into the bright morning sun. Max had reversed the vehicle and was sitting, as instructed, in the driver's seat. Without hesitating, Klopp opened the passenger door, placed the aluminium case in the foot well, and climbed in.

"Drive!" he shouted.

"Where to Sir?" came the reply.

"Windhoek!" shrieked Klopp impatiently "Drive now!"

18

Chapter Eighteen: Green

The huge off-road tyres spun in the gravel as I took the left turn onto the C28 road. I gunned the powerful engine until I had reached a speed of 100 km per hour. The road surface was heavily rutted and the entire vehicle juddered and shook violently as I drove. After fifteen minutes I glanced in the rear-view mirror to see that the massive dunes of the coastal region were out of sight and I was now completely surrounded by a bleak and dystopian wasteland. On a few occasions, I tried to push the vehicle harder and get my speed to 120 km per hour, but it resulted in a dangerous loss of control at the wheel which was compounded by the occasional hidden stretch of deep sand that caused the vehicle to swerve precariously. At one point the truck almost rolled and it was then that that I decided it was best to proceed with caution. *Slowly slowly catch the monkey Green*. The terrible heat of the desert came on with a vengeance as I drove. It was exactly the same as I had experienced at the mine and the memory of it brought on a sense of foreboding and extreme isolation. The rays of the burning sun above reflected off the countless flakes of silica in the desert sand. They stung my eyes even through my sunglasses. It was half an hour later when I stopped to answer the call of nature. As I stood relieving myself, I pulled my phone from my pocket to check for network coverage. I was surprised to find that even at that distance there were still four bars of signal. I could only put it down to the fact that there was literally nothing standing between the mobile base stations at Walvis Bay and where I stood. I knew for a fact that due to distance this would not be the case for much longer, but it sparked an idea in my mind. I climbed back into the cab and removed the laptop from its case. The vehicle was fitted with an AC inverter which provided power for such devices. I plugged it in and set it up on the passenger seat. Next, I connected my phone to the computer using a USB cable. The process took five minutes but when I was done I was effectively online. I knew I was wasting precious time but curiosity had gotten the better of me and, while I still could, I could not help taking a look at the movements of Klopp's vehicle. The mobile internet was a lot slower than normal Wi-Fi and the tracking program took three minutes to load. I drank from one of the water bottles and chewed on a stick of biltong as I waited.

Once the program had loaded I clicked on the icon for the tracking device in the black Mercedes of Heinrich Klopp. I pulled another stick of biltong out of the bag as I waited for the heavily pixelated screen to load and clear. When it finally cleared it was not the usual image of the mine I had become used to. Instead, the screen showed the vehicle was surrounded by an endless flat landscape of desert. More importantly, the image showed the vehicle was moving, and doing so at great speed. I quickly screwed the top back onto the water bottle and sat forward to take a closer look. There was not a single landmark on the screen that I recognized. Using the mouse pad I zoomed out of the picture to get a clear idea of the vehicle's location. It was only when I did this that I saw it clearly. Heinrich Klopp was travelling north through the desert towards the C28 road. The scale on the map showed he had travelled some 80 km since leaving the mine and he had roughly another 80 km to go until he would reach the turn-off.

"He's on the move" I whispered to myself. "He's making a run for it."

I hurriedly lit a cigarette as I pondered what to do. I knew I was roughly 100 km from the turn-off to the mine. *He has only two courses when he gets to the crossroads at the C28. He will have to either head my way towards the coast or make a run for Windhoek. Those are the only options he has. If he comes my way, I'll spot him immediately. If he heads for the capital, I'll find him using the tracker. Either way, you need to get going now Green!* I slammed the engine into gear and the tyres kicked up a cloud of dust behind me as I went. The fact that Heinrich Klopp was making a run for it had the instant effect of awakening me to the urgency of the situation. The feelings of exhaustion were gone as was the stinging in my eyes. The confrontation would happen, and perhaps sooner than I had anticipated. I glanced at the speedometer to see I was travelling at 100 km per hour once again.

Keep it steady Green. Keep it steady.

19

Chapter Nineteen: Klopp

Heinrich Klopp gritted his teeth furiously as he waited for the security guard to open the boom at the entrance to the mine. Even at that early hour of the morning, there were beads of sweat forming on his forehead and on that of his driver, Max Chawora. When finally, they were through and had begun their journey down the long 160 km stretch to the C28 road, he sat back and breathed a sigh of relief. With his jaw muscles bulging he stared straight ahead at the great expanse of emptiness and thought. *It will be a seven or eight-hour drive to Windhoek. I will pay Max off and send him back to the mine. I will lie low and get a flight out of the country tomorrow. Everything will be fine.*

"Faster Max!" he blurted out at the confused-looking man "Put your foot down!"

Heinrich Klopp had never once made this journey by road. He had always flown to and from his work at the Apex mine. The powerful black Mercedes SUV rattled and juddered over the rutted surface leaving a cloud of pale talcum behind it. It was a great relief, however, to have left the mine and the terrible torment he had suffered from the Englishman, Green. He glanced at his phone to see there was no signal at all. *Ja, schweinhund.* He thought. *We will see who has fixed who.* With his mind racing and fighting extreme fatigue, he sat in stony silence as they drove through the morning. Occasionally Max would glance at him and then quickly look away in fear. The very fact that he was doing this began to annoy Klopp. It was as if he was questioning his authority, and in his mind, this amounted to massive insubordination. It was only after forty-five minutes of solid driving that he finally spoke.

"We will drive to Windhoek, Max," he said. "I have some extremely important business there. You will drop me at a location I will choose, and then return to the mine. Of course, you will be paid very well. Is that clear?"

"Yes sir," said Max nervously. "No problem."

Heinrich Klopp started to relax. In his mind, he finally had a sense of purpose and direction instead of the dreadful feelings of paranoia and loss. The worry and stress were gradually subsiding and the knowledge that he had the giant diamond and the firearm strapped to his belt was reassuring too. He took a deep breath and stared out at the sparkling white expanse of hard-packed sand to his left. His exhaustion was countered by the adrenalin pumping through his veins. It was a classic case of fight or flight, and he was in full flight mode. It was twenty silent minutes later that he saw a cloud of dust on the horizon. There was no doubt it was from an approaching vehicle. Heinrich Klopp sat forward suddenly and screwed his eyes to see through the glare. His right hand unconsciously touched the butt of the Luger pistol on his belt. It turned out to be simply a fuel tanker destined for the mine and he sat back with a sigh of relief as they passed it. It was some time later when they finally reached the lonely crossroads at the C28. Without saying a word, Max slowed the vehicle and turned right towards the Boshua Pass and Windhoek. This point in the journey was a milestone for Heinrich Klopp. In his mind, he was one step closer to freedom and he smirked to himself as Max engaged high gear once again. He had no idea that there was another vehicle, driven by his tormentor, racing towards him from behind. It was a full hour later that the featureless expanse of the desert began to change slightly. They passed the occasional rocky outcrop and clumps of Welwitschia and strange grotesque Quiver trees. Suddenly there was a misty blue haze on the horizon and Heinrich Klopp sat forward in his seat to study it.

"The mountains of The Boshua Pass sir" said Max "We are almost there."

"Good," replied Klopp. "Very good."

The sun glared in the perfectly blue sky above as the shapes of the hills and mountains of the pass became more defined. With every passing kilometre, Heinrich Klopp's confidence grew. The terrible wastelands of the open desert were behind him and ahead lay the green belt, the capital, and freedom. It was when finally, they reached the foot of the mountains that the surface of the road suddenly changed from sandy gravel to larger stones. The going was rough and occasionally one of them would flick up from the tyres into the wheel arches noisily. The thin road weaved and snaked its way upwards into the hills. There were gnarled, stunted trees growing on the sunburnt rocky slopes and Max slowed the vehicle to negotiate the many sharp corners and terrifying drop-offs as they climbed. It was five minutes later when Heinrich Klopp noticed Max slowing the vehicle more than usual and looking in the rear-view mirror repeatedly. This loss of speed annoyed him and this was compounded when he heard the incessant hooting of a vehicle behind him. He spun around in his seat to see a large Toyota Land Cruiser bearing up on them fast. Blind panic filled his mind as he realized Max had slowed down further and had pulled over to the left to allow the vehicle to pass them.

"What are you doing?" he screamed "Do not let it pass!"

But it was too late. The large Toyota was almost parallel with them on the thin road and Max sat wide-eyed and confused as to what to what exactly was going on. The gap between the tyres of the black Mercedes and the deadly three-hundred-foot drop-off was down to inches.

Heinrich Klopp's eyes flicked towards the driver of the other vehicle. The passenger window of the cab was open and the man at the wheel was shouting something inaudible and pointing straight at him. Despite the heat, the face of the man struck a bolt of cold terror through Heinrich Klopp's body. It was the face of the man that had tormented him and completely destroyed his life's work. It was the face of Jason Green.

20

Chapter Twenty: Green

The turbo diesel engine of the Toyota roared under the hood as I engaged high gear. I had pushed my speed up to 120 km per hour and as a result, the steering felt a lot lighter. Instead of feeling each individual rut in the road surface I now heard a constant hum beneath me. But the added speed came with a marked loss of control. On four occasions the front wheels became embedded in thick sand and the vehicle lurched away to the side resulting in me losing control completely and bouncing off dangerously into the desert. The added concentration needed to maintain a semblance of safety at that speed caused me to start sweating despite the blast of the air conditioning. It was forty minutes of intense speed later that I glanced at the tracker to see that Heinrich Klopp had reached the C28 turn-off and had indeed turned right towards The Boshua Pass and Windhoek. I had hoped he would turn left and I would intercept him earlier but there was nothing for it. *Keep going Green but keep it on the road for Christ's sake.* The baking sun in the cloudless sky overhead burned the skin of my arms as I drove and I drank frequently from the water bottle. My pursuit of Heinrich Klopp had turned into an extremely dangerous high-speed chase but it was one I was not prepared to lose. It was not long after that I finally lost the signal on my phone. The tracker screen went blank and I realized then that it would only start working again when I got close to the capital. I was effectively driving blind with absolutely no idea where Klopp was. It was a worry but I consoled myself with the knowledge that there really wasn't anywhere to go except east. It was a full two hours later that I noticed the surrounding landscape begin to change. I recalled from my two flights over the area that this was more than likely the end of the badlands of the desert and that I was approaching the mountains of The Boshua Pass. This was confirmed thirty minutes later when the rugged hills of the pass revealed themselves through the heat haze on the horizon. Since leaving the coast I had not seen a single other vehicle on the road. The sheer scale of the desert and the complete and total isolation were both hauntingly beautiful and deadly at the same time.

Eventually, I reached the foot of the mountains and swung around to the left to begin the ascent. The sound of the tyres on the surface changed noticeably as did their grip as the vehicle began climbing. The road was narrow, steep, rocky, and dangerous, with sharp hairpin corners and sheer drop-offs. *Don't fuck up here Green. Take it easy.* It was after ten minutes of nerve-racking twists and turns that I saw the dust of the vehicle in front of me. Whatever it was, it had just made a turn to the right around a sharp corner on the slope. *That's him. It's got to be!* I dropped a gear and spun the wheels on the rocky surface to catch the as-yet-unseen vehicle. It was only when I made it around the bend on the slope that I saw it. It was covered in a fine layer of white dust but there was no mistaking the black Mercedes of Heinrich Klopp. *Gotcha you bastard!* I came up behind it dangerously fast and began hooting as I approached. It came as a surprise to see the vehicle slow down and attempt to pull over to the left to allow me to pass. I pushed the switch to bring the passenger window down as I approached in a cloud of dust and flying rocks. But it was only when I was parallel with the vehicle that I saw there were two occupants. The fat, sweaty face of the mine foreman, Max, stared at me with wide fearful eyes. In the passenger seat next to him sat Heinrich Klopp. His cold blue eyes were bloodshot and wide with shock. I pointed at him with my left hand and tried to yell over the sound of the engines and the crunching of the rocks under the tyres.

"You murdering scum!" I shouted. "I've got you now!"

At that moment Klopp reached over and spun the steering wheel of the Mercedes to the right. The two vehicles slammed into each other with an ear-piercing metallic screech. The Toyota was forced into the side of the hill and although I tried to brake, I could not avoid the large boulder that lay in the shallow gulley to my right. The front right of the vehicle bounced violently upwards and my head slammed into the sidewall of the cab.

The heavy Toyota came down on its two left wheels and I had to swing the steering wheel sharply to the left to avoid rolling. This caused me to swerve dangerously close to the precipitous drop on the side of the road. With stars in my eyes from the blow to my head, I managed to put the vehicle straight once again but the Mercedes was now thirty metres ahead of me and gaining speed. It was then I saw Klopp with the gun. He had opened the passenger window, turned in his seat, and was firing wildly at me using what looked like the Luger pistol. Through the noise, dust and confusion, I watched as his right hand jerked repeatedly from the recoil. The first bullet hit the left side mirror of the vehicle. It exploded with a crash of splintering glass. The second shot slammed into the left pillar near the windscreen with a deep metallic thud. Still, I pushed the Toyota to catch them but it was the third shot that finally grounded me. It hit the left front tyre which exploded immediately. The sudden loss of traction caused the steering wheel to spin suddenly and once again I found myself on a path towards the deadly drop to the left. I braked as hard as I could and with a deafening crunch on the stones below, the Toyota finally came to rest at the edge. I sat there stunned, blinking in a cloud of choking dust, and watched as the black Mercedes rounded a bend and disappeared. There was a high-pitched ringing in my ears as I opened the door and stumbled out onto the rocky surface of the mountain pass. I walked around the front of the vehicle and looked at the blown and ripped front left tyre.

"Fuck!" I shouted out loud as a peaceful silence descended on the scene.

The front left of the vehicle was hanging clean over the edge of the road and the drop-off. It would have been impossible, and extremely foolhardy to attempt to reverse, let alone change the wheel in situ. One slip of the tyres on the rocky surface and the vehicle would surely tumble off the edge. I stood with my hands on my hips as I pondered my next move.

The winch. It's the only thing for it. I walked around to the back of the vehicle and retrieved the equipment. There was the winch remote, several tree straps, extensions, and bow shackles, but I figured I could get away with simply using the straps. Carrying one of the longer tree straps, I walked over to the safe side of the road and found a fallen boulder similar to the one I had hit earlier. It was the size of a small armchair and I knew full well it weighed a lot more than the vehicle. *Perfect.* I unrolled the heavy yellow strap, tossed it over the boulder, and yanked at it to check it had set. Next, I walked back to the vehicle and attached the winch remote to the powerful five-tonne device at the front near the bumper. Using the remote I put the winch into a free spool and pulled the high-tensile nylon rope away from the barrel. It unwound easily and I pulled it across the road until I reached the two ends of the strap. Using the hook, I attached the rope to the strap and walked back to where I had left the remote on the bonnet of the Toyota. I activated the winch motor and it immediately took up the slack. Multiple tiny puffs of dust blew from along the rope as the tension increased until finally, I heard the reassuring crunch of the stones beneath the vehicle as it was pulled safely back from the edge of the abyss below. Once the Toyota was safely back in the centre of the road I disengaged the winch and re-packed the equipment. The process had taken me a full forty minutes in total. All the while I was painfully aware that Klopp was putting valuable miles between us and I still had the job of replacing the front left wheel. The process was hard and took a further thirty minutes. By the time I had finished the sun was high in the sky and I was filthy with dust, grease, and sweat. With a grunt, I tossed the heavy, ruined wheel into the back of the Toyota, slammed the door, and stood back to light a cigarette. I climbed back into the driver's seat, closed the door, and started the engine. *This man will stop at nothing Green. He is spooked and extremely dangerous. Be very careful.*

21

Chapter Twenty-One: Klopp

"What were you thinking Max?!" shrieked Klopp as he righted himself in his seat.

The rotund and normally docile man driving the Mercedes was shaking violently and sweat ran in rivulets down his shiny black head.

"We could have been killed!" Klopp continued.

Max shifted his fat sweaty hands on the steering wheel as he drove and appeared lost for words. It was then that Heinrich Klopp detected the faint smell of human excrement in the cab. The incident on the mountain pass had been so terrifying it had caused Max Chawora to lose control of his bowels.

"Please sir!" said Max, close to tears "What is going on?"

Heinrich Klopp took a moment to think of a suitable response. With the pistol still in his right hand he turned in his seat and looked behind the vehicle as it sped off. They had reached the top of the pass, the air had cooled, and the road had flattened out somewhat. After another quick glance behind him, he spoke.

"That man is trying to kill me, Max," said Klopp. "To kill us both in fact. This is why we must get to Windhoek in one piece. As soon as we are there, everything will be fine, I promise."

His words seemed to calm the man slightly and he nodded vigorously in understanding.

"Okay sir," he replied. "I will get us to Windhoek as fast as I can. I hope he will not catch us."

"If you make good speed Max, there is no chance of that," said Klopp. "His front tyre was blown out and the vehicle is more than likely stuck where it stopped. Keep your speed up and we will be there in three hours."

Max Chawora blinked twice and looked at the rear-view mirror nervously as he depressed the accelerator pedal.

"Okay sir," he said.

Heinrich Klopp was faced with a terrible dilemma. His plan of leaving Namibia with the diamond through Windhoek International Airport was now far too dangerous. Green would surely be expecting this. In his mind, he strongly suspected the Mercedes had been fitted with a tracking device. He also knew the Englishman, Green, was extremely determined, and would more than likely get mobile and resume the chase very quickly. *No.* He thought. *I will make another plan.*

He pulled his phone from his pocket and checked for a signal. As expected, there was nothing, and he didn't expect there to be any until they reached the outskirts of the capital. With another glance behind him, he sat back and tried to think. He was feeling a mixture of emotions. There was a sense of elation. Elation at having stopped the Englishman in his tracks, and very nearly having killed him. *God, that would have been so sweet.* But there was also a deep fear. *This man is extremely determined and far from stupid. Do not underestimate him.* The thin dirt road wound its way through the rugged hills of the green belt above the desert for another two hundred and fifty kilometres. The journey took exactly three hours during which both Heinrich Klopp and Max kept a fearful eye on the road behind them. To their relief, at no stage did they see the dreaded Toyota approaching.

It was 3.00 pm. exactly when, at last, Heinrich Klopp found he had a bar of mobile signal on his phone. He wasted no time in calling a local car hire firm in the capital to book a vehicle.

"No," he said to whoever was on the line. "Just a normal sedan. I will not be travelling on anything but tar roads."

Max Chawora listened as the conversation continued. Finally, it was done and Heinrich Klopp turned to him to speak.

"Max, you will drop me at Regency Car Hire on Independence Avenue," he said. "I will give you some money for a hotel, fuel, and expenses. I will also give you a very generous bonus for helping me today. You will then travel back to the mine tomorrow and you will say nothing to anyone about what has happened today. Is that clear?"

Max Chawora was relieved beyond words. Ever since leaving the mine in the early hours of the morning, he had been worried. And since the terrifying run-in on the pass, he had been literally petrified. Not to mention the slight accident he had had in his pants at the time. As far as he was concerned, the further he got away from his boss the better. He had always known the man was a crook. He had even been complicit in a few shady deals with him, but that day it had gone too far.

"Yes sir," he said with relief. "No problem."

"Good."

Next, Heinrich Klopp called a travel agency in the city. Max listened to the conversation as he drove. Klopp seemed annoyed that the lady he usually dealt with was absent but he finally ended up talking to one of the junior agents.

"My name is Mr Klopp from Apex Resources," he spoke slowly and clearly. "My company has an account with you. I would like to book a flight from Livingstone to Johannesburg tomorrow afternoon."

There was a pause as the agent checked her computer. Heinrich Klopp tapped his leg with his free hand repeatedly, clearly impatient at having been made to wait.

"Yes of course Livingstone in Zambia!" he snapped into the phone. "Where else would it be?"

There was another long pause as he waited for the agent. All the while Max Chawora listened carefully as he drove.

"4.00 pm tomorrow, Livingstone to Johannesburg," said Klopp. "Is that confirmed now?"

There was another brief pause as the agent spoke again.

"Thank you," said Klopp. "Yes, charge it to the Apex account. Thank you. Goodbye"

Heinrich Klopp took a deep breath and turned in his seat to check for the dreaded Toyota. The road behind was clear. The Englishman was nowhere to be seen.

Up ahead the trees and buildings of the capital were finally visible on the horizon. They had finally made it, literally from the middle of nowhere, to civilization. The short drive from the outskirts of the city to Independence Avenue in the centre was quick in the pre-rush hour traffic. Max parked in a specially allocated bay outside the car hire premises. Heinrich Klopp attached the single handcuff of the aluminium diamond transport case to his left wrist and looked furtively around the busy street for any sign of trouble. As he opened the passenger door he spoke.

"Remain here with my bags Max," he said. "I will return shortly."

"Yes sir."

Fifteen minutes later Klopp emerged from the offices of the car hire firm driving a nondescript cream-coloured Toyota Camry. He parked next to the dust-covered black Mercedes. With the metal briefcase still attached to his left wrist, he alighted from the vehicle and opened the back of the Mercedes. He removed the two heavy bags of his belongings and placed them in the boot of the new car. Finally, he walked back to the passenger side of the Mercedes and climbed in.

"Max," he said pulling his wallet from his pocket. "I am going to give you $1000 in cash. This is for you to do as you please. You must, however, return to the mine by tomorrow and never say a word to anyone about what you have seen today. The man who was chasing us is a killer, and he will do anything to get to me. He will be looking for you as well. I advise you to go and find a place to rest now and do nothing until tomorrow"

"Okay sir," Max replied as he took the folded wad of notes. "Understood."

Without a word, Klopp got out and swiftly walked around to his new vehicle. Max Chawora watched as his boss reversed carefully onto the busy road and drove off. He looked at the wad of notes in his hand and his spirits lifted immediately. It was more money than he had ever seen in his life. Although his job title as foreman would indicate he held a senior position, the actual pay for locals in Namibian dollars was relatively low. To him, it was an incredible payday and he immediately forgot the terrible events of the journey. For Max Chawora, there were only two things on his mind. Beer and women. And he would have both.

22

Chapter Twenty-Two: Green

It was 4.15 pm. by the time my phone first showed a mobile signal. The drive had been long and I had driven like a man possessed, but apart from a few times where I had almost gone off the road, it had been largely uneventful. I had hoped that Klopp and Max might have run into trouble and that I would meet them en route, but apart from a lone bus, I saw no other vehicles. Feeling exhausted, I pulled over in the late afternoon sunshine to take a look at the tracker on my laptop. I lit a cigarette as I waited for the screen to clear then leant over to study the movements of Heinrich Klopp. The thin blue line showed clearly on the map of the city and the times were logged in a section to the left of the screen. The black Mercedes had travelled to an address in the centre of town and had parked there for twenty minutes before moving off again to a location roughly thirty kilometres west. I screwed up my stinging eyes as I read the street name. *Independence Avenue. What were you doing there Klopp? I think I need to take a look.* I stepped out of the vehicle briefly to splash my face with water before heading off. By the time I reached the city, it was rush hour and it took a full forty minutes to get through the traffic to the address on Independence Avenue. I parked in the exact spot the Mercedes had been earlier that day. The heavy traffic and the noise of the city were jarring and somehow alien after the solitude and emptiness of the desert. My nerves were frayed and my temper on a short fuse due to the lack of sleep and tension. The offices of Regency Car Hire were closed but I sat for a moment as I tried to imagine what might have taken place. There were many possibilities, but in the end, I realized there was no point speculating. The only real option was to follow the tracker to the Mercedes and take it from there. Although I had been snacking on the sticks of biltong, I was starving hungry, so I pulled into a drive-through takeaway restaurant to get a burger. I pulled over and parked on the side of the busy road as I ate, all the while watching the screen of the computer. It was twilight in the city and the traffic began to thin out. The Mercedes had been in the same spot for some time in what appeared to be some rural growth point.

There were no street names and the surrounding map indicated very little on the screen. Thankfully it was only 30 km away down the main Swakopmund road and then two kilometres off the highway. When I was done with the food I threw the packaging into the foot well in the rear and pulled away. It was completely dark by the time I had crossed the city and reached the highway. The food had made me feel drowsy so I stopped at a service station and bought a travel flask which I filled with hot black coffee. The anticipation of what I might find awoke me and my body buzzed with caffeine and adrenalin. It was twenty-four kilometres further to the turn off where I headed right onto a dirt road. It led to a small rural village complete with mud huts, a couple of general dealers' shops, and a thriving bar or shebeen in the centre. The exterior walls of the place were decorated with multi-coloured fairy lights and several cars were parked outside. As I drove past I heard loud distorted Sungura music and drunken laughter coming from the inner courtyard of the establishment. Several emaciated, scantily clad prostitutes milled around the entrance clutching bottles of beer and trying their best to stay upright on their high heels. *I can't imagine Heinrich Klopp frequenting such a place. There's no fucking way Green.* A light breeze blew litter and dust around the car park and for a moment I panicked thinking the Mercedes was no longer there. But the tracker was working perfectly, so it came as a relief when I found the dusty Mercedes parked at the far end of the line of vehicles near a flat-top Acacia tree. I drove around the back of the building and parked my own vehicle in the dark out of sight near a general store. Before leaving I removed a Stanley knife from the tool kit in the back. I pocketed it and locked the vehicle activating the alarm at the same time. I walked through the warm dark evening, keeping to the perimeter of the car park to stay out of sight. I found a safe spot at which to wait in the darkness near the Acacia tree. As I watched the proceedings at the shebeen I became more and more convinced that Klopp was not actually there. *This is a dirty rural whore house. Definitely not his style at all Green. But, you never know, and there's nothing for it. You have no choice, you'll have to wait.* The punters came and went, some on foot, but most of them in cars.

It appeared the establishment was popular with the residents of Windhoek as the music and laughter never stopped. I smoked occasionally, cupping the cigarette in my hand to avoid being seen in the darkness. My fatigued mind was plagued by doubts and fears as the hours dragged on. It was 9.45 pm when I finally saw the portly figure of Max Chawora stumble out of the shebeen entrance. Instantly I became awake and hyper-alert. His shirt was hanging loosely and he carried a large brown bottle of beer in his left hand. Clearly drunk, he stumbled along the wall of the establishment using his right hand to steady himself against the wall until he reached the corner nearest where I was hiding. Once there, he stopped in his tracks as if lost, and swayed on his feet as he looked around. For a brief moment, I thought he might have seen me hiding in the dark near the Acacia tree, but in fact, he had simply seen the Mercedes. He stood and downed the last of the beer before throwing the empty bottle on the ground nearby. The bottle smashed noisily, but this was drowned out by the racket of the repetitive music coming from the bar. Max Chawora turned where he stood, undid the front of his trousers, and urinated on the broken glass below. When he was done he zipped up and shuffled off towards the Mercedes. *No sign of Klopp, as I thought. Where the fuck is he? I'll find out.* Crouching low, I crept through the darkness up to the thick gnarled trunk of the tree. I pulled the Stanley knife from my pocket and slid the blade out to a length of five centimetres. My arms and legs buzzed with adrenalin as I reached the tree and poked my head around in the darkness to watch. The man was drunk but I had no idea if he was armed or not. Given what had happened earlier, he might have been, and I would need to exercise caution. Max Chawora shuffled his portly frame through the darkness towards the driver's door of the Mercedes, not two metres from where I stood. He grunted and hummed to himself as he moved. The first thing I smelt was the beer swiftly followed by his body odour. He brought a set of keys from his pocket and pushed the immobiliser on the fob. The vehicle alarm bleeped once and the hazard lights flashed yellow in the darkness as I heard the doors unlock.

It was as he reached for the door handle that I made my move. I sprang forward silently from behind, put my arm around his head and pulled his body roughly towards my own. I covered his mouth with my left hand and brought the razor-sharp blade to his throat with my right, exerting just enough pressure to ensure he knew it was there, but not enough to break the skin.

"You make a sound, I'll cut your fucking throat," I whispered in his ear through gritted teeth. "Do you understand me?"

The man let out a high-pitched muffled squeal as I swung his body away from the vehicle to face the darkness behind.

"Shut up!" I hissed in his ear "Walk now!"

THE STAR OF THE DESERT

I frog-marched the drunken man into the darkness and around the perimeter of the car park. He stumbled on a few occasions, but I held him upright and forced him forward until we reached the rear of the parked Toyota. Keeping the blade to his throat I searched him using my left hand. Apart from his phone and a thick wad of cash, he was clean. Keeping the blade to his throat, I opened the back of the vehicle and shoved him inside roughly. I needed to get us both away from where we were. There were too many people around and I knew that if he squealed it would raise the alarm immediately. I held the man by the scruff of his shirt as he lay in the back of the vehicle face down. With my right hand, I rummaged in the toolbox until I found the battery jumper cables. I leant over and spoke in his ear.

"I repeat, make a sound and I'll kill you," I whispered.

The process of hog-tying the man with the cables took less than a minute. When I was done he was completely immobilized with his hands and feet bound behind him. I quickly slammed the back door and jumped into the driver's seat. I drove slowly past the back of the shebeen and the other buildings until I reached the dirt road that led to the highway. Finally, there was no one around and I was free to question him.

"Where is he, Max?" I shouted from the front. "Where is Klopp?"

"Fuck you," he replied from the back slurring his words. "I will tell you nothing!"

"Oh you'll talk," I said "Believe me, you'll talk."

I drove through the darkness until I reached the highway where I took a right. I had wanted to stop and question him on the road to the shebeen but there was too much vehicular traffic moving to and from the place. *Find a quiet place, Green. Somewhere you won't be disturbed.* It was three kilometres further down the road that I saw a dirt road on the left. The moon had risen enough for me to see that the dried grass had almost covered the entrance and it looked to me like it hadn't seen traffic for years. In the back, Max grunted and burped as we trundled over the rocks and through the trees. Apart from reeking of beer and body odour, I became aware of the distinct smell of human excrement on him.

Eventually, I came across a flat area of ground near the track and pulled up near a grove of trees. The moon had turned the surrounding grass into a pale silver colour and the trees cast ghostly shadows on the ground. I stopped the engine, got out, and walked around to the back of the vehicle.

"Right Max," I said as I swung the door open, pulled him around and flipped him onto his side. "You and I are going to have a nice chat. Where is Klopp?"

I leant down to look him in the face. The portly man smiled at me drunkenly in the moonlight and once again I became aware of the stink that emanated from him.

"Fuck you," he said with a sneer. "I will tell you nothing"

With that, he spat at me. A heavy globule of sticky saliva splattered on my cheek and I instinctively recoiled. Unfortunately for Max Chawora, this marked a turning point in the interrogation and the end of my patience. I raised my right fist and slammed it heavily into the side of his face. It landed with a meaty crack and his head thumped into the carpeted steel in the rear of the Toyota. His eyes glazed over immediately and a thin trickle of blood ran out of the corner of his mouth. It looked black in the moonlight. The man groaned softly as I flipped his body over and gripped him by the back of his trousers and the collar of his shirt. I felt the small of my back aching with pain as I carried the semi-conscious body around to the front of the vehicle. I dropped him in a dusty heap in the beam of the headlights near a young Mopane tree. I walked swiftly back to the rear of the vehicle and retrieved the winch remote I had used earlier.

I plugged it into the winch and immediately engaged the free spool. The thick nylon rope came away easily and I pulled it out and around the trunk of the tree leaving plenty of slack. I clipped the rope onto itself using the spring-loaded hook and walked back to the man lying on the sandy soil in the headlights. I lifted his head and wrapped the rope loosely once around his neck.

"Where is he?" I said still squatting near the man.

"Fuck off," he slurred.

I stood up and walked swiftly to the winch remote. The powerful five-tonne device emitted a steady whine as the rope constricted. At the time, I was sure that the man had no idea what was actually happening to him. However, he soon found out as the nylon noose tightened around his neck and lifted his head from the ground. There was a brief choking sound before his windpipe was completely blocked and his bound body was dragged by the neck until he was in a kneeling position. Max Chawora's body began to vibrate uncontrollably. His sweaty, rotund head swelled up and his terrified eyes bulged grotesquely as the powerful winch pulled. I stopped the winch and watched with interest as I pulled the cigarettes from my pocket and lit one. Unable to make a sound, the man's body bucked and flicked dust in the headlights. It was only when I exhaled a second time that I released the winch into a free spool. Max Chawora fell with a thud and I walked over and squatted nearby as I loosened the rope from his neck. His breathing came in short violent bursts and his wide unblinking eyes stared at me in complete and total horror.

"I'm not going to ask you again, Max," I said quietly. "Where is Klopp?"

"Livingstone!" he gasped. "He has gone to Livingstone in Zambia. By the Victoria Falls."

"What vehicle is he using?" I said quietly.

"A Toyota Camry. A hire car," he replied, his voice croaking. "Cream in colour. Namibian plates. He has booked a flight from there to Johannesburg tomorrow at 4.00 pm. It's the truth, sir!"

"I believe you," I said as I untied the battery jumper cable from his hands and feet.

I reached for his pocket, removed his phone, and crushed the cigarette out under my foot as I stood up. It took only a minute to unhook the rope from the tree and wind it back onto the winch. All the while Max Chawora lay where he had fallen in the sand. He watched me with fearful eyes as I worked. Although seriously shaken, I knew he would be fine. I climbed into the driver's seat of the Toyota and took one last look at him before starting the engine.

"You'll have some time to think on the walk back to your vehicle," I said quietly. "I strongly advise you against attempting to contact Mr Klopp. Goodbye, Max."

23

Chapter Twenty-Three: Klopp

Heinrich Klopp was a driven man. He had been that way all his life. He was driven by greed, money, lust and power. But now he was driven by fear. It was a raw, primitive fear. A fear of arrest, a fear of incarceration, and a fear of the dogged and indefatigable Englishman, Green. On his way out of the city, he had stopped at a pharmacy and bought a large bottle of Adderall tablets. The staff in the shop had been bemused by the strange behaviour of the man, not to mention the aluminium briefcase handcuffed to his wrist. He had left the city in the hired vehicle at dusk and headed north on the B1 highway. He had started taking the pills as he left the city, downing them with gulps of bottled water that he had bought at a service station. The powerful amphetamines belonged to a class of drugs known as stimulants. They are commonly used by truck drivers and shift workers and Heinrich Klopp knew they would keep him awake for the long journey through the night. Already his body was in mild shock from lack of sleep but, in his mind, there was no other option. He had to get away and out of the country safely. But the dextroamphetamine coursing through his veins had common and dangerous side effects. It is well known that these side effects caused intermittent episodes of euphoria, aggression, general confusion, and extreme paranoia. All of these side effects began to affect him two hours later by the time he reached the small town of Otjiwarongo. There had been a police roadblock in the darkness on the outskirts of the town. The officers were simply checking vehicle licences and waving most of the traffic through. Heinrich Klopp had snapped at a junior officer accusing him of delaying and harassing tourists. The officer tried to explain politely that they were merely checking license discs, but Klopp's brief episode of aggression was in full swing. Eventually, he was waved through and continued on his journey. The distance between Windhoek and the

THE STAR OF THE DESERT

border with Zambia at the Katima Mulilo bridge was over nine hundred kilometres. From there it was another two hundred to the tourist town of Livingstone in Zambia near the Victoria Falls.

Heinrich Klopp figured he could make the entire journey in thirteen hours or less. The roads at night would be quiet and he would be able to maintain a good speed throughout. It was an hour later, on the hill approaching the tiny outpost of Otavi, that the hallucinations started. The yellow lights on the main street seemed to wobble, almost vibrating in his vision. In his mind it was curious, but in no way alarming. This blurred and wobbly perception of light continued through the nearby outposts of Kombat and Grootfontein, until he had passed them and was once again back into the open, dark countryside. But simply passing these small towns in no way meant his strange visions were over. The moonlight in the trees on the hills played new tricks on his mind. He saw faces. Multiple faces. Huge menacing faces where in fact there were none. On occasion, Heinrich Klopp would shriek out loud and blink wildly as he drove past them. Every half hour he would stop and wash his face with water to rid himself of them, but they always returned. It was three hours later when he reached the remote outpost of Rundu near the Angolan border. There was a feeling of smug satisfaction as he realized he had passed the halfway mark on his epic journey. He stopped briefly at a service station to fill up on petrol. The sleepy attendant watched his shaking hands with puzzled curiosity as he handed over the payment in cash. From there he turned east and headed towards the Caprivi Strip. This narrow stretch of national park ran between Botswana to the South and Angola and Zambia to the North. By the time Heinrich Klopp began this second stage of the journey, it was 1.00 am. He had no idea that his body was visibly twitching and he ground his teeth constantly as he drove. Feelings of great euphoria came in waves and on occasion he would laugh out loud to himself hysterically. He constantly looked at the aluminium briefcase that lay in the foot well of the passenger seat. *There you are my beauty*. He thought repeatedly. *My salvation*. The Caprivi game park was teeming with wildlife and on two occasions he almost collided with small groups of sleeping Cape Buffalo on the road in the darkness. It was at exactly 5.10 am. when he finally cleared Namibian customs at the dusty Katima Mulilo border post.

The border officials regarded him with genuine concern as he stood there gurning and shaking at the immigration cubicle. The sun had risen fully as he crossed the 900-metre concrete bridge over the great Zambezi River into Zambia. Heinrich Klopp was filled with a sense of great triumph. His plan had been executed with razor-sharp precision and soon he would be safely in the tourist town of Livingstone awaiting his flight to Johannesburg and freedom. It was at 8.00 am. two hours after clearing Zambian customs at the Sesheke border post, that he finally pulled into the Guest House in Livingstone. Carrying only the aluminium briefcase, he walked into the small air-conditioned reception and announced his arrival. His pupils were dilated and his hand trembled as he filled in the registration form. Once completed, the receptionist led him to his room. It was situated in a lush tropical garden near a miniature stone replica of the nearby Victoria Falls.

"This will be fine," he snapped at the receptionist as she showed him the facilities in the room. "Thank you."

Heinrich Klopp lay on the bed and stared at the ceiling clutching the briefcase to his chest with both hands. His jaw muscles bulged as he ground his teeth but he was wide awake. *I have done it. I have escaped, and now I will be free.*

"Ja," he said to himself with a wry smile. "Du hast gewonnen." You have won.

24

CHAPTER TWENTY-FOUR: GREEN

I tossed Max's phone out of the window as I approached the city and pulled over under a street light near the university. The time was 10.30 pm. and I needed to consult my own phone to get an idea of the journey that lay ahead. It was only after consulting the map that I realized the distance. It would be a staggering 1200 km. trip with a border crossing to the tourist town of Livingstone in Zambia. The Toyota was fully kitted out for such a journey and I had more than enough fuel on board. I switched on the interior light and looked in the mirror. The solemn face that looked back at me was haggard and unshaven with dark purple smears beneath the eyes. I had been awake for more than thirty-six hours. I looked back at the map on the screen on the phone but the very thought of the drive ahead was daunting. I closed my eyes briefly and in my mind, I saw the smiling faces of Danny and Temba. Both of them murdered, and their young lives ended by Mr Heinrich Klopp. The thought of him actually getting away with it turned my stomach. *No Green. You cannot allow that. He must be stopped at all costs.* I opened my eyes, plugged the phone into the charger, engaged first gear and pulled off into the night. There was very little traffic and the drive through the city was easy at that late hour. I pulled into a service station on the north side to replenish my flask with coffee. The first two hours were easier than I had expected. I arrived at the small town of Otjiwarongo at 12.30 am. and it was an effort to slow down to the official speed limit in the deserted streets. It was another hour to the tiny outpost of Otavi which was the turn-off to the Etosha National Park. Keeping an eye on the map on my phone, I passed through the old abandoned mining town of Kombat eventually emerging at Grootfontein. I stopped once again to stretch my legs and fill up with coffee at the only service station in town. It was the next three hours on the lonely stretch to Rundu in the North that were the worst. The moonlight played tricks on my mind and the shadows of the trees on the hills looked like skeletal hands reaching out for me. At times it felt as if I was driving in a never-ending tunnel of weird patterns and ghostly shapes.

I fell asleep at the wheel on one occasion, only waking when the Toyota left the road and veered onto the rough stone surface of the verge to my left. I stopped the vehicle, washed my face, drank some coffee and continued. I found that smoking helped me stay awake and I had gone through two packs by the time I reached the town of Rundu on the Angola border. In my mind, I held the image of Klopp's face. It spurred me on and gave me the stamina I needed to continue. The African sun rose on a new day as I took the right turn into the Caprivi Strip. The surrounding vegetation was completely different from that of Windhoek. It was now thick, lush green bush, similar to that of my destination in the Zambezi Valley. I reached the border post at Katima Mulilo at exactly 10.00 am. My body ached and I was almost delirious with fatigue by the time I drove across the bridge into Zambia. The process of clearing customs and immigration took a full hour and I paid a bribe of $30 to a policeman who objected to my smashed side mirror. The road to Livingstone was heavily potholed but the concentration needed to avoid them helped me stay awake as the heat of the day increased. It was 12.30 by the time I finally arrived at Livingstone. The small town was bustling with craft markets, curio vendors, guest houses and tourists. The landscape sloped downwards to where I knew the mighty Zambezi flowed. The sudden civilization was somehow alien and slightly overwhelming at first. I drove down the tree-lined main street past old colonial buildings, government offices, and supermarkets. There were multiple billboards advertising safaris, white water rafting, and scenic flights over the falls. I realised then that any attempt to locate Klopp before his departure at the airport would more than likely be futile. His was an international flight and he would need to be there at least two hours before 4.00 pm. *You need to go. Head for the airport now Green. He might already be there.* I pulled into a service station and got directions from the attendant. The drive took me north through the town past the Protea Hotel until I reached the clearly marked airport road on the left. The road passed a residential suburb until opening out to a wide flat glade of scrubby bush. Eventually, I reached the security fence of the airport grounds and directional signs were placed above huge advertising billboards that spanned the road.

The turn-off to the car park was on the right and up ahead I saw the small terminal building with its control tower. The car park was set out in parallel rows to the front of the building and thankfully there were very few cars there at the time. I drove up and down each row looking for a cream Toyota Camry but there was not one to be seen. I parked the vehicle and walked into the terminal building headed for the information desk.

"Good afternoon," I said to the lady behind the desk. "I wanted to ask about the 4.00 pm. flight to Johannesburg."

"Sorry sir" she replied as she checked her computer screen. "The check-in desk will only open at 2.00 pm. An hour from now."

I thanked her and walked off to take a look around. There were several souvenir shops and an upstairs bar with a viewing platform of the runway. I needed to be certain that Klopp wasn't lurking around waiting in some hidden corner of the terminal. Once I was sure he hadn't arrived I walked back out to the car park and climbed into the Toyota. I glanced at my watch as I drove out. It was just after 1.00 pm. It had been a hell of a journey, I had cut it fine, but I was there. I took a slow drive out of the airport complex and made a U-turn eight hundred metres from the entrance. There was a thatched structure on the left with several locals selling sculptures and curios. I parked the Toyota just beyond it making sure I had a clear view of the approaching vehicles. There was a strict speed limit on the approach to the airport and I knew that would work in my favour. Several cars passed as I sat and I could see the occupants clearly from my vantage point. *Good. Now you wait, Green. Wait and watch.*

CHAPTER TWENTY-FIVE: KLOPP

Although he tried, sleep never came for Heinrich Klopp. The powerful amphetamines pumping through his system prevented it. Instead, he lay there on the bed with the aluminium case never more than a few inches from his side. Occasionally he would get up, pour a glass of water, and swallow another couple of pills. On three occasions he removed the giant diamond from the case and lay there studying it before another wave of paranoia would wash over him and he would hurriedly lock it away again. His entire body was buzzing pleasantly and he spent the time planning and picturing what the future might hold. There were moments of extreme enthusiasm and happiness followed by periods of desperate lows and fears where any noise in the garden outside would cause him to leap to his feet and peer through the curtains and the door. There was a bowl of fresh fruit near the coffee machine on the sideboard but for some reason, he had no appetite. His plan was to keep the aluminium case attached to his left wrist until he reached the airport car park. Once there he would remove the giant stone and put it in his hand luggage. Tourists in Africa were fond of buying cheap stone sculptures and the diamond would look no different in the X-ray machine at security. He would abandon the aluminium case in the vehicle and check his other bags in as usual. It was only a two-hour flight to Johannesburg and once there he would have plenty of time and space to plan his next move. Heinrich Klopp spent the final hour pacing the room and flicking through random channels on the television. It was at 1.15 pm when he pulled his phone from his pocket and Googled the directions from the guest house to the airport. When that was done, he checked his pocket to confirm the two tiny keys for the handcuff were still there. Slowly and methodically, he attached the single handcuff on the silver chain of the case to his left wrist. The reassuring clicks of the locking mechanism pleased him and he made sure that it was attached firmly. Heinrich Klopp sat on the edge of the bed and prepared to leave. In his mind, everything was perfectly in place and the final part of his plan would be executed with similar precision to the last. He stood up and walked out of the room into the blazing afternoon sun in the tropical garden.

He walked swiftly towards the car park glancing from side to side as he went, and his wide eyes did not go unnoticed by the old Matabele gardener who was clearing leaves from the pond nearby. With his drug-addled mind alert to every movement and sound, he climbed into the dusty Toyota Camry and placed the aluminium case on the passenger seat next to him. The engine started on the first attempt and he reversed carefully out of the driveway and onto the street beyond. The drive was largely uneventful apart from a particularly annoying incident with a slow-moving overland truck. The dirty-looking young tourists on board were waving to the locals and causing a minor traffic jam. Heinrich Klopp slammed his fist angrily on the hooter of the car as he overtook, mumbling to himself in annoyance. A few minutes later he saw the sign that marked the turn off to the airport. He took the left turn calmly and drove through the tree-lined residential suburb. Eventually, the landscape opened up into flat bush and he increased his speed. It was with an incredible sense of elation and joy that he saw the airport building in the distance to his right. He had no idea that a dusty Toyota Land Cruiser had just pulled out from behind him and was following closely. Heinrich Klopp smiled to himself and began to hum The Ride of The Valkyries by the great German composer Richard Wagner. He tapped his hands on the steering wheel to its triumphant beat as he took the right turn towards the airport. It was when he was only fifty metres from the entrance to the car park that he glanced in his rear-view mirror. What he saw gave him the shock of his life. He blinked repeatedly, telling himself he must be seeing things. Another one of the hallucinations perhaps. But there was no mistaking it. The man following in the vehicle behind him was the Englishman, Jason Green.

"Schweinhund!" he screamed in total disbelief.

Heinrich Klopp could not believe his eyes. As if to add insult to injury, the man driving in the vehicle behind him smiled and waved.

"Schweinhund!" he screamed repeatedly as he pounded his right fist into the steering wheel.

In a wild panic, Heinrich Klopp floored the accelerator of the small car. He knew that if he entered the car park he would be trapped. Up ahead at the entrance was a small roundabout. It represented his only option for escape. The tyres of the car howled on the tarmac as he made the turn at breakneck speed and sped off with the Land Cruiser in hot pursuit.

26

Chapter Twenty-Six: Green

It was just before 2.00 pm. when I saw the potential vehicle approaching. I had been waiting in my spot behind the craft stall for almost an hour, studying each and every vehicle as it passed. I glanced at my watch and realized the timing was perfect for his arrival. Many Toyotas had passed, some cream in colour as well, but it was the thick layer of dust on this particular one that piqued my interest. My own vehicle was coated in the same. The speed limit on the approach to the airport allowed me to scrutinize the drivers and passengers of each vehicle and I was 100% certain I had not seen Klopp in any of them. It was only when the car was within thirty metres that it was confirmed. His square head and brutal Germanic features were unmistakable. Heinrich Klopp sat slightly forward in his seat and stared ahead at the road with wide eyes. He drove straight past me without seeing a thing and I immediately pulled out behind him. Instantly my body was charged with adrenalin and any feelings of fatigue were forgotten. I followed from a distance at first only closing the gap after he had made the right turn into the airport complex. *You fucker. I've got you now*. It was perhaps fifty metres before the entrance to the car park that I saw his eyes in the rear-view mirror. I watched as his head moved slightly and his eyes blinked repeatedly in disbelief. He had recognized me. There was no doubt that this gave me a small amount of pleasure and I smiled and waved at him with my left hand. I was sure I saw him mouthing some unheard words in the mirror and I watched as he struck the steering wheel repeatedly in frustration. Instantly he dropped a gear and raced ahead towards the entrance to the car park. I did exactly the same but it was only then that I realized my mistake. The small roundabout offered him an escape route that I had overlooked. *Fuck!* The small car raced around in front of me and I had no choice but to follow. The small petrol motor of the Camry offered a great deal more acceleration than my own turbo diesel which wheezed and roared as I took it around the island to the centre of the roundabout. Heinrich Klopp floored his accelerator and took off like a bat out of hell. By the time he reached the turning towards Livingstone, he was travelling at 100 km. per hour. My own tyres squealed in protest as I rounded the same bend behind him.

"Fuck!" I said to myself through gritted teeth. "How could you fuck up like this Green?"

Heinrich Klopp pushed the small petrol engine until it screamed and hit 130 km. per hour. This was fine on the open road and I was able to keep up but I could hardly believe it when he entered the built-up residential area nearer the town and failed to slow down at all. I watched in horror as he swung into oncoming traffic as he overtook a minibus full of tourists. The shocked bus driver pulled over to the left and I used the opportunity to drop a gear and floor the accelerator. Up ahead I could hear the manic hooting of the Camry as he fought to put distance between us. I gained on him slightly only to hear the tyres screeching as he swung the wheel and took the right turn into town. He did so at full tilt leaving thick lines of steaming rubber on the tarmac. Heinrich Klopp never slowed down once. He drove like an absolute lunatic, weaving dangerously between the cars and trucks on the two lanes leading into town. I gritted my teeth as I fought to keep up as we approached the four-way intersection with the main street. Once again, I heard the manic hooting and I watched in astonishment as a group of locals scattered to avoid him as he made a left turn. One woman had been carrying a basket of fruit on her head in the African fashion. She lost it in her haste to get out of the path of the Camry and her load of mangoes was left scattered and rolling in the middle of the street. *Fucking hell! I don't want to see anyone killed here.* I slowed my own speed down slightly to make the turn safely. Deep down I was afraid of losing him and after such a journey that was something I was not about to allow to happen. I made the left turn onto the main street with a hundred astonished faces of locals and tourists watching me. Up ahead I saw the Camry weaving through the traffic once again and running multiple give ways. *Jesus Christ Green. This is going badly wrong now!* In his mad panic, Heinrich Klopp had made distance. The powerful turbo diesel roared and I too hooted wildly at the traffic and pedestrians as I desperately tried to catch up. It was roughly 1.5 km further that I saw the Camry swing wildly to the right and head down toward the riverfront.

My own tyres howled as I made the corner and I shifted in the seat to see where he had gone. Heinrich Klopp had reached the end of the road. Ahead of him lay the mighty

Zambezi River and the many luxury hotels that lined its banks. From where I was, I could see that he had only two options. Left towards the falls or, right along the riverfront. At that moment a fully loaded school bus crossed the road in front of me. I slammed my foot on the brake and waited as I watched the wide eyes of the startled school kids on the bus as they passed. The Land Cruiser leapt forward once they had gone, its powerful engine screaming under the hood in front of me. I almost lost control as I made the turn at the bottom of the slope. To my right, a succession of luxury hotels lined the banks of the mighty Zambezi. Tall Queen Palms and bright green luminous barked fever trees grew from their lush green lawns. Several security guards had rushed out to see what the commotion was. I sat forward in my seat in an effort to spot the Camry but the road ahead was empty. Heinrich Klopp was nowhere to be seen.

"Fuck!" I shouted out loud as I pounded the steering wheel in frustration.

I dropped a gear, revved the engine, and sped off.

"He's got to be close by," I said to myself through gritted teeth. "He didn't have time to get far."

A feeling of desperate panic set in as I passed the last of the hotels. The grounds of The Stanley Waterfront Hotel ended with a fence of heavy black gum poles. Beyond that, I saw only bush and the dark green swirls of the great river. The road ahead led only to a dead end at the various viewing points of the great Victoria Falls. *You've lost him, Green. After everything you've only gone and lost him.*

It was then that I saw the stone pillars of the gateway to the right. They had been partially obscured by dried grass and bush. There was a faded sign on one of them that read 'Stanley Waterfront Sunset Cruise'. It caught my attention as I approached and then I saw the dust. The Toyota Camry was winding its way through the Acacia trees on the dirt road heading towards the riverbank. Moored at a wide jetty, jutting out into the river, were two double-decker river cruise boats. Each large enough to accommodate thirty people, they were both in the process of being re-stocked for the evening cruise. I swung the steering wheel to follow on in and the bumper at the rear of the vehicle clipped the stone pillar. The sound of tearing metal filled the cab but I carried on regardless. Heinrich Klopp pulled into the parking area at the front of the jetty. In his haste, he must have used the handbrake as the car slid sideways on the dirt and came to rest near a small ablution block to the side. My own front-right tyre hit a protruding tree root as I skidded on the dirt around a group of trees. The front of the vehicle bucked and I fought to regain control as it came down. It was as I was making my final approach towards the jetty that I saw Heinrich Klopp leap from his vehicle. He carried the same aluminium briefcase I had seen him use at the Apex mine in Namibia. It was attached to his left wrist on a silver chain with the handcuff. I watched as he sprinted up the concrete stairs of the jetty looking back at me as I approached. There were two workers in blue overalls working on the pier. One was loading the cruiser to the right with crates of beer while the other was at the far end attempting to load a couple of fuel tanks into a small tender boat that was attached by a rope to the jetty. The first man saw Klopp coming and wisely stepped on board the cruiser to avoid him. The second man had not seen him and was only alerted to his presence by the thundering footfalls on the wooden surface as he approached. The man stood up from his work with a surprised look on his face. Heinrich Klopp ran into him at full tilt. He hit the man squarely in the chest with the briefcase. The blow sent him tumbling into the water below and he wailed in terror as he fell. The Land Cruiser skidded to a halt in a cloud of red dust near the front of the jetty. I leapt out and sprinted up the concrete steps of the jetty.

By the time I reached the wooden decking, Heinrich Klopp had climbed down into the small tender boat and was busy untying it from the concrete pillar it was attached to. I tore down the jetty only to see he had succeeded in freeing the small boat and had pushed it out into the powerful current of the river beyond. He was busy pulling at the rope start of the small, two-stroke outboard motor at the rear. He paused as he saw me running towards the end of the pier and smiled.

"Schweinhund!" he shrieked before bursting into peals of hysterical laughter.

The powerful current was taking the boat downstream rapidly. Heinrich Klopp's high-pitched cackling stopped when he realized I was not slowing down. I reached the end of the pier at full speed and dived forward into the air with my arms outstretched. My body hit the water with a loud crack and I immediately swam as hard as I could towards the drifting boat. I felt the unstoppable current pulling at me as I went. In the small boat, Heinrich Klopp frantically searched for a weapon. He grabbed the first thing that came to hand. The portable steel fuel tank was old and its red paint was chipped and faded. I saw it flying through the air towards me and immediately I ducked underwater. It landed heavily on my back and winded me, but I carried on pulling with my arms and kicking my legs. By then we had drifted far out into the river and more than a hundred metres downstream. I was beginning to tire. I forced one final burst of strength from my arms and finally, my right hand landed on the gunwale at the side of the aluminium hull.

I lifted my head to see Klopp frantically rummaging in the rear of the boat for another weapon. He rose holding a heavy wooden oar in his right hand.

"Schweinhund!" he roared as he brought it down towards my head.

I ducked under the water, letting go of the boat for just long enough to avoid the impact. The sound underwater reminded me of a giant gong in an old Kung Fu movie. I brought my head up and gripped the side of the boat once again. Heinrich Klopp's face was engorged and purple with rage. Once again, he drew the heavy oar behind him and brought it down towards me with savage force. Again I submerged myself and waited for the sound of the impact. It came as expected but there was another sound this time, as if something heavy had fallen in the boat. I lifted my head from the swirling green of the water to see he had swung the oar so hard he had lost his footing and fallen forward towards me. I gripped the side of the aluminium hull and brought my right foot up out of the water. It connected with his temple as he fell and sent him sprawling to the other side of the boat. The briefcase and chain attached to his left wrist rattled and clattered in the boat as he fell. It was as I pulled myself onto the boat that I first became aware of the voices shouting from the riverbank. At the time I ignored them as I had more important business to attend to. Heinrich Klopp lay in the centre of the boat with a slightly confused look on his face. Soaking wet and dripping with water I lunged for him where he lay and gripped him by his collar. Once again, I heard the voices shouting from the riverbank but again I ignored them. I looked at his face as I brought my right fist up above my head. It was as if all of the rage that had been pent up inside me was about to burst. My fist slammed into his face four times, and as each blow landed, I shouted.

"Eins, zwei, drei, Klopp!

"Eins, zwei, drei, Klopp!" I growled as another four heavy blows struck him.

Heinrich Klopp moaned softly and a strange smile formed on his lips as he lay in the bottom of the boat.

I saw a mixture of blood and saliva filling the gaps between his perfect teeth and suddenly I was confused. I paused with my fist still raised and looked down at his body. It was then that I saw the bulge in his trousers. *What the fuck?* I could not believe my eyes. The man was enjoying the beating. I sat back panting heavily and it was then I heard the manic shouting from the riverbank once again. I lifted my gaze to see the boat had drifted close to eight hundred metres from the jetty. I had no idea that the powerful current had carried us far out into the river and we were speeding towards the edge of the largest waterfall in the world. *Jesus Christ Green!* Suddenly my world changed. It was as if everything was happening in slow motion. Even the rabid cries from the running men on the riverbank seemed to fade away. Heinrich Klopp's left hand lay at the side of the boat near the outrigger normally used to secure the oar while rowing. The aluminium briefcase lay nearby, still attached to his wrist by the heavy silver chain. I lifted the chain and wrapped it twice around the metal base of the outrigger. At the bottom of the boat, Klopp moaned again as I did so. I stood up and slammed the heel of my shoe onto the outrigger. The metal bent with the force of the blow but it was not enough. Once again I stomped with all of my weight onto the smooth metal. This time it worked and both sides of it lay flat against the gunwale. I looked up to see there was less than two hundred metres to the edge of the falls. Up ahead, a thin spur of land jutted out of the water. It was covered with blackened rocks and surrounded by reeds. I paused as the boat sped towards it but it was only when we were parallel that I realized it was at least ten metres away. I stepped onto the side of the hull and launched myself into the frothing water. The current was unlike anything I had ever felt and it seemed like I was carried away like a leaf in a storm. I thrashed desperately in the boiling confusion of it all until my right hand found a clump of reeds and I pulled myself to safety. Panting wildly, I pulled my aching body onto a pile of rocks at the far end of the island and looked up. The boat drifted away steadily, almost peacefully. It was as if it was a living being that had accepted its fate and was simply allowing itself to be taken.

I blinked the water from my eyes as I watched. It was then that the upper body of Heinrich Klopp popped up like a jack in the box. His square head jerked from side to side like an automaton as he realized the gravity of the situation. Our eyes met and I heard his scream clearly above the roar of the falls.

"Nein!" he screamed. "No!"

His mouth was like a bloody hole in his head as he yanked savagely at the chain on his wrist. But his efforts were futile. The silver chain was immovable on the bent metal of the outrigger.

"Nein!" he screamed again, his eyes like lasers of pure hate.

I watched his mouth open as he screamed a third time, but I could no longer hear him.

THE STAR OF THE DESERT

The boat and its occupant were gradually enveloped by the smoke that thunders at the edge of the great Victoria Falls, and Heinrich Klopp disappeared forever.

27

Chapter Twenty-Seven: Cape Town, Two Days Later.

There was a cool breeze coming in from the ocean as I walked from the taxi drop-off point into the V&A Waterfront complex in the heart of Cape Town. The sky above was perfectly blue and hordes of relaxed-looking tourists and locals wandered the many shops, restaurants, and museums of the working docks. Behind me, the stunning backdrop of Table Mountain was resplendent, glittering green and grey in the mid-day sun. The masts and rigging of hundreds of colourful boats swayed lazily in the ocean beyond. A marimba band playing under the shade of an oak tree nearby pounded out a repetitive rhythm that pulsed through the air like a heartbeat. I had been picked up from the tiny island above the Victoria Falls by a young rafting guide on a jet-ski. He had dropped me safely on the riverbank near the viewing points where I melted into the crowds and disappeared. An hour later I had collected my belongings from the Toyota and headed to a back-packers' lodge on the outskirts of town. The body of Heinrich Klopp was never found, although one of his shoes was picked up the following day at rapid number four in the gorge beneath the falls. His body had been smashed to pieces by the hundred-metre drop and the enormous force of the 625 million litres of water that flowed over the edge every minute. What was left of him was swiftly consumed by the ravenous crocodiles and tigerfish in the gorge below. The briefcase attached to his wrist was ripped away, and pulverised, and the giant diamond was lost forever. I caught a direct flight to Cape Town the following morning and booked into The Blueberry Guest House in Kalk Bay. I glanced at my watch as I walked into the main square of the waterfront. I had made contact with Danny Meyer's girlfriend, Charmaine, through Facebook and she had agreed to meet me at a coffee shop the following day. I had said nothing at the time, only that I was a friend of his and I had something to give her. I spotted the logo of the coffee shop on the blue canvas awning that covered its verandah and made my way through the crowds towards it. I climbed the steps up to the faux wooden decking and stood in the shade of the wide awning to scan the tables. Most of them were occupied by small groups and families but at the table at the far corner, a young woman was sitting alone.

She wore a light yellow and white summer dress and her long blonde hair was tied back in a ponytail. *It has to be her Green*. As I approached, I saw her take a sip from a tall glass of iced tea. She placed the glass back on the table and stared wistfully out towards the ocean. She glanced at me as I approached and I knew then it was her. Her clear blue eyes were vacant with grief.

"Charmaine?" I asked.

"Yes," she replied as she stood and offered her hand. "Mr Green?"

"Thank you for seeing me," I said as I sat down in front of her. "I know this must be a very difficult time for you."

Her eyes dropped to the table briefly as if she didn't know what to say. I knew then there was no point in beating around the bush.

"I was a friend of Danny's," I said. "I was aboard his plane when it came down."

She sat forward slightly, brought her right hand up and placed it just below her throat.

"But..." she said with a confused frown.

"What you have heard is not true," I said firmly. "There were three people aboard that plane and I was one of them. I tried to get him out but I couldn't. I'm sorry, Charmaine."

She stared at me and I knew then that she believed me.

"He gave me some things and made me swear I would give them to you."

I took the khaki envelope from my pocket and placed it on the table.

"These are the title deeds for the smallholding in Stellenbosch," I said. "He told me he wanted to build a house there."

She blinked as she stared at the envelope.

"But there's something else," I said as I took the tiny black jewellery box from my pocket.

I placed the box on the table and opened the top. The single diamond sparkled in the sunlight as I pushed it towards her. She brought her hand to her mouth in shock and I saw the tears welling in her eyes.

"He loved you very much," I said quietly. "He was going to ask you to marry him."

I sat and watched her for a few seconds then slowly stood up to leave. I put my hand on her shoulder lightly and I saw the tears running down her face as she looked up at me.

"Look after yourself," I said.

THE END.

THE STAR OF THE DESERT

Dear Reader,

I'm guessing if you are reading this, it means you have finished this book. If so, I really hope you enjoyed it! I would like to ask you to please take a minute to leave a review on Amazon & Goodreads. Reviews are vitally important for independent authors and help me reach new readers. All the books in the Jason Green series are stand-alone novels. If you would like to continue with the series, you can find it by clicking here:

https://geni.us/QCVsT24

Please feel free to follow me or contact me through my Facebook page at https://www.facebook.com/gordonwallisauthor,

I love hearing from my readers!

Thanks again, Gordon.

Printed in Great Britain
by Amazon